TAKING A SHOT
AT LOVE

What Reviewers Say About KC Richardson's Work

A Call Away

"…the romance between both characters was nice and gave me all the feels by the end. I really think this is the kind of novel you take on holiday and read by the pool. I look forward to seeing what's coming up next for KC Richardson."—*Les Reveur*

New Beginnings

"Pure and simple, this is a sweet slow-burn romance. It's cozy and warm. At its heart, *New Beginnings* by KC Richardson is a story about soul mates that fall in love. …If you're looking for a sweet romance, the kind of romance that you can curl-up with as a fire crackles in your fireplace, then this could be your book. It's a simple love story that leaves you feeling good."
—*Lesbian Review*

Courageous Love

"Richardson aptly captures the myriad emotions and sometimes irrational thought processes of a young woman with a possibly fatal disease, as well as the torment inherent in the idea of losing another loved one to the same illness. This sensitively told and realistically plotted story will grab readers by the heartstrings and not let them go."—*Publishers Weekly*

Visit us at www.boldstrokesbooks.com

By the Author

New Beginnings

Courageous Love

A Call Away

Taking a Shot at Love

TAKING A SHOT AT LOVE

by

KC Richardson

2020

Credits
Editor: Cindy Cresap
Production Design: Susan Ramundo
Cover Design By Sheri (hindsightgraphics@gmail.com)
Cover Photo By Inger Richardson

Acknowledgments

A huge thank you goes to Radclyffe, Sandy Lowe, and everyone at Bold Strokes Books involved in helping produce outstanding books. Special thanks go to my editor, Cindy Cresap, who always teaches me something new. Editing is my favorite part of writing because I always learn something new, and in Cindy, I have a patient teacher.

Thank you to my fantastic beta readers, Inger, Dawn, and Sue. Because of your insight, I was able to turn in a pretty decent first draft.

Huge shout-outs go to Lynnette Beers-McCormick and Carol Jue. Lynnette allowed me to shadow her for a day in the life of a college English professor. Lynnette and Aurora Rey answered my "what if" questions of college life, and I greatly appreciated their help. If I got anything wrong, it's because of my error. Carol introduced me to the internal life of a college basketball coach. Even though I played college basketball, I really had no idea what the coaches did other than make our lives miserable by making us run so much in practice. Coach, thank you for welcoming me back into the Chapman University family. I love my Panthers.

Thank you to my good friends Lisa, Ngina, and Athena. Their brainstorming gave me some great ideas for this story, including the names of a couple of characters and what pole dancing is all about. I'll let you, the reader, wonder what I mean by that.

My wife, Inger Richardson, gave me the setting and idea for this story, and I'm so glad that she also helped me with the "what-ifs" in the storyline. She also used her extraordinary photography talents and took the picture of the fountain on this book cover.

Finally, I want to thank you, the readers, for your continued support in my writing endeavors by buying my books, leaving reviews, and sending me messages on Facebook, Twitter, and email. You inspire me to keep writing, and I hope you enjoy reading this book as much as I enjoyed writing it.

Dedication

To my wife for believing in second chances.
I love you for life.

CHAPTER ONE

Celeste came strutting out in her clear, six-inch platform high heels, metallic rave multicolor green booty shorts that hugged her ass, a matching skintight camisole with a sheer white blouse over it, the bottom of it in a knot at her belly button. Her wavy hair was teased high, her heavy black eyeliner gave her cat eyes, and her deep, dark red lipstick made her lips look plump, like she'd spent the past few days making out with her lover. The sultry music was deep and slow, and she felt it deep in her soul. This was her place of worship and the brass pole was her shrine.

She grabbed the pole, looked over her shoulder, and caught the attention of her audience as she slowly stroked it up and down. Now that she was in command, she'd have her way with them, captivating them by climbing up the pole, swinging around while holding on with only one leg hooked around it. This was her favorite dance partner, the one that would let her lead, the one that would support Celeste in any move she'd want to make. When her feet were firmly back on the ground, she squatted with her back to the pole, legs spread apart, giving the audience a sliver of hope to see what she had hidden behind the shiny fabric.

She crawled along the floor, sleek, like a prowling tiger, looking for a poor soul to prey upon. No, none of them were worthy. She ran her fingers slowly through her hair, lifting it off her neck, thrusting out her chest. She let her hands linger down her body, over her breasts, until one hand grazed over her covered mound. This performance always made her a little hot, a little turned on, and tonight was no different. The thrill it gave her, to do something outside her comfort zone, as well as getting the crowd willing to obey her every command, was why she did this. When the music ended, Celeste felt like she'd climaxed and was ready for a cigarette that she'd never smoke. The applause, hoots, and hollers from the audience and her classmates brought her out of her reverie. Her pole dancing class's showcase was, for her, a success. For the rest of the evening, she'd enjoy being seen as a sexy, lustful woman. Tomorrow, she'd return to her public persona.

❖

The solid oak door to the grand residence opened.

"Celeste, it's so wonderful to see you. Thank you for coming."

Celeste Bouchard, professor in the English department, almost laughed since this soiree was mandatory for all faculty at Glassell University. Even if she didn't want to be, she had to be there. Fortunately for her, she wanted to be there. The president of the university went all-out to provide the faculty of his university delicious food, expensive wine, and a melodic string quartet to entertain his guests. Though only a small, private university, Glassell really had a lot to offer, not only to the students, but also the staff.

"Gerald, thank you for having me. How was your summer? You're looking very tan."

Gerald Prescott, President of Glassell University, stepped aside and allowed Celeste to enter the marble-floored foyer. He was an elegant looking gentleman in his late sixties, and he had a kind smile that reached his eyes when he greeted her. She could hear the low murmur of conversation and soft music coming from the grand room at the end of the hall.

"Margaret and I just returned a week ago from Hawaii. We took our children and grandchildren to Oahu for a week. While the kids were busy surfing and snorkeling, Margaret and I sat on the lanai and read the entire time. It was just the thing I needed before starting a new school year. But now, I'm well-rested and hoping for an exciting year."

"As am I."

The doorbell interrupted them and Celeste excused herself. "I'm going to mingle. I'll talk to you soon."

The echo of Celeste's heels on the marble floor followed her down the hallway where the walls were adorned with original artwork, Gerald's personal museum, and into the room where her fellow professors had gathered. No matter how young or old, people always seemed to gather in their own cliques. She noted the athletic director talking to a few men and women, presumably coaches. There was one particular woman in that group who caught Celeste's eye, but she wasn't about to go interrupt a group of jocks. She'd learned her lesson when she was in high school that she had nothing in common with them even if they did give her the time of day.

She continued to the bar area and asked for a glass of pinot noir. She took a sip and fingered the pearl necklace she wore as she looked around the room to see if she knew anyone she felt comfortable talking to. She had no qualms about standing in front of a classroom and imparting her knowledge to students, but in a social setting, she'd always felt a little awkward and inept. She was trying to overcome that, but it was a slow process. She spotted her ex trying to hold court over a group of uptight looking men. Her ex's loud cackle caused Celeste to wince and turn the other way. For the thousandth time, she wondered what she ever saw in Jackie Stone. The very thought of her gave Celeste a sour taste in her mouth.

Celeste caught someone trying to get her attention, and she was relieved to see it was her closest friend in the English department, and her life, Olivia Daniels. Celeste gave a small wave and made her way to Olivia and kissed her on the cheek. Celeste and Olivia had gone to graduate school together and became study partners, then best friends. It was Olivia who submitted her name to the dean of the English department at Glassell University and why she was now a professor there.

"I'm so glad to see a friendly face tonight."

"Celeste, who wouldn't be friendly here besides your ex-psycho?"

Celeste touched the side of her nose and pointed at Olivia, indicating that was exactly who she was talking about. "You know this is only my third year here so I don't know as many people here as you do. I thought maybe you could introduce me to a few of them in the other departments. I'm ready to mingle amongst the other groups this year." Celeste held up her glass and winked at Olivia.

"I'll be happy to, but after Gerald gives his welcome back speech." Olivia looked at her watch. "It should be any time now. By the way, can I tell you how sexy your routine was last night in our pole dancing showcase? My word, I was so worked up that Carl got very lucky when I got home last night."

Celeste could feel her face get hot, and she looked away. She still had a little trouble accepting praise when it came to pole dancing, but she loved it and thrived at it. "Thank you, I think. But please, let's talk about something else while we're at a school function. The last thing I need is that image in my head." Olivia snickered.

Celeste and Olivia started to talk about their hopes for the upcoming semester when Gerald tapped a knife to his wine glass to get everyone's attention.

"Good evening. I'd like to thank you all for coming." Gerald only spoke for ten minutes, highlighting some events that would be happening on campus in the upcoming school year, including homecoming activities, and what he expected out of the staff and students. During his speech, Celeste looked over to the "coach group" and found the lone woman looking back at her. Celeste quickly looked away, then slowly glanced back at the woman who offered a smile and a small wave. Celeste was tempted to look behind her to make sure that smile wasn't meant for someone else. She wasn't used to women looking her way, especially ones who were that gorgeous. She lifted her wine glass as a small greeting and was rewarded by a bigger smile. Celeste grinned and bowed her head, suddenly feeling bashful. She looked back at the woman who was now paying attention to Gerald, and it gave Celeste an opportunity to look at her more closely. She was tall, trim, looked to be in good shape. She wore a light blue button-down shirt, black slacks, and black loafers. Nothing too stylish, but she looked good.

Too bad they worked in the same university. After the disastrous ending to her last relationship with Jackie, she vowed never to get involved with anyone she worked with ever again. She did not need a repeat of being subjected to the rumor mill, or having her romantic life public knowledge amongst the students and faculty. She was brought back to the present at the sound of polite clapping, and she set her glass down to join in.

Olivia touched Celeste's shoulder. "I'm going to get a refill of my wine, and then I'll introduce you to some of the professors I know."

Once Olivia stepped away, Celeste saw the woman she'd been admiring start to walk toward her. Her heart did a little flutter, and she again began fingering her pearls at the thought of meeting the handsome woman she could never get involved with. She let out a gasp when Jackie stepped in her line of sight to the other woman and ruined her view.

"You look beautiful tonight, Celeste. But then again, I always thought you looked beautiful."

Celeste attempted to keep her face expressionless and her voice quiet. "Is that why you called me a fat cow when I broke up with you?" Celeste could feel her body tense when she recalled that very moment and how shamed she felt. That moment took up a lot of time in her mind and at times, she felt she still wasn't over it. Sometimes she felt that she would hear those words in her mind for the rest of her life. The need to flee took over, but Celeste would be damned if she let Jackie know how affected she was just by her presence.

Looking appropriately embarrassed, Jackie slightly blushed. "I didn't mean it. I was just upset that you were ending things. I thought we were really good together."

Celeste's annoyance flared and her blood simmered with anger. Not wanting to rehash everything she'd already said to Jackie, she ignored that last comment. "What do you want, Jackie?" The faster she could get rid of Jackie, the quicker her lungs would ease and make it easier for Celeste to breathe.

"Nothing. I just wanted to come say hello and ask how your summer was."

"My summer was pleasant. Now if you'll excuse me, I'm going to find Olivia."

Celeste turned but was stopped by Jackie's hand gripping her arm. Jackie's face was scrunched up, and Celeste wondered what she ever saw in her. Her mind flashed back to the first time Jackie gripped her arm in anger, and the bruises she'd left. Jackie had an excuse that first time, and the times after, until Celeste finally stopped accepting her excuses and apologies.

"Why are you being such a bitch?" The fire in Jackie's eyes that once excited Celeste in the beginning of their relationship now made her more cautious. She tried to keep the tremble from her hands and her voice when she finally spoke.

"Get your hand off me and don't ever touch me again." Celeste issued the command through clenched teeth, and she felt her nostrils flare.

Celeste's warning made it through Jackie's dense skull and she let go, allowing Celeste to walk away. She found Olivia walking toward her, and she must have noticed something was wrong. She could feel her heart pounding through her chest, and she really needed some fresh air.

"Are you all right? You look white as a sheet."

"I just had words with Jackie. Look, I want to get out of here. I don't want to be anywhere she is."

"Of course. Why don't you and I go grab a bite to eat and we can just chill out."

"I don't want to take you away from the party, Olivia."

"Nonsense. I'm not a fan of these gatherings anyway. I'd much rather spend some quiet time with my friend, indulging in nachos and beer."

Celeste couldn't help but grin and was secretly pleased that she wouldn't have to be alone so soon after her run-in with Jackie. Thankfully, despite GU being a small campus, Celeste's building was across campus from Jackie's so they didn't see each other much. "You're on. I'll even let you order them with jalapenos. And I think tonight might call for tequila and margaritas."

After they said good-bye to Gerald, they made their way out of the grand room. Celeste didn't see the attractive woman, but she did see Jackie watch her go and her eyes were shooting daggers at Celeste every step of the way.

Celeste and Olivia went to their favorite Mexican restaurant by the campus and were seated right away. Once the school year started, there was usually a wait to get a table. The restaurant had once been a church in its previous life, and the seats for the booths were the old pews. Some of the original stained-glass windows were still present, and the food was so good, it made the customer want to thank God. Their server dropped off a basket of chips and two bowls of salsa, the one food combination Celeste had trouble saying no to. Because of that, she'd decided she would order a salad with grilled chicken and light dressing on the side. The server took their drink order and left them to their chips.

"So, what did Jackie have to say?"

Celeste bitterly laughed. "Nothing important and nothing I wanted to hear." Celeste had tried to put her confrontation out of her mind. In fact, at times like these, she wished she had short-term memory loss, but only of the time she and Jackie dated.

Celeste scooped some salsa onto her chip and popped it in her mouth. Olivia stared at her until Celeste was done chewing. Olivia knew the whole story, from beginning to end, of the relationship between Celeste and Jackie, including the abuse Celeste had suffered at the words and hands of Jackie. It was only through Celeste's pleading and tears that Olivia hadn't said anything to Gerald.

"Okay. She said I looked beautiful and wanted to know how my summer was, but when I turned to leave, she grabbed my arm and called me a bitch."

"Damn her! It's not bad enough she spread lies about you but now she has to harass you? You might want to talk to Gerald about that if she continues. And if you don't, I will." The chip in Olivia's hand broke from holding on a little too hard, and it crumbled into the salsa. "Well, shit." Olivia took her spoon and dug out the broken pieces of chip.

Celeste reached across the table and squeezed Olivia's hand. "I love that you're almost as upset as I am about Jackie, but trust me, she's not worth your time or energy. I don't want Gerald, or anyone else, to know what happened between us. I'm embarrassed enough as it is. Thank you for sticking with me last year when she was spreading those lies."

Olivia's features softened, and Celeste felt a lump form in her throat. There were many reasons why Celeste was grateful that she took the teaching position at GU, but her friendship with Olivia topped the list. Jackie? Well, she didn't make the list at all. In fact, she'd made a different list altogether.

"You're my best friend and one of the most respected and loved professors in the English department. Maybe on the entire campus."

"It's not that big of a campus." Celeste winked before putting another chip in her mouth.

"You know, for the elegance and grace you show to the world, you sure are a smart-ass."

Celeste giggled and she felt good. It felt like it'd been forever since she felt this happy despite having a run-in with Jackie. She felt excited about the school year—not just with teaching, but she felt she was in store for something magical this year. She was coming up on her last year in her forties and she felt like she was finally starting to hit her groove.

Chapter Two

Lisa Tobias walked through the front door of the university-owned house she shared with her best friend and assistant coach, Athena Chang, who was sitting on the couch watching a WNBA game. Lisa threw her keys and wallet on the small wooden table near the door, said hi to Athena, then continued to her bedroom to get out of her clothes and into her basketball shorts and T-shirt.

After she was more comfortable, she grabbed a beer from the refrigerator and joined Athena on the couch.

"Who's winning?"

"Sparks. Parker is going off tonight."

"Mmm." Lisa leaned forward and plucked a few cold fries from Athena's discarded dinner.

The game ended and Athena muted the television. "How did tonight go?"

"Not bad. Good turnout. I talked to the athletic director about ordering new uniforms for the team. He said it was a good possibility for next year if we do well enough." That definitely hadn't been an issue at her last coaching position. She had coached at a large Division I university, and the school spared no expense for any of the athletic teams. New uniforms, new shoes, new practice gear, travel sweats and luggage, state-of-the-art facilities. Getting the coaching job at GU had definitely been an adjustment, even if she was glad just to have a coaching position at this point. The uniforms her team had were over five years old. It was like pulling teeth to get the team new travel sweats. Her argument was that her team was representing GU and they should look good doing it, even if they were boarding a budget airline.

"I don't think that will be a problem. We had a pretty decent recruiting class. And with the four juniors, two seniors, and three sophomores, we'll have more than enough talent to bring the freshmen up to speed."

"That's what I'm thinking too as long as all the players keep their grades up. We almost lost Emily Logan for the fall semester. Thankfully, she pulled up her GPA with her two summer school classes. She's been put on academic probation though so we really need to stay on top of her. I just don't understand it. She's really smart and has the intelligence to get all As but something happened last spring to make her tank some of her grades. Did you ever find out what happened?"

"No, she was tight-lipped, only saying she'd try harder."

"We're going to have to talk to her about that or I may just threaten to bench her if she doesn't work harder in class."

Athena nodded. "How else was tonight? I noticed you're home early and couldn't get out of those clothes fast enough."

Lisa laughed. "You know how it is. Fancy appetizers, fine wine, which I don't drink, and all the scholarly people talking about their upcoming lectures that I have no interest in."

"So, you hung out with the coaches." Athena knew Lisa too well, and it came out as a statement and not a question. Lisa had half a mind to send Athena in her place next year, if they were still at the school, just so she could understand the suffering a head coach had to endure for the greater good.

"Yep. We were all bragging on our teams and putting together a friendly wager on which team would finish with the best conference standings. The baseball coach feels like he's going to win the bet, and he just might. They had a great season last year. I feel we have a decent shot at finishing in the top three of our conference. This is only our second year here, but I felt we inherited a pretty good team. And with the players we were able to bring in, I'm hoping they all gel by the time conference starts. We start preseason conditioning in two weeks, but I want the ladies to start practicing on the court together. We can put the seniors in charge of that since we can't have an 'official' practice until mid-October."

"I'm excited about this team and our season, Ice."

Lisa smiled at the nickname Athena gave her way back when they were college teammates. The team had been on the road, and they were in their hotel room after a game. Athena had sprained her ankle and needed ice, but the ice machine at the hotel only had cubed ice and Athena wanted it crushed. In an effort to shut her up, Lisa dropped the bag of ice on the floor and stomped on it a few times. She picked up the bag and handed it to Athena and said, "There's your crushed fucking ice." Athena and their trainer burst out in laughter, and that night Athena gave Lisa her nickname. She had to admit that she liked it better than her previous nickname of LT. So boring. "Ice" had a much funnier story associated with it. She had one other nickname, Tobi, short for her last name, but Athena was the only one who called her Ice.

"We'll give our conference a run for their money, that's for sure." Athena went to the kitchen and brought back two more beers.

"Thanks." They tapped the glass bottle necks together and took a drink. "I saw a gorgeous woman at the party tonight. I don't know her name or what she does, but she's a real looker." Lisa recalled the moment the woman walked into the room wearing a blouse that was one button away from exposing just enough cleavage, a skirt that fit her like a glove, and high heels that gave a delicious shape to her calves. Lisa noticed the string of pearls around the woman's neck and thought that she looked like the type of woman who should wear pearls and diamonds. The way her hips moved with every step certainly got Lisa's attention.

"You didn't talk to her?"

"No. I made eye contact across the room, and she smiled back at me during the president's speech. I was about to make my way over when another woman took her attention. I changed directions to go to the bar, but when I returned, she was gone. Just as well. I need to focus on this season and the team. I'm never going to get back to a Division I school if we don't have a good record and do well in conference."

"I don't know, Ice. I kind of like it here. I like the small campus and the old town feel. It just feels homey to me."

"Athena, as much as I love having you coach with me, if you have a better offer that presents itself, I'd expect you to take it. Same goes for me. If I can get back to a higher-ranking school to coach, I'm going to take it. If I get a better offer and I accept, and if you want to stay here, I'd totally give you my recommendation for the head coach position. I'd miss the hell out of you, but I'd be happy for you."

Athena took a gulp from her beer and stared at the television screen. "We don't have to talk about that now."

Lisa could see she hit a nerve with Athena. The thought of not having Athena by her side on the bench made Lisa a little sick to her stomach, but she'd never hold her back or stop her from leaving if she wanted something different. They'd been best friends since their college days and Lisa knew Athena like the back of her hand. She only wanted the best for her.

"Anyways, tell me more about this woman who caught your eye."

Lisa closed her eyes to conjure up the image of what had to be one of the most beautiful women she'd ever seen. "Do you know that actress on that lawyer show you like so much? She kind of looks like her."

"No shit? She's hot."

"I know. She was a lot shorter than me but had all the right curves in all the right places. She wore these heels that would break my ankles, but they made her legs look shapely. She wore a skirt and a blouse and carried herself with an air of sophistication."

Athena burst out in laughter. "You're such a dude. You have no sense of female fashion."

"And you do?" Lisa threw a fry at Athena and she fell over on the couch. "I don't know what they call that style of skirt or heels. I've been wearing slacks and loafers too long."

"No, you've been wearing basketball sweats and high tops for too long."

"Whatever, Chang." Lisa joined Athena in cracking up. "I've never seen her before so I have no idea what department she's in. The woman who was talking to her after the speech though? She looks like she plays for our team so it gives me hope that the other one does too."

"What does it matter if you have plans on leaving here? And I thought you wanted to focus on the season. That means no outside distractions."

Lisa shrugged. "You never know, buddy. You never know." It had been a while since Lisa had dated anyone, and at forty-six, she wasn't getting any younger. She'd like to find a woman to spend her life with, but she would have to be understanding about Lisa's schedule and travel. If she could find someone who looked like the woman she saw earlier who supported her coaching career, then she would definitely date her.

Chapter Three

Celeste met Olivia in the locker room on campus early Monday morning to get ready for a fitness program that was being started for students and faculty. It was to include exercise classes and nutritional information run by some of the athletic coaches and professors in the health department. That was one of the benefits of working for a small university—the development of programs such as this one to promote good health. It was only the second week of the semester, but it was very easy to get caught up in poor health habits. There would be lots of sitting or standing in one position, meals on the go, or forgetting to eat altogether.

"I really appreciate you doing this program with me, Liv."

"Don't mention it. I think this is a great program the university is putting on. Hopefully, it has a good turnout so it will be continued. It's great that we're doing this together so we can encourage each other and have fun."

Celeste wrapped her arms around her and agreed. "Come on. Let's get into the gym and see who else is doing this."

They walked up the stairs and through the doors of the gym, surprised to find so many people gathered, a good mix of faculty and students. Suddenly self-conscious about working out in front of so many people, Celeste tugged the hem of her T-shirt over her black yoga pants in an effort to hide her butt. She felt like she was back in high school in PE class—the kid being picked last for teams, the one with no coordination or athletic ability.

Olivia leaned in as she took Celeste's arm to lead her farther into the gym. "I know what you're thinking, but there's no need to be embarrassed. You look like a warrior ready to work out and we're all here for the same common goal."

Celeste smiled and waved to a couple of her former students and spoke quietly out of the corner of her mouth. "How do you always know what I'm thinking? Am I that transparent?"

"No, but I've known you for a very long time, and I know the changes you've made to live a healthier lifestyle. You are awesome, my sweet friend, and we're going to have a great time."

The shrill sound of a whistle made them jump and turn to the offending sound. Celeste quietly gasped when she saw the woman from the faculty mixer. She stepped to the side until she was behind another person, not wanting the woman to see her.

"Good morning. Thank you for coming out to our first class. When I initially took this idea to President Prescott, I was thinking it was going to be a small gathering that would meet once a week to go for a walk, maybe do some light resistance exercises. But as I started to tell some of my colleagues, they volunteered to run some of the meetings. We'll be doing various exercises and nutrition classes that hopefully will be fun and informative for all of you. I'm taken aback by the turnout we have for our first class, and I'm excited to get started. Remember, this is totally voluntary and you can choose what classes you want to attend, but I'm hoping that most of you will want to come out every week.

"My name is Lisa Tobias and I'm the coach of the women's basketball team. With me today is my assistant coach, Athena Chang, and we're here to answer any and all questions. Does anyone have any questions?"

Celeste saw an older woman raise her hand.

"Yes, I have a hip replacement, and I want to make sure this is safe for me to do."

"Absolutely. These workouts can accommodate everyone, and we can always modify something if it's too difficult."

Celeste was impressed that Coach Tobias had considered different levels of fitness. She felt herself start to relax and her muscles loosen. She wasn't completely new to exercise, but her workouts consisted of a smaller, more intimate group. She had been worried that she wouldn't be able to keep up or that everyone would be athletic and in shape. But she saw plenty of people who had a similar shape as her, all ages, shapes, and sizes. And as a bonus, she'd get to occasionally look at Coach Tobias.

Lisa Tobias was very good-looking with wide-set eyes, strong angular jaw, and a straight nose. Her dark brown hair was pulled back in a ponytail, she had on sweat pants, a GU hoodie sweatshirt, and a whistle draped around her neck.

"I'll leave a stack of papers with the weekly schedule by the door so you can grab one on your way out. For our first class, we're just going to walk around the campus. It's a good way to get familiar with the grounds for our new students and faculty if we have any in our group."

A few people raised their hands and Lisa clapped. "Excellent. Welcome to GU. Okay, people, let's head outside and meet in front of the fountain."

The group started to make their way to the door like a herd of sheep. Celeste saw the coaches standing by the table that held the schedule and they were greeting everyone. Celeste felt her pulse increase and felt her face getting hot. Lisa was going to see her. In yoga pants. Granted, they were new but still. She looked around the crowd, looking for an escape route. Would Lisa even recognize her from the other night? Celeste guided Olivia in front of her and lowered her head, trying to hide behind her, but she caught Lisa's eye and Lisa's face lit up.

"Hi. Thanks for coming." The coach's voice sounded like she was excited to see her, but she didn't give any indication that she recognized her so Celeste tried to hide the tremor in her voice.

"Hello." Celeste said nothing else as she grabbed a copy of the schedule and increased her pace to catch up to Olivia. *Whew. Dodged that bullet.*

❖

"That's her. That's the chick I was telling you about, the one I saw at the party." Lisa nudged Athena sharply in the ribs. She thought she'd caught a glimpse of her when she was talking to the class, but she was standing behind an older man, and she couldn't be sure it was her. Lisa was starting her second year on campus, and she'd never seen her before the faculty mixer more than a week ago. Now she'd seen her twice. Even though the woman had been in workout clothes this morning, Lisa thought she looked just as beautiful and sexy as she did dressed up at the mixer.

"Lisa, she is no chick. She is one hundred percent woman. She's too much for you."

"Eff off, Chang," Lisa said with a smile so Athena would know she was just joking.

"And you were right. She does look a lot like that actress. Do you know anything about her?"

Lisa shook her head.

"You want me to find out?"

Lisa laughed. "We're not in elementary school. I'm quite capable of talking to a woman and asking her questions if I'm interested in knowing something. But I already told you, I'm not interested. I need to focus on this season and our team."

"There's no reason why you couldn't socialize with her just because you don't want to date. Maybe the three of us could go get a beer or something at the pub down the street."

"Athena, you think she looks like a woman who would frequent a dive pub and drink a beer? I see her more of a wine bar type of woman who would eat fancy little appetizers. She's definitely not a wings and beer woman like we are. We're hot dogs and French fries and she's champagne and caviar." They walked out the door and to the group waiting near the fountain. "We'll talk about this later." Which meant Lisa hoped Athena would forget about it or just drop the subject. She knew better though. Athena was like a dog with a bone when she thought something was a good idea.

Lisa called the group around and gave them instructions to walk around the square block, then follow the path through campus. She encouraged the group to try to raise their heart rate during the walk and maybe work up a bit of sweat.

Lisa didn't have much of an opportunity to appreciate the beauty of the campus or the history. She was usually in her office or the gym area. The college was formed in the late 1800s and moved to its current location in 1914. Memorial Hall was the oldest building standing on campus and was full of history. Lisa loved learning the history of every school she played or coached at. She'd had to admit that of all the universities she'd been affiliated with, Glassell University charmed her the most. Even though it was a small school, some famous people had walked through its hallowed halls—activists, Holocaust survivors, actors, musicians. Lisa was honored to be a part of the university.

But she wanted more. More notoriety, more prestige, more money. She had her eye on the prize and she'd work hard to get there. The better the record she could get at GU, the better the opportunity she'd have to coach at a larger university.

"Okay, people. I'll lead the walk and Coach Chang will be in the back. If you have any questions or concerns just raise your hand and one of us will help."

Lisa started walking, and an older gentleman, a professor in the history department, moved to Lisa's side and started asking her questions about the team, and where she'd coached before. He expressed interest in coming out to support the team, and it touched her. The team had decent attendance the previous season for their home games, but Lisa encouraged them to invite their friends and professors. She made it a point to introduce herself to the shop owners in Old Town, a charming area near the campus that provided an array of stores, coffee houses, and restaurants. It didn't take long for some of the townspeople to recognize her and ask how she was.

It helped that Lisa and Athena lived within walking distance of Old Town and the school. They would often eat dinner out or grab a beer at the pub. The nights at the pub were the ones she enjoyed the most. She and Athena would sit at the bar with some of the regulars and talk sports. She even got some of the old timers' interest piqued in women's basketball. She bribed them by telling them if they made it to one of her games, she'd buy them all a round after the game. Who didn't want free beer?

Lisa looked back and caught Athena's thumbs-up to let her know everything was good and there hadn't been any problems. They made their way along the cement walkway that was surrounded by grassy knolls and tall lecture halls. There were a couple of water features and multiple sculptures scattered throughout campus. Since it was early morning, there weren't many students milling about just yet, and the smell of wet grass that was watered overnight was turning into a warm soil smell. The small Southern California town would continue to have high temperatures until mid-October, and it was already starting to warm up. She waved at a couple of maintenance workers who were raising the flags of the different countries represented by the student population.

The walk was over all too quickly, but Lisa enjoyed getting to know a few of the professors and students. One of the professors who'd been at the school for over thirty years gave her a history lesson of some of the buildings so not only did she get people exercising but she also learned more about the campus.

"That's a wrap, people. Thank you for getting up so early and taking a walk with me. I hope you'll return next week. Coach Mulligan from the men's tennis team will be in charge of the next workout. I hope you'll spread the word and get more of your friends to join us. Have a great week."

Everybody waved and went off in different directions. Lisa felt a little deflated when the stunning woman didn't even give Lisa a second glance. Nothing she could do about it now. Lisa and Athena gave each other a high-five and headed back to their shared office to get ready for their conditioning session with the team later that afternoon.

CHAPTER FOUR

The squeaking and squealing of the rubber soles on the hardwood floor echoed throughout the gym. The slap of the ball on skin when a player caught a pass, another player cut to the basket, saying she was open, and the thud of the ball hitting the bleachers as it was knocked out of bounds. The pass was too late. The shrill of the whistle brought everything and everyone to a halt.

"Brooks! You have to anticipate that cut. Evans could have had an easy layup, but because you were late getting the pass to her, we gave up two points."

"Sorry, Coach."

"Run it again."

The door to the gym opened and the team's starting point guard, and league's assist leader, jogged onto the court, tucking her jersey into her shorts. Lisa looked at her watch and blew her whistle again.

"Everybody on the baseline."

"Coach, I'm sorry I'm late, but I was waiting to talk to my professor."

"You know the rules, Logan. If anyone is late, the whole team runs. On the baseline."

The groans coming from the players irritated Lisa, but she understood. She did the same thing when she was a player, but she'd been in a foul mood from the time she woke up and she was just feeling a little off. "Down to the end of the court and back under fifteen seconds. Anyone over, the team runs again." The pounding of feet on the floor was almost in sync, and it made an awesome thundering sound like a herd of elephants running through the African plains. She didn't want to take too much time from practice, but it was important that she upheld the rules, even if it was for a good reason. She didn't want to give her team an inch for fear of them trying to take a mile. She blew her whistle and the ladies took off. When they reached the far end of the court, Athena yelled for them to hustle. The last player crossed the baseline and used the wall to stop herself. Lisa looked at her watch. Fourteen seconds. Just made it. The team ran four more down and backs then Lisa gave them a short break to get a sip of water.

"Okay, ladies. Let's resume the play." The five defenders matched up as the starting offense ran through the plays. The familiar sounds of a college basketball practice soothed Lisa's insides as she inhaled the smell of leather, sweat, and wood. The sound of the ball hitting the floor, the swish of the net as the ball dropped through the basket, the yelling of players to guide or congratulate their teammates. The gym was her home. It was her heaven. Even with the stress of recruiting, planning practices, and preparing for games, nothing else came remotely close to fulfilling the satisfaction Lisa got from seeing a play executed perfectly, all the hard work the players and coaches put in to become one team. They won together, they lost together.

Two hours later, Lisa sent her team to the showers and/or training room for treatment. She and Athena walked into their office and hung up their whistles. Athena sat at her desk, already prepping for the next day's practice. She placed her pen down, leaned back in her chair, and crossed her ankle over her knee.

"How do you think practice went?"

Lisa mirrored Athena's sitting posture and added her hands placed behind her head, fingers interlaced. She looked up at the ceiling and let out a deep breath. "Not bad for just the third organized practice of the season. The ladies really started playing well toward the end of the last season and have worked really hard during conditioning the past six weeks. I think we're going to have a pretty good season, especially if we can get everyone's timing down so they play as a cohesive unit. I want them to be able to anticipate what their teammates are going to do. The more they play together, the sooner that will come."

The knock on the door brought their attention to Emily Logan, their star point guard, standing in the doorway. Her brown hair was still wet from her shower, and she was wearing her gray, thick cotton post-practice sweats.

"What's up, Logan?"

Emily stood in the doorway and fiddled with her drawstring from her sweat pants. "I wanted to apologize again for being late, Coach. I'm having some trouble in my English class and I wanted to talk to my professor about it, but there were other students before me and they were taking too long. I'll try to catch her in her office hours to talk about it, but I just wanted you to know I wasn't goofing off or brushing off practice."

Lisa waved her in and pointed to the chair in front of her desk. She always emphasized an open-door policy with her players and would do anything she could to help them if they were having any kind of trouble. Sometimes it had to do with a boyfriend or girlfriend, but mostly their troubles came from classes. Lisa's college coach always made academics come first because the odds of becoming a professional player were a long shot so her players needed an education and their degree. Lisa beat those odds by becoming a professional player overseas, but she'd had just enough serious injuries to cut her career short. Because she took her studies seriously when she was going to school, she was able to make a good living as a college coach.

"What are you having trouble with?"

"Everything, Coach. I just can't seem to do anything right. I've failed a couple of quizzes, and my paper I just turned in got red-inked. I get what she's lecturing on, but when it comes to the assignments, I'm not understanding the questions, or I think I'm answering them correctly but they turn out to be wrong. She's a tough professor, but I shouldn't be doing this bad. I'm putting in my time to study so I don't get it."

"How are your other classes going? You having trouble with them too?"

"Nah. I'm doing okay. At least I'm passing them all."

"All right, Logan. I'll see what I can do to get you some help. Keep working hard in class and it will all work out, okay?"

"'K. Thanks, Coach."

"One more thing, Logan. As captain of this team, your teammates are looking to you as their leader, which means you have to set a good example, including getting to practice on time, or even early, and being ready to play. Do you understand?"

"Yes, Coach. It won't happen again."

"All right then. Have a good night and we'll see you tomorrow."

Once Emily left, Lisa asked Athena to pull up Emily's class schedule. Her English class had been scheduled right before practice started, and her professor's name was Celeste Bouchard.

"I need you to start practice without me tomorrow, Athena. I need to go talk to Professor Bouchard."

Celeste walked into her empty classroom ten minutes before class was set to start. The silence was blissful, and she knew it would be short-lived. Her students in her Critical Thinking class would begin filtering in—some talking, others thumbing the keyboard on their smartphone to get in one last text before class started. Today's students were a lot different from when she did her undergraduate studies. They all looked so...*young.* Hardly any of her students took notes with a pen and paper. They were all done on voice recorders or small laptops. They seemed to be more preoccupied as well. Of course, there were a lot more electronics available now. Celeste never had to worry about texting or social media or cyber bullying or cyber anything. Computers were barely a thing when she went to college. She didn't have her own. She had to go to the computer lab with her floppy disc and do her assignments with thirty other people in the lab. Or it would be done on a typewriter. Did they even make those anymore? She was pretty sure they were probably in one of the Smithsonian museums. She chuckled to herself as she woke her computer and loaded up her PowerPoint for that day's lesson.

This was her only lower level class, and it was made up primarily of eighteen- and nineteen-year-olds. Rowdy eighteen- and nineteen-year-olds. She wasn't sure if it was the excitement of being on their own or the responsibility resting on their young shoulders, but every manner their parents had probably taught them stayed outside that door once they walked through. They weren't even a third of the way through the semester and she already knew who the troublemakers were. She stood behind the podium in the corner and watched her students arrive. She looked at the clock, and at one, she began.

"Ladies and gentlemen, please put your phones on silent and put them away. We have a lot of material to cover today before you take your quiz. Before you leave class, make sure you turn in the one-page summary of the film we watched last week. Does anyone have any questions? I want to remind you that your final paper is due the week before your finals, and it's worth forty percent of your grade. It needs to be between twenty and thirty pages, and it can be on any subject you like, but it needs to be well thought out and have correct punctuation."

Celeste began her lecture from behind the podium, but it didn't take her long to start making her way through the aisles and rows of desks. She stopped occasionally next to a student to make sure they were taking notes and not just doodling. One of the things she loved most about teaching at a smaller university was the smaller class size. She was able to learn the students' names instead of just seeing them as numbers. It was all more personal, and she felt she could connect with her students better. It was also more conducive to having the students interact in class.

She noticed one of her student-athletes furiously writing in her notebook. One of the few she'd seen actually *write.* The young lady, Emily Logan Celeste believed to be her name, always showed up to class in her team-appointed practice gear, her hair up in a ponytail, and her duffel bag intruding on the aisle next to her desk. Judging by the grades she'd received so far, she appeared to be a subpar student. She was probably using college as a way to continue playing her sport. She wouldn't be the first and most likely wouldn't be the last. It was difficult for Celeste to drum up any kind of sympathy for the student-athletes who thought just because they played a sport that their professors would automatically give them a passing grade. *I saw that too many times at my previous university. I just want them to get something out of my class, something that might benefit them later in life.*

Celeste nudged Emily's gym bag with the pointy toe of her black pumps, and Celeste felt a little thrill at the chagrined look on Emily's face as she bent down and moved it completely under her desk. Participating in class was something Celeste had always felt was important for the student's learning and grasping the subject of discussion. So important, in fact, that it went toward part of the grade, but Emily never raised her hand, and Celeste never put her on the spot. If a student wasn't going to put forth the effort, why should she?

Once class ended, a handful of students congregated around her wanting to discuss something or another. She saw Emily standing behind the group, but after a few minutes, she hiked her gym bag over her shoulder and left the room. Celeste had wondered what Emily had wanted to talk to her about. It must not have been that important since she didn't stay. Emily hadn't taken advantage of Celeste's office hours either. Truthfully, not many students did. They'd bombard her after class rather than see her in her office. Celeste didn't mind though. As long as she didn't have another pressing commitment or another class didn't need the room, she would stay as long as there were students who needed help. She appreciated students who wanted to do well.

Twenty minutes later, she walked across the campus quad, passing by the library and gymnasium, until she reached the building that held her office. Her Critical Thinking class was the only one of hers that wasn't in that building so it wasn't much of an inconvenience, and she enjoyed being able to get out of the building and enjoy the fresh air. She occasionally saw friends walking and talking animatedly, a boyfriend and girlfriend holding hands on their way to a class, and in the beautiful Southern California sunshine, there were always more than a few students doing their homework while sitting under a tree or near a fountain. She unlocked her door and turned on the lights before she sat at her desk to start grading the quizzes.

CHAPTER FIVE

Celeste looked up in time to see a dark figure on the other side of the tempered glass of her office door. She told the figure to come in after they tapped on the glass. She gasped when Coach Tobias opened the door. The look of surprise on the coach's face quickly turned to one of pleasure, which gave Celeste a tiny flutter to see the handsome coach standing in *her* doorway.

"Professor Bouchard?"

"Yes, Coach Tobias, how may I help you?"

Lisa stood in the doorway, leaning against the frame with a look of delight on her face and her hands in the pockets of her sweatpants. Lord, she was a good-looking woman. She was tall with a trim, athletic build that was evident despite being dressed in sweats. And if she recalled correctly, Lisa wore a more fitted outfit the night of the mixer. Initial lust flickered in the pit of her belly being in such close proximity to Lisa. Celeste quickly tamped down those feelings and assumed her professional demeanor.

Lisa stepped into the office and extended her hand across the desk to shake Celeste's. "I'm so glad to finally know your name. I saw you at the faculty mixer and again at the exercise class, but I didn't get a chance to actually meet you."

"Yes, I had to run both times, but I enjoyed the class. I think that was a great idea you had to get the students and faculty involved in learning how to take care of themselves through nutrition and exercise."

"Thank you. It's so easy to get caught up in eating late night pizza while studying. At least that's how it was for me when I was in college. I was fortunate enough to have basketball to keep my weight steady, but not everyone has that desire to exercise and it's easy to gain weight."

Celeste recalled her own struggles all her life with her weight. She had been the one Lisa spoke of—late night snacking, eating the rich foods her French father would prepare, being sedentary. It wasn't until in her late thirties that Celeste had a health scare that got her on track to leading a healthier lifestyle. Even though she was still considered overweight, she was healthy, and that was important to her.

"I'm sorry. I'm going on and on."

"No, that's quite all right. What can I do for you, Coach?"

Lisa smiled and Celeste thought she saw a slight dimple form.

"Please, call me Lisa. I have a player in one of your classes and she's informed me her grade isn't good. She's my starting point guard, and a lot of our team's success depends on her leading our team. I have a team rule that if any of our players gets a failing grade in any class, she's suspended from the team until she can raise her grade point average. You see why I came to you for help."

Celeste could feel the heat rising in her body, and it wasn't from the deep timbre in Lisa's voice. She clenched her fists. Same story, different school. "Yes, I think I do, Coach Tobias. And you can forget it. Every student in my class gets the grade they earn. I don't care if she's the daughter of the president, I'm not going to raise a grade just so your team can be successful."

"Celeste—"

"Professor Bouchard."

"Fine, *Professor.* That's not what I was asking." Lisa stood up in a hurry and leaned over Celeste's desk, less than a foot away from her own face, and Celeste was tempted to lean back in her chair, but she wouldn't give the coach the satisfaction of letting her think she was intimidated.

Celeste clenched her jaw again, as did Lisa, and she felt her facial muscles tense. She was about to tell Lisa that she knew the game and she would never be a willing participant.

"I would never ask for a grade my player didn't earn. I wanted to know if you had anyone you could recommend to help tutor Emily. But forget it. I can see you're not willing to help. Obviously, this has happened to you before, but that's not how I run my team. I'll find someone to help Emily myself and I'll make sure she does better in your class. Good-bye, Professor."

Celeste startled when the door slammed behind Coach Tobias. *Well, that was rude. How dare she raise her voice to me in my office then slam the door.* She smoothed her hands down her silk blouse then over her hair. She stood, mostly because she didn't know what else to do. She had half a mind to go after her and give her a piece of her mind, but she was still in a bit of shock from Lisa's reaction. She went to the window where she saw Lisa walking quickly across the quad, presumably toward the gym. Lisa looked tight as a bow, striding with a purpose. And damn it. There were those lustful stirrings again. She stared out the window until Lisa was out of sight, then sat back down. She tapped her fingers on her desk as she was deep in thought. Maybe she did jump the gun and accuse the coach of being like all the others who'd asked her to change a player's grade so they could play. Ms. Logan did attend every class and she'd never been tardy. Maybe she was trying and just not getting it. Celeste let out a deep breath, then looked up Emily Logan's school email address and sent her a note.

❖

"Goddamn, that woman is infuriating!" Lisa entered her office and Athena stopped typing on her keyboard.

"You're back already? I figured you'd still be talking to Logan's English professor. I was just about to head to the gym."

"I went to talk to her and she accused me of wanting her to give Logan an unearned grade. She has no idea how important it is to me that my girls are more successful in the classroom than on the court. Hell, these kids aren't going to play at the professional level. Even if one did, she wouldn't get paid enough, not like the men. Our kids need to get their degree. I promised their parents that I would look after them. They need to get what the professors are trying to teach them. I'm so pissed right now, I can't even see straight."

Athena placed her whistle around her neck and grabbed the list of drills the team was going to do in practice. "I want to hear all about it, Ice. But I need to get to the gym and you need to cool down before you come to practice, otherwise you'll take out your frustrations on the team. Take some deep breaths, do a quick meditation, then come in when you're ready."

"Thanks, Athena. I'll be there soon."

Lisa paced the small space of her office while mumbling under her breath. Thankfully, Athena had shut the door so nobody else in the athletic department would witness Lisa's rambling. Just who in the hell did Celeste Bouchard think she was? Lisa had always been honest, always, always played by the rules, and never looked for shortcuts. She worked hard on the court and even harder in the classroom when she was a student, and that was what she demanded from her team. All she wanted was someone who could help her point guard understand and perform better in her English class.

Lisa took a few more deep breaths before grabbing her whistle and heading to the gym. When she walked in, the team was lying on the floor at midcourt in a circle and they were meditating. This was a practice Athena thought was important for the team so they could empty their minds of school, boyfriends and girlfriends, family, and all the other crap that might prevent them from being one hundred percent solely focused on practice. For the next two hours, the girls belonged to Lisa and Athena, and they would be getting ready for their home opener that coming weekend.

Athena gave Lisa a nod, indicating that their meditation session could come to an end.

"Okay, ladies, let's run through our offense." Lisa called out the probable starting five and the defense. "Logan, take it to the right." Lisa and Athena stood off to the side, analyzing every movement, every screen set, and had the team run it over and over until they were satisfied.

"Great job, ladies. Grab some water. Logan, I need to have a word." Athena walked away as Emily jogged over to Lisa. "I went to speak to your English professor today."

"I know, Coach. She emailed me right before practice and told me to come see her tomorrow during her office hours. She's going to work with me to figure out why I'm having such a hard time in her class."

Lisa was speechless but didn't want to let Logan in on her surprise.

"Well, that's good. Keep me up to date on your progress or if you need further help."

"I will, Coach. Thanks for going to bat for me."

"Every time, Logan. I made a promise to you and your parents that I'd look out for you."

Emily joined her teammates on the baseline to wait for Lisa to call out the next drill. Lisa felt a little satisfaction and a little relief that Celeste Bouchard reached out to Logan to help her. Maybe she wasn't so bad after all, but the jury was still out on that.

CHAPTER SIX

Celeste had been looking forward to this all week. She sat on the hardwood floor in her black Lycra shorts, strapping up her high-heeled platform shoes. When she had first started pole dancing a few years ago, she had been self-conscious about her body and did her best to hide it under baggy clothes. That made it even harder to pole dance. Since taking the classes, she'd become more comfortable with her body and she'd been able to embrace her sensuality. Celeste had never been crazy about exercising, but she had tried it when she worked at her previous university, and she loved it. The pole dancing had become not only her exercise but also a way of clearing her mind. When she moved to her new town, she found a new studio and talked Olivia into going with her. They'd been going to their Thursday night class almost every week, and Celeste had a pole installed in her home so she could work out anytime she wanted.

Olivia came rushing into the gym and dropped her gym bag on the floor before stripping out of her sweats. She wore an outfit similar to Celeste's and similar shoes, just in a different color.

"Sorry I'm late, but I had to meet with a student after class."

"No problem. I got here just a few minutes before you. Are we still on for the juice bar after class?"

"Absolutely, if by juice bar you meant having a glass of wine."

Celeste laughed. "Was your day that bad?"

"No, I'm just kidding. We're not dressed for a place like that anyways. Maybe we could hit up a wine bar this weekend though. But yes, we can get a smoothie."

The instructor started the music, getting the students' attention, and she started with her choreography. By the time class ended, Celeste was sweating but felt energized and strong. When she had first started taking the class, she wasn't even strong enough to work with the pole. She just learned the moves and practiced on the floor and against the wall. The first time she used the pole, she fell on her ass, but she got right back up and tried it again with the encouragement of her classmates. Because she stuck with it, she improved her flexibility and strength, and best of all, she formed close, lasting friendships with women she never would have met.

Celeste and Olivia said good-bye to the class and walked down the sidewalk to the Jamba Juice and ordered strawberry-banana smoothies with a protein shot. This was Celeste's weekly Thursday night dinner whether she bought it or made one at home. She was never hungry after working out, but she had to refuel her body somehow.

They sat at a table after they received their drinks. Celeste played with her straw for a moment. "So, I had a visit from Coach Tobias on Tuesday afternoon."

Olivia scrunched her eyebrows together. "Coach Tobias?"

"Yeah, the one who did our first fitness class. The walk around the campus. Remember?"

"Oh, yeah. The hottie."

Celeste smirked. "I hadn't noticed." She took a sip through the straw.

"Uh-huh. Anyways, what did she want?"

"She has a player from her team in one of my classes and the student isn't doing too well. She apparently wanted to know if I knew of a tutor that could help her."

"Apparently?"

"Yes, well, I misunderstood. I thought she was asking me to raise the student's grade."

"Tell me you didn't accuse her of asking you to cheat."

Celeste winced. She knew she'd been in the wrong, and she really needed to contact Coach Tobias to apologize. "I may have."

"Celeste! What on earth were you thinking? That's a serious accusation you made."

"I know. I know. Look, this happened to me a few times at the last university I worked. You know that sort of thing happens."

"Not at our school, it doesn't. These kids aren't going to play professional sports, and they needed at least a 3.5 GPA to get accepted here. These kids are not unintelligent. Most of the students here will graduate."

"I'm just wary when a coach comes to talk to me rather than the student, but I know I made a mistake, and I'll apologize to the coach for jumping to conclusions."

"How did the coach react? I know if it had been me, I would've been really upset."

"Yes, she was angry. She slammed my door when she practically stomped out of my office. I was surprised none of the other professors came to see what was going on."

"You make sure you apologize to the coach, Celeste. The sooner, the better."

The rest of their time together was peaceful and they hugged each other in the parking lot when they said good-bye. During her drive home, Celeste rehearsed what she would say when she called the coach the next day.

❖

Celeste was finishing up with Emily the following morning. They had spent the better part of an hour going over the assignments they'd covered so far, what she'd been doing wrong, and what Celeste had been looking for. What it came down to was the way Celeste had been explaining in class, Emily somehow had a difficult time expressing her thoughts on paper. They had agreed that before Emily turned in an assignment, Celeste would take a look to make sure Emily got the concept. From their short time together, Celeste had an opportunity to get to know her student a little better. She did seem like an intelligent young lady who really did want to learn. They would meet a few more times to make sure Emily was truly getting what Celeste was trying to teach.

"Great job today, Emily. I'm confident that you'll be able to pick your grade up. Forget about your scores thus far and focus on the rest of the semester. And promise me that from now on, if you're having a problem in a class, talk to your professor. We want you to succeed. Do you have an idea for your final paper?"

Emily avoided Celeste's gaze and fiddled with the hem of her shirt. "Yeah, but I'm not sure if I'm ready to write it, you know, Professor?"

"I don't think so, Emily. Can you tell me what you mean?"

Emily's face turned red and tears welled up in her eyes, but she remained quiet.

"Emily, whatever it is, you're safe with me. I won't judge you." She would've judged her probably just a few weeks ago, but now Celeste had gotten to know Emily and she thought she was a good kid.

"I was thinking about writing my paper on what it's like to be a young lesbian growing up in a small town and in a family where that wouldn't be accepted."

Celeste moved from behind her desk and sat in the chair next to Emily. She placed her hand on Emily's shoulder and waited until Emily looked up to say something. "I think that would be a great topic. You never know when the information you have might help somebody else. Would you be writing it from your own personal knowledge?"

Emily looked away again, and this time, the tears fell freely. Emily could only nod.

"Emily, look at me." Celeste waited until Emily's red, puffy eyes met hers. "I'm here for you if you want to talk about anything. You'll always be safe with me. Do your parents know?"

Emily shook her head. "They're very strict in their religious teachings, and I've heard the way they talk about sinners. I'm afraid they'd send me to conversion therapy."

Now her tears were falling harder, and Celeste's heart broke for the young lady who was crying on her shoulder. "We can certainly discuss your fears about that, and they are definitely valid. Are you out here? Does Coach Tobias know?"

Emily shook her head and cried harder. "I don't want to do anything that would disappoint her. I was seeing a girl last year in the spring. She was my first girlfriend, and I was crazy about her. She broke up with me toward the end of the semester last spring and it completely wrecked me. I tanked most of my finals and I barely passed my classes. Then I had to go home for the summer with a broken heart and pretend I was fine so my family wouldn't ask questions."

"That must have been very difficult for you." Celeste handed Emily some tissue and got her a bottle of water from the mini fridge she had in her office. "If you wanted to talk to Coach Tobias about this, I'm sure she'd be very supportive. If you don't, I'm always here for you. Your secret is safe with me, Emily."

"Yes, ma'am. Thank you for helping me."

"Any time. And, Emily, you can call me Celeste."

"No, ma'am, I can't. My father would be very disappointed in me if I called someone in authority by their first name."

That comment took Celeste by surprise, but she tried to keep a straight face and just nodded. She'd wondered what kind of household Emily had grown up in, and Celeste hoped that Emily would confide in her if need be. "By chance, do you know if your coach is in her office?"

Emily's eyes widened like she was going to the firing squad.

"Don't worry, it has nothing to do with you. I owe her an apology from something I misunderstood."

Emily looked confused. "She should be. We have practice at two today, but she's usually in her office all day with Coach Chang going over basketball things."

Celeste smothered a smile. There were times when her students reminded her that even though they were legally adults, some still talked and behaved like teenagers. Emily exited the office and Celeste picked up the phone to call Coach Tobias. She started to dial, then placed the handset back on the receiver. She really should apologize in person.

❖

"There. Right there. Did you see that fake?" Lisa pointed at the television screen where she and Athena were studying game tape of the team they were scheduled to play the next day. She always watched their opponents play so she could get her team prepared in the practice before the game. If her team lost, it would be because the other team was better. It would never be due to lack of preparation.

"Yeah, I see it. We'll have to go over that with Wilson. She loves going for that fake, and we need to get her to stop." Athena wrote it down on her list for practice later that day. The tap on the door made them both turn. Lisa was tempted to tell the visitor to go away, but she decided against that.

"What can I do for you, Professor?"

"I was wondering if I could have a word with you."

Athena stood and pulled her wallet out of her desk. "I'm going to grab a sandwich. You want anything?"

"Yes. My usual, please."

Athena held out her hand. "Hi, I'm Athena Chang."

"Hello, I'm Celeste Bouchard."

Athena nodded as she invited Celeste into their office, then behind Celeste's back, Athena gave Lisa a thumbs-up and mouthed "wow." Lisa gave a subtle shake of her head, indicating to Athena to drop it. Lisa had told Athena the other day that Emily's English professor was the one she'd found so attractive… and so irritating.

"What can I do for you, Professor?"

Celeste took a couple of steps deeper into the office. "I wanted to apologize for our misunderstanding the other day."

"I'm pretty sure it was *your* misunderstanding, Professor. You were the one who thought I was trying to cheat."

Lisa felt a small pinch of satisfaction when Celeste looked down at her feet before meeting Lisa's glare. "You're right. I assumed one thing before I got the facts. That was very wrong of me, and I wanted to apologize in person. I also wanted to let you know I met with Emily a little earlier, and I think we figured out what's happening and how we can fix it."

Lisa gestured to the chair for Celeste to take a seat, and she rolled her chair back behind her desk. She crossed her ankle over her knee and steepled her fingers. She took a moment to observe Celeste, who was dressed in a blouse and skirt. A pencil skirt, Lisa thought they were called. See? She knew a little about fashion. Celeste's dark brown hair fell a few inches below her shoulders in ringlets, and Lisa wondered what it would be like to run her fingers through her hair. Was it as soft and luxurious as it looked? Would it feel like silk between her fingers? What would it feel like brushing across Lisa's chest?

She cleared her throat and prayed her face wasn't turning beet red. "Oh, really? She worried me toward the end of last spring because her grades fell, and I know what a good student she is. Then to see her start off poorly in your class, I really grew concerned."

"I don't want to betray Emily's trust, Coach, but I think she might be having some personal issues. She talked to me about it, but if she comes to you, she's going to need reassurance that she's not disappointing you."

"Disappointing me? Why would she think that?"

"Like I said, Coach, I don't want to betray her, but I'll encourage her to talk to you about it."

Celeste re-crossed her legs and her skirt hiked up just enough to make Lisa's heart rate increase. Man, did someone turn up the heat? She felt she might break out in a sweat at any time. She'd heard what Celeste had said, but she had trouble concentrating on anything except for Celeste's bare, creamy legs that taunted her.

"I'll meet with her a few more times, but I think she's catching on. She gave me permission to keep you informed of her progress if you wanted. She was very concerned about not letting you down."

"I appreciate you taking the time to help her, and I accept your apology."

Lisa saw Celeste looking at the television where she'd paused the video. The faint scent of Celeste's perfume was starting to make its way to Lisa's senses, and it was having a softening effect on her. She felt some of the tension leave her shoulders, and she started to relax.

"Athena and I were just watching a game tape of tomorrow's opponent."

"Oh, I'm sorry I interrupted." Celeste stood and Lisa followed suit.

Lisa extended her hand, and when Celeste's hand met hers, Lisa paid close attention to how it felt in hers. Soft. The skin was soft against her own palm, and it looked dainty and elegant in Lisa's larger hand. Warm. Celeste's hand was warm but not sweaty, unlike Lisa's. Damn sweaty palms.

"I appreciate you coming by, Professor Bouchard. If you're not busy tomorrow, come to our home opener. We play Claremont University at one tomorrow."

"I'll see if I can make it, Coach Tobias. And call me Celeste."

"All right, Celeste, as long as you call me Lisa."

Celeste gave her a small smile. Wait. Did she just quickly check Lisa out? Maybe. Or maybe Lisa just *wanted* Celeste to be checking her out. She left Lisa's office, and Lisa inhaled deeply to get one more whiff of Celeste's perfume. Celeste. Lisa loved the way Celeste's name rolled off her tongue.

Chapter Seven

L isa stood with her arms crossed, closely scrutinizing the opposing team during warm-ups. She and Athena had gone over the game tape numerous times, and her team was prepared to guard the offense, break the full-court press, and make the proper cuts to the basket to hopefully score some easy layups. What Lisa was looking for now was to see who the hot shooter was for the opposing team. The player who was making most of her shots from the outside was who she put her best defensive player on to guard.

The buzzer rang and the players jogged to their respective benches. A recorded rendition of the national anthem played, and Lisa sang the words softly while her right hand rested over her heart. As the daughter of a Marine and cousin of an Army Ranger, the words of the anthem, and what it represented, were important and never failed to choke her up a little. After the song ended, the announcer introduced the lineup for both teams. In Lisa's first year as head coach at Glassell University, it took her a little by surprise when she first heard the introductions. All her adult life, as a player and a coach, she had played mostly in arenas with a state-of-the-art sound system. The sound system at GU sounded like a cheap karaoke machine, and most of the time, she couldn't understand what the announcer was saying. As expensive as it was to attend the university, one would think they could spare some money to do an upgrade. She had mentioned it more than once to the athletic director, who said he'd look into it, and quite frankly, it was embarrassing. Many times, she'd seen the opposing team looking at each other, wondering what the heck was being said.

Lisa's team won the tip-off and immediately scored the first basket. Her team got off to a fast start, and the opposing coach had to quickly call a timeout. Three minutes had gone by and GU was up by eight points. That timeout apparently settled down the opposing team, and they quickly scored three baskets to get within two. Lisa felt it was way too early to start getting nervous, but she wanted to nip this streak in the bud. She quickly changed up the type of defense her team was playing in hopes it would throw the opposing team off. Instead, the opposing team set a perfect screen and their best shooter scored a three. Lisa stomped her foot and yelled to the referee that she wanted a timeout. When her players sat on the bench, she squatted in front of them and started yelling to be heard over the crowd noise.

"You ladies need to start playing with some intensity. You're just standing around while the other team has their way with you and they are scoring easy baskets." She pointed at her players on the bench individually. "If you don't start playing hard, I'll put in other players who will. I want you to run the play, Panther, and after we score, I want you to full-court press." The buzzer sounded and the players ran back out onto the court, ran the play, and scored their first basket in four minutes of play. For the rest of the game, her team played with a greater intensity, and they won by twelve points. Lisa and the rest of the team lined up to congratulate their opponents, and before she walked out of the gym, she looked up into the stands to see Celeste walking up the stairs. Lisa grinned and felt oddly pleased that Celeste came to the game.

❖

Celeste arrived at the game a few minutes late and had trouble deciding where she would sit. This was the first game she had attended at Glassell University, and she was surprised to see the smattering of people in the stands. She'd guessed that there were about two hundred people in attendance, but she thought there would be more. Actually, she didn't really know what to expect. She had never been athletic, never had gone to any games or matches when she was in high school or college, and all she had to go on was what she had seen on television. When she had seen games on TV, the gym always seemed bigger, the bleachers always full. This would definitely be a new experience for her, seeing a live game. She walked down four rows of bleachers and squeezed past a few people, then took a seat on the hardwood plank. It didn't take long to feel the energy from the players and spectators.

It was hard to pay attention to the game when Celeste had difficulty taking her eyes off Coach Tobias. She was dressed similarly to what she had worn to the faculty mixer—black slacks, a cardinal button-down blouse, and black loafers. Her hair was down and she stood with a strong posture, looking like she was about to jump out of her skin. One moment, she had her arms crossed over her chest. The next, she was pointing toward a group of players and yelling something Celeste couldn't understand.

Throughout the game, Celeste had a different picture of who she thought Lisa was. The two interactions she'd had on campus with Lisa had given Celeste the impression that she was pretty laid-back. However, seeing the coach side of Lisa gave Celeste a little flutter deep in her belly. She found it extremely sexy to see the butch coach so riled up and animated. Celeste felt herself get warm and wondered if it was from the activity in the gym or the effects Lisa had on her. She used her program to fan herself but quickly put it down when she noticed nobody else was doing it. She was at the age where she could pass it off as a hot flash, but she didn't want anyone to know about that either.

Celeste managed to turn her focus back to the game and found herself clapping when Emily scored a basket. From that point on, it wasn't too difficult to stay focused on the actual game except for the time when Lisa had called the timeout. Celeste finally got to see Lisa's face when she was talking to her team sitting on the bench. She could see the fire in Lisa's eyes and her eyebrows scrunched when she was emphasizing her point. Celeste felt the heat rise in her own body, and she unscrewed the cap off her water bottle and took a drink to try to cool down. There were so many things about Lisa that turned Celeste on— her intensity was off the charts—but she appeared to be in total control. Her strong jaw looked more angular when she clenched her teeth. The sleeves rolled up to her elbows showed off her muscular forearms. Her slacks showed the definition of Lisa's behind. Her eyes were eagle-eyed sharp. Despite feeling warm, Celeste shivered.

Celeste had to admit that she didn't know all that much about basketball, but she was finding this game, and the coach, extremely exciting. The constant running up and down the court, passes swinging from one side to the other, and the all-out hustle of these ladies was impressive. She had already decided that this would not be her only game she would attend. The added bonus was being able to observe Lisa in a different environment and see a different personality. Lisa didn't look half bad in her baggie basketball sweats, but she was off the charts hot wearing her nice coaching clothes. Oh yes, indeed, she would definitely be attending more games. The final buzzer rang indicating the game had ended, and she spotted Emily waving to her. Celeste waved back and gave her a thumbs-up before walking back up the bleachers to leave the gym. Celeste resisted the urge to turn around for one last look at Lisa because the last thing she needed was an image of Lisa in her mind before she went to sleep. Who was she kidding? She already knew the image of Lisa would be floating in her mind. Damn it.

❖

Once the post-game meeting ended, Lisa dismissed the team so they could shower and get their treatment by their trainer. Lisa and Athena said good-bye to their two volunteer coaches and headed back to their office. Lisa felt really good about this win. There were times when the team got sloppy, but considering it was their first game of the season, she was pleased overall by her team's hustle.

"I think we need to do a few passing drills tomorrow in practice. The girls were getting pretty sloppy at one point with their ball handling. I know it's early in the season, but we need to get that under control."

Athena nodded and wrote it down on her pad of paper. "I think we also need to work on some rebounding. The post players did a good job of blocking out, but our guards need to hit the boards as well."

The audio-video guy brought a copy of the game to their office. Athena thanked him and put the disc in the DVD player. A few minutes into analyzing the game, Athena nudged Lisa's shoulder with her elbow. "So, did you see Professor Bouchard in the stands tonight?"

Lisa feigned surprise. "No. Was she there?"

"You are so full of shit. You saw her and you know it."

Lisa pointed at the screen. "Did you see Watson just standing around when the shot went up? She needs to get more aggressive on the boards."

"I see what you're doing there. I'll let it go for now, but just so you know, this conversation will be revisited."

Ugh, that dog with a bone. Yes, Lisa had definitely seen Celeste in the stands, but she actually felt her there before she even saw her, which was a new sensation for her. Fortunately, Lisa was able to keep Celeste in the far corners of her mind so she could concentrate on the team and the game. She hoped Celeste would come to more of the games, and she felt like a teenage girl when she hoped she'd impressed her with her coaching skills.

By the time they finished watching the first half it was already ten o'clock. "Come on, Lisa, let's finish this up tomorrow. I just want to get in my comfortable clothes and chill out in front of the TV for a while."

Lisa agreed, grabbed her keys out of her desk, and turned out the lights before locking the door. Yes, she'd have plenty of time tomorrow to go over the game. Tonight, she'd think about Celeste sitting in the stands cheering on her team.

CHAPTER EIGHT

Celeste opened the door to her office early Monday morning and turned on her computer. She was going over her lesson plan for that day when she heard a knock on the door. She looked up and was happy to see Olivia standing there with her briefcase in her hand.

"Well, this is a nice surprise. What are you doing here so early?"

Olivia smiled as she walked farther into Celeste's office. "I wanted to catch you before you got too busy. There's something I wanted to run by you." Olivia handed over a piece of paper that looked to be an ad of some kind. Celeste perused the information and looked up at Olivia with wide eyes.

"What's this about?"

"There's a pole dancing showcase in Las Vegas for all skill levels. I thought it would be fun for you to do."

"Me? Why me?"

Olivia sat in the chair in front of Celeste's desk and pointed at the paper that Celeste was still holding. "Because you're so good at it, and it would push your comfort level. Isn't that what you've been wanting to do? Try new things?"

"Well, yes, but I think this might be too much. What if someone sees me?"

"Like who? It's in Vegas, baby."

Celeste laughed at Olivia's childish play. "What happens in Vegas, stays in Vegas?"

"Exactly. Tell you what, if you do it, I'll do it. It will be fun. We can do a girls' weekend."

Celeste took a deep breath and let it out slowly. Before she could change her mind, she agreed. She had promised herself when she turned forty that she was going to push her comfort level and try new things. Now that she was approaching fifty, she could look back and remember that she'd gone zip-lining, skydiving, and learned how to scuba just to name a few out of her comfort zone activities. But performing a pole routine in front of a large number of people was really pushing her boundaries. She felt a little sick to her stomach thinking about it, but also a little thrilled. The thought of choreographing her own routine and performing it in front of people she didn't know gave her a little bit of a tingly feeling throughout her body. The competition was in three weeks, and today was the deadline to sign up.

"Okay, we're going to do this." Celeste went to the competition's website, and as Olivia stood behind her looking over her shoulder, Celeste completed the online registration while her heart was threatening to beat out of her chest.

"Now it's your turn." Celeste stood and allowed Olivia to sit in her chair to complete her own registration. When she was done, Olivia looked at Celeste like a deer caught in headlights, then squealed as she stood, and they hugged while giggling like school girls.

"This is going to be so much fun." Olivia gathered her briefcase and slung the strap over her shoulder. "I'll book us a room at the host hotel and email you the itinerary."

Once Celeste was alone in her office, she sat at her desk with her face in her hands, wondering if she had just completely lost her mind. She shook her head and smiled, thankful she had a friend like Olivia who would go on that ride with her. She was finally going to do a larger showcase, and in a town like Las

Vegas. She wouldn't say it was a dream come true, but it certainly ticked off another box on her bucket list.

Celeste's daydream was interrupted by another knock on her door. She felt nauseous when she saw Jackie standing in her doorway, acting like she was gifting Celeste with her mere presence.

"Hi, beautiful. What's happening?" Jackie stepped inside Celeste's office uninvited and moved closer to her desk. Celeste slid the ad for the showcase into the top drawer before Jackie could see it.

"What do you want, Jackie? I have papers to grade and I don't have time to deal with you."

Jackie placed her hand over her chest like Celeste had hurt her feelings. "Come on, baby. Don't act like that."

"I don't have time for this, Jackie. Why can't you just leave me alone?"

"We belong together, Celeste. Why can't you see that?"

"Why can't you see that I want nothing to do with you? Get out of my office. I'm done trying to be nice."

Jackie's face turned red and Celeste thought steam might come out her ears. There was another knock on the door, and Celeste's further interaction with Jackie was saved by one of her students.

"Professor, is this a bad time?"

"No, Robert. Professor Stone was just leaving."

Jackie quickly transformed her face from angry to professional, and she left the office.

"Come on in, Robert. What can I help you with?"

Celeste was able to slow her heart rate while Robert was talking to her about an assignment. What was it going to take to get Jackie to leave her alone?

Later that afternoon, when she'd dismissed her class, Celeste called Emily up to her desk. She felt bad that Emily looked like she was about to face a firing squad. Celeste smothered a smile because what she had to show Emily would certainly turn that frown upside down.

"Emily, I have something for you." She handed over Emily's last paper she had turned in. Emily's smile could've lit the entire room when she saw the grade at the top of her paper.

"A-minus? That's so awesome. Thanks, Professor."

"No need to thank me. You handed in a well thought out paper that hit all the points. Nice job."

Emily turned to leave but stopped when Celeste called her back over.

"I also wanted to tell you I went to your game the other night, and I was very impressed. You and your team played an exciting game. I have just one question. Why aren't you as outgoing in the classroom as you are on the court?"

Emily scuffed her sneaker on the floor and looked at her feet before lifting her head and meeting Celeste's gaze. "I grew up in a conservative family in a conservative town, and I was never encouraged to be outgoing or speak my mind. It took a lot of work on Coach Tobias's part to get me to step into a leadership role on the team. I'm still not all that comfortable with being outspoken when I think about it, but when I'm playing, I don't have time to think. I just act and react."

Celeste nodded. "I see how speaking up in class or asking for help would be difficult for you then. But, Emily, remember this. Your opinion matters. Your thoughts matter. You matter. What you have to offer might help someone else who might be afraid to speak up. Do you understand what I'm saying?"

"Yes, ma'am. Thank you. I'll keep working on it."

"And what about the other matter we talked about? How are you doing?"

"I'm doing okay. I'm thinking about telling Coach, but I'm so nervous. I don't want to disappoint her."

"I don't think that will happen if you tell her you're a lesbian. If it would help, I can go with you."

"Thanks, Professor. I'll think about that."

"Very well, then. Have a great day and I'll see you next time." Celeste smiled as she watched Emily walk out of her classroom with her head held high and a bounce in her step.

The following day, Celeste was in her office grading exams when she heard a clearing of a throat. She looked up to see Lisa standing in her doorway, looking all kinds of yummy in her khaki shorts and black polo shirt with the GU mascot over the left chest. Her dark hair was pulled back in a ponytail and her sunglasses perched on top of her head. Judging from the smirk on Lisa's face Celeste guessed that Lisa caught her actually cruising her. Lisa had a bit of swagger to her step as she walked toward Celeste. Yep. Lisa caught her. Celeste could feel the heat rise in her cheeks. For goodness sake. She was a sophisticated college professor. Cruising? Really? She just hoped that Lisa didn't call her out on it.

"I hope I'm not interrupting anything."

"No, no. Not at all. Come in, Coach Tobias."

Lisa smiled at Celeste and once again, Celeste felt warm. "I thought I told you to call me Lisa."

Celeste again felt herself blush and quickly wondered why she behaved like a schoolgirl in Lisa's presence.

"Anyways, I wanted to thank you for supporting our team last week. I hope you had a good time and you liked what you saw."

Celeste flashed back to that evening, the intensity of Lisa's actions and how damn good she looked in her slacks. The double entendre didn't go unnoticed. Yes, indeed, she really liked what she saw.

"I was very impressed with what I saw." *Stop flirting with her.* "It was my first live college basketball game, and your team looked really good."

Lisa looked pretty pleased with herself, and Celeste found that extremely sexy.

"Well, I hope you'll come to more games. Also, Logan gave me the good news on the grade she received. I really want to thank you for helping her out. We realize you're busy with your classes and other students, so it means a lot to all of us that you took the time to help her."

Celeste could feel her facial features soften. "It was my pleasure. I want all of my students to succeed, and if I can help, I will."

Lisa sat there staring at Celeste for what felt like forever. It was like Lisa was studying her or was trying to figure her out. Celeste was tempted to break their eye contact until Lisa stood to leave.

"Well, I have to get back to work. Hope to see you at another game. Have a good day." Lisa didn't give Celeste a chance to respond, and Celeste didn't know if she was grateful or perturbed.

Celeste studied Lisa's backside as she let herself out of Celeste's office. She shook her head to disengage her stare, and she returned her attention back to grading her exams.

CHAPTER NINE

Celeste had to up her fitness program. She took two pole classes a week and did her weekly wellness day that the university offered, but she needed a little more in order to firm up her body before the pole competition. She'd decided to swim three mornings a week. The school had a pool that was available to students and faculty when it wasn't being used by the aquatic sports teams. Celeste figured there'd be little chance in running into one of her students if she went first thing in the morning. She'd gone to a sporting goods store the night before and bought a racing suit, goggles, a cap, and a kickboard. When she got home, she tried everything on and stood in front of a full-length mirror. At first, she thought she looked ridiculous, but then she'd remembered what her therapist had told her when she was having negative body image issues. Her therapist told her there was nothing ridiculous about taking care of her body. Everyone had to start somewhere and at least she was doing her best to live a healthy life.

She had turned to the side to see part of her backside in the mirror. She'd had to admit that her behind was looking pretty good from pole. This week's subject for the school's healthy living class was going to be on weightlifting—proper lifting techniques, how to determine weight for one's goals, and orientation on the weight machines. Celeste was excited about that class because she'd never lifted weights in her life, and she struck a pose to see how big her biceps were. Hmm. Not much there. Yet. There was a little bit of muscle from doing her pole classes, but there was nothing wrong with adding a little more.

So, there she was, walking into the locker room near the pool at five forty-five a.m. She opened her duffel bag and donned her swimsuit, cap, and goggles. She grabbed her kickboard and towel before locking up her bag in a locker. She was tempted to wrap the towel around her body for the walk to the pool but figured she probably wouldn't see anyone at that time of morning.

Once she reached the pool deck, she spotted only one person in the pool. She placed her kickboard on the side, sat on the edge, and lowered herself into the tepid water. Initially, Celeste lost her breath, then she took a few shuddering breaths before she acclimated to the water temperature. She grabbed her kickboard and off she went. The other swimmer was in the lane next to hers doing the freestyle stroke, and when she reached the end, she did a flip turn. Celeste had her head above water, goggles on her forehead, and she marveled at how graceful the other swimmer was.

Celeste had completed six laps with the kickboard and was sorely tempted to call it a session. It was just her first time, after all. She sighed, disappointed in her lack of discipline, and decided that she needed to continue to reach her fitness goals she set for herself. She knew she wouldn't reach them in one day, but she also knew she would never reach them if she didn't push herself. She placed the kickboard on the side of the pool and was about to pull her goggles down when the other swimmer came to a stop next to her. Celeste wanted to compliment the other person on their swimming style. The swimmer pulled her goggles off and flashed a look of surprise followed by a wide smile.

"Well, good morning, Celeste. Fancy running into you here."

Was that a jab Lisa made to her regarding her non-athletic looking body? Despite the cool temperature of the pool, Celeste could feel her face get hot. How dare Lisa insult her like that.

"Why? Don't I look like I can swim?" Celeste heard the fire in her words as they escaped her mouth.

Lisa held up her hand. "Whoa. All I meant is that usually I'm the only one here at this time. I didn't mean anything by it." Lisa placed both hands on the edge of the pool and pushed herself out of the water and onto the deck. Celeste was shocked, and if she was being honest, a little turned on by the muscle striations in Lisa's arms, shoulders, and back. Lord, she had a fantastic body.

"Enjoy your swim." Lisa turned and headed toward the locker room, and Celeste was embarrassed when she heard the sarcasm in Lisa's voice. Just great. Celeste owed Lisa another apology. Why did she keep jumping to conclusions when it came to Lisa? And what did it matter what Lisa thought of Celeste? It's not like they were friends or anything. They just happened to work at the same school. Celeste wasn't used to getting compliments from strangers, or they had an agenda like Jackie. Obviously, Celeste still had some work to do on herself, especially when it came to Lisa.

Celeste was tempted to get out of the pool and go apologize, but two things stopped her. First, she really needed to think about what to say to Lisa other than she was sorry, and swimming some laps would allow her to do that. Second, she was more than a little apprehensive to see Lisa in her swimsuit or worse, naked. Up close. By themselves. Nobody else around. Yeah, that would be a very bad idea. The thought of Lisa naked gave Celeste a tingle that developed into a throb. She squeezed her legs together to ease the ache, then she pulled her goggles down and started her laps.

❖

"What is that woman's problem? She's got a serious stick up her ass when it comes to me," Lisa mumbled to herself as she made her way to the locker room. She opened her locker, and removed her shampoo, conditioner, and body wash before she slammed her locker shut and headed to the showers. She turned the water as hot as she could stand it to ward off the chill from the cool air hitting her wet skin. She angrily scrubbed her head and body while continuing to talk to herself about what a miserable woman that Celeste Bouchard was and that she had some real issues that couldn't have anything to do with Lisa. She barely knew her for Christ's sake.

She stood with her face under the water spray and felt her tension finally start to ease away. She turned off the water and toweled herself dry as she walked back to her locker to get dressed and was surprised to see Celeste in the same aisle. She looked up and saw Lisa standing there completely naked. Celeste averted her eyes and looked down. Lisa shook her head and twisted her lock through the combination then pulled her locker door open and threw her towel and swimsuit in a plastic bag. Lisa applied her deodorant, combed her hair, and began applying lotion to her body.

"I didn't know you'd still be here."

Celeste's words didn't get a response from Lisa, who put one foot on the bench Celeste was sitting on and continued to rub the lotion into her leg. She took her time, and out of the corner of her eye, she could see Celeste struggle to not look her way, failing miserably. It gave Lisa a little perverse satisfaction to make Celeste uncomfortable after the way she spoke to Lisa earlier. It was too early in the morning to deal with Celeste's surliness. She was about to switch legs when she heard Celeste's sharp intake of breath and saw her face away from Lisa.

"Would you please put on some clothes?"

"Why? What's the problem? We're both women with the same parts."

Lisa's lack of modesty had a lot to do with growing up in athletics, showering and being naked along with her teammates in the locker room. To her, it was no big deal. But then she realized that Celeste probably didn't grow up that way. Lisa thought Celeste had a beautiful curvy body, but she had it covered with a towel so she figured Celeste was shy. Even though Lisa didn't feel like Celeste deserved it, Lisa decided to give her a break.

"Fine." Lisa pulled her sports bra over her head and her underwear up her legs. She added khaki shorts and a GU team polo. "You can turn around now." Celeste turned and Lisa found her blushed cheeks adorable. Lisa sat on the bench and put on her socks and shoes, then gathered her things out of the locker and closed it. She was about to leave when Celeste said her name.

"I'm sorry."

Lisa tilted her head. "About what?" Lisa wasn't going to make it easier for Celeste.

"For jumping to conclusions earlier in the pool. It was presumptuous of me to think you were insulting me."

"Celeste, I would never insult you, or anyone else for that matter. I'm not sure what's happened in your past to make you so skeptical, but I hope it's something you can overcome." Lisa walked out of the locker room leaving Celeste sitting on the bench, wrapped in a towel and her own arms.

❖

Celeste could feel the tears sting her eyes the moment Lisa walked out the door. Sure, she was angry with herself for speaking to Lisa the way she did, but she was also embarrassed that she got caught looking at Lisa's amazingly sexy naked body. The moment Lisa came back into the locker room with the towel in her hand, Celeste thought her eyes would actually pop out of her head. Lisa's skin was still damp and pink, and it made her own body damp and pink. Well, a particular body part. There was a masculine scent that floated by her. Cedar wood? Sage? Whatever it was, it would always bring up the memory of Lisa standing butt-naked, right next to her, slowly rubbing lotion into her beautiful body. Whew! Celeste fanned herself and blew out a long breath. That memory would lead to many, many fantasies, Celeste was sure. Despite the chill in the air, her body was on fire and it needed extinguishing. She headed to the shower and washed the chlorine off her body and out of her hair. Celeste took her time getting ready, partly because her office hours didn't start for another few hours and partly so she could think about what she'd say to Lisa when she went to apologize.

Once she was dressed and presentable for her day, she went to Lisa's office. Lisa sat at her desk, apparently in deep thought since she didn't acknowledge Celeste standing in the doorway until she cleared her throat. Lisa looked directly at Celeste, then dropped the pen she was fiddling with on the desk with a little bit of force.

"What is it, Celeste? I'm kind of busy here." Lisa sounded tired, maybe a little frustrated or irritated, and Celeste knew she was probably to blame for some, if not all of that. She almost told Lisa that she didn't look busy, but she was there to apologize, not antagonize her more. And she really needed to figure out what it was about Lisa that had her so off balance to the point that she'd been rude.

"May I buy you breakfast?"

"No, I don't think so. But thanks anyway."

Celeste felt like the wind was taken out of her sails, but she tried again. "Please, Lisa. I'd like to apologize to you."

"We don't need to go to breakfast for that. You can say what you came to say right here."

Wow. Lisa was really going to make Celeste work for it. Obviously, she was really upset with Celeste. Okay, if she had to work harder, she would. She stepped farther into Lisa's office and closed the door behind her to give them some privacy. Celeste noted Lisa's office smelled like her, that familiar scent from earlier. Celeste took a deep breath and stood before Lisa's desk.

"I'm sorry."

"Yes, you mentioned that."

Celeste sat uninvited in the chair across from Lisa. "Okay, here it is. I've never been athletic, and as a child, I was really overweight, so I was always picked last and teased for what I looked like and my lack of coordination. I guess I'm still holding on to those insults, and I'm sensitive to things people tell me about how I look or about exercising. I go back in time to the playground in school. I realize now you weren't insulting me, but it's just instinct for me to think you were."

"I wasn't insulting you, Celeste. On the contrary. I was actually impressed that you were at the pool that early. It takes a lot of discipline to get up that early to work out. The only reason I'm up that early is because it's the only free time I have to work out."

That surprised Celeste. She'd thought that Lisa would have plenty of time to spare. She was just a coach, after all. Practices and games were only, what? Two hours?

"Besides, we're mature adults, not children. The adults I know aren't petty and insulting."

Obviously, Lisa hadn't met Jackie Stone. Jackie gave new meaning to immature and vindictive. There was more to Celeste's story, but she didn't know Lisa well enough to give her more. Celeste smoothed her hands down her skirt, which caused Lisa to look in that direction. Lisa bit the inside corner of her mouth before bringing her eyes upward to meet Celeste's. *Hmm. That was interesting.*

"Anyways, thank you for your time, Lisa, and again, I'm sorry."

Lisa stuck her hands in the pockets of her shorts and shrugged. "Thanks for the talk. And for what it's worth, I think you look great."

Celeste couldn't help but cruise Lisa from head to toe, admiring every inch of her. As she made her way back out the door, she added a little extra sway in her hips, hoping Lisa enjoyed the view.

❖

Athena walked into the office and Lisa didn't even notice her. It wasn't until Athena shut her desk drawer a little too loudly that Lisa finally looked up from her computer screen.

"Oh, hey. When did you get here?"

"Just now. What are you doing?"

Lisa quickly minimized the screen she'd been looking at for the past hour, since Celeste had sauntered out of her office, leaving Lisa a little mesmerized. Getting involved with anyone was not on her current to-do list, but Lisa wanted to know more about Celeste. The screen that was currently on display had the travel itinerary for a basketball tournament in Las Vegas that they'd be participating in in a couple of weeks. The screen she'd minimized was a Google search of Celeste. It mostly contained her academic life and LinkedIn page. Lisa had read everything she could find on Celeste. She was impressed by the student reviews she'd been given. All four and five stars. There were many comments talking about how fair she was with grading, that she could make the most boring subject interesting, and how available she was to her students. Lisa could see that given how helpful she'd been with Emily.

Lisa clicked on images of Celeste at school events, standing in front of the whiteboard in a classroom, and her faculty picture. One picture in particular caught Lisa's attention. Celeste was in a black dress, her dark hair in an updo, and wearing subtle makeup, and she was on the arm of a butch woman wearing a black tux. They were both smiling, but the butch's eyes weren't kind like Celeste's. In fact, they looked downright sinister. She looked familiar to Lisa, but she couldn't place her and there wasn't a name associated with the photo. She had an irrational need to punch that butch in the throat and wipe the smirk off her face that made her look like she owned Celeste and anyone who was interested in her could just fuck off. Lisa had never been a jealous person, but that woman made Lisa clench her teeth.

Lisa clicked on one picture that showed Celeste's entire body that eased the hardness in her stomach from seeing Celeste with that other woman. This particular photo caused a hardening in a different body part below her stomach. Lisa wasn't exactly sure what it was about Celeste that drove her crazy in more ways than she could mention. One moment, she wanted to strangle her. The next, she wanted to give up, and the next, she wanted to pin her up against the wall and kiss her breathless. If Lisa was able to help Celeste peel back the layers that made her so judgmental, she was sure it would be the pin her against the wall scenario that Lisa would go with.

"Lisa?"

"What? Oh. I was just checking our itinerary for the Vegas tournament."

"I can't wait. That's going to be so much fun. I haven't been to Vegas in forever."

"Athena, we're going there for basketball, not to party."

"Come on, Ice. I know that. Basketball is fun, but when we're not playing or having a team function, we can go have a little different type of fun."

"We'll see how it goes, but I really want us to make a good showing."

"So you can get a job offer at a Division I school?"

Lisa sighed and removed her reading glasses she wore whenever she had to look at the computer or game tapes for a prolonged period of time. "Athena, I would love to go back to Division I, but my primary responsibility is to our team and Glassell University. I don't appreciate you insinuating otherwise."

Athena plopped down in her chair. "You're right. I'm sorry, Lisa."

"It's okay, but you and I have been friends over half our lives and I've never been selfish when it comes to basketball."

"I know. Again, I'm sorry."

Lisa nodded, indicating that the conversation was over. They'd already had this conversation, and she didn't feel the need to rehash it. Especially since it made Athena shut down and get quiet—the complete opposite of her normal demeanor.

"So, since we're only a four-and-a-half-hour drive from Vegas, we'll take three of the school's vans. We'll stay at a hotel casino near the arena where we'll be playing." Lisa told Athena what schools would be there and who they were scheduled to play. It was going to be a good test to see how well the team would do during the season. They would be playing schools they'd never played before. But first, they had four more non-conference games to play before the tournament. They'd won their first two games, but the team looked sloppy in those wins. Lisa had planned on the team working on making better passes and blocking out for rebounds in that afternoon's practice.

Later in the day, Lisa and Athena met their two volunteer assistant coaches before practice. They were an integral part in helping Lisa and Athena see things they might not be paying attention to because their focus was elsewhere. They also kept statistics during the game which helped Lisa know which one of her players was in foul trouble or which opposing player needed tougher defense.

"Hey, guys. There are a few things we need to work on today. Chris, I want you to hit the boards hard. We're going to work on boxing out. And, Joe, I'm going to have you try to steal passes during a passing drill. The girls will run sprints if they continue to be sloppy."

Lisa and Athena had gone through that when they were players, having to run as punishment. It might seem barbaric to people who didn't play sports, but honestly, there was no greater motivator. It was an age-old ploy that would continue for generations to come.

"All right. Let's get this party started."

The coaches walked into the gym to find their players shooting around. Athena gathered them in a circle at midcourt and led them through their five-minute meditation practice then through their warm-ups.

Lisa split the team into offense and defense to run through a few of their plays. A moment later, she blew her whistle. "Mac, you have to run your player into the screen so you can get free for your shot. Run it again." They ran the play, and again, the defender got through the screen. Lisa blew her whistle to stop playing again. "Mac! Was I not speaking English? What part of having to run your player into the screen did you not understand?" A few of the players giggled, but Lisa shut them down with a glare. "Run it again and stop being sloppy." The third time was the charm as Mac did what Lisa told her. She got free and made her jump shot, which brought cheers from the players on the sideline. Lisa threw her arms in the air. "Well, will you look at that. It actually worked." Lisa grabbed Mac by the shoulders and playfully shook her.

Mac laughed and exaggerated her shake. "Got it, Coach."

"Run it again." Lisa blew her whistle and the players continued to run through the three offensive plays they used against different defenses. Right before practice was over, Lisa called the players and coaches into a circle, and everyone threw their arms over the shoulders of the person next to them.

"Decent practice tonight, ladies. We looked a little lazy at times and we need to work on that. Remember, however you play in practice is how you'll play in the games. It's important to stay focused and keep your head in the game even during practices. Does anyone have any comments or questions?" When everyone remained quiet, Lisa continued. "Okay, the vans leave tomorrow at four p.m. so I want you all here no later than three fifty p.m. See you tomorrow."

Once the players were gone and they had the equipment put away, Lisa grabbed her wallet out of her desk drawer. "I'm going to grab a bite to eat at the café. You want to come?"

Athena shook her head. "I brought some food. I have a few calls to make before we start watching film."

"Right. See you in about an hour then."

Lisa stood waiting for her grilled chicken sandwich to be made. The campus café served some pretty good food. She glanced around the room and saw Celeste sitting by herself, eating a salad and checking her phone. Lisa contemplated pretending not to see Celeste and grab her food to go, but she decided to be a mature adult and say hi. She dressed her sandwich and carried the tray over to Celeste's table. She stood there for a few seconds before Celeste finally looked up and startled.

Lisa fought back a small laugh. "Hi. Am I interrupting?" For a moment, Lisa felt like a schoolgirl trying to get a seat at the lunch table next to the head cheerleader.

Celeste put her phone to sleep. "No, not at all. Would you like to have a seat?"

"Yes, thank you." Lisa put her food and drink on the table, returned the tray, and sat down. She eyed Celeste's salad that included a lot of different vegetables, sliced hardboiled egg, legumes, and grilled chicken. "Wow, that salad looks fantastic."

Celeste looked it over as if studying the contents. "Yes, they have a wonderful salad bar here."

Lisa watched Celeste spear some lettuce and a mushroom then dip it in a paper container filled with dressing before putting it in her mouth. Lisa had never seen that done before. "Can I ask you a question?"

"I don't know. Can you?" Celeste smirked then winked at Lisa, letting her know she was teasing.

"Damn English professors," Lisa muttered under her breath.

Celeste laughed and placed her hand on top of Lisa's, causing a pleasant fluttering deep in her belly. "I'm just kidding."

"*May* I ask you a question?" Lisa smiled good-naturedly. "Why dip your salad into the dressing? Wouldn't it be faster just to pour it on?"

Celeste removed her hand and Lisa felt the loss immediately. "It's a trick I learned in Weight Watchers. I just want the flavor from the dressing, but too much of it is pretty high in calories and fat."

"Wow. I had no idea. I thought salad was healthy."

"Technically, it is, but the dressing can make it fattening."

They took a couple of bites of their food then continued their conversation.

"Are you done for the day or are you teaching tonight?"

Celeste wiped her mouth. "I have a class tonight from seven to ten. A creative writing class. How about you? Did you have practice already?"

"Yeah, we finished about a half hour ago. I'm just grabbing some dinner and fresh air before Athena and I go over game film tonight."

"Game film?"

Celeste looked genuinely interested although Lisa found it incredibly boring. Maybe because she'd been doing it for more than half her adult life. It was a necessary evil though if she wanted to know what the other team was going to do. "We send someone to film a game of our next opponent so we can see their plays, how they play defense, that sort of thing to help us prepare for a game against them. We've already gone over it in practice, but Athena and I like to go through it one more time the night before the game to make sure we haven't forgotten anything."

Celeste scrunched her eyebrows together, and Lisa thought she'd lost her. "Isn't that cheating?"

Lisa laughed. "Not really. All the teams do it. We're just preparing to see how they play."

"Are you playing here tomorrow night? I'd like to go."

"No, we're playing on the road. I can email you a copy of our schedule though if you'd like."

"I would like, thank you. I really enjoyed it the last time I went."

"Okay then." Lisa sat back and studied Celeste. Celeste looked back at her, the connection between them electrifying and undeniable, and it took a power Lisa didn't know she had to break that force. Lisa cleared her throat. "So, how's Logan doing in your class?"

Celeste had an amused look on her face. "Logan?"

"Sorry, habit. I usually call my players by their last name or by a nickname. They know I'm upset with them when I call them by their first name."

"Like when your mom calls you by your full name?"

Lisa laughed. "Exactly. Let's try this again. How is Emily doing in your class?"

"Much better. She seems to be getting the hang of the assignments, and she's getting better at coming to me if she has a question."

"Good. I probably shouldn't tell you this, but she told me in the beginning of the semester that she was afraid of you."

"Afraid of me?" Celeste put her hand on her chest and was clearly surprised. "Why would she be afraid of me?"

"She thought you didn't like her, that that was why she was getting bad grades."

Celeste would never admit that she'd never had a soft spot for collegiate athletes, especially now that she'd gotten to know Emily and some of the other athletes in her classes. Just because she'd had a few bad experiences at her last job didn't mean all student athletes were like that. She was ashamed at how she initially acted, that she never took the opportunity to get to know them, but she was proud of herself for overcoming that.

"I'll admit that I didn't know her, but now I'm learning more and I think she's a nice young lady. We've had a couple of really nice talks outside of class. She's a great kid. Hard worker too."

"Yes, on and off the court. What other classes do you teach besides Creative Writing?"

"Well, I teach upper level Creative Writing. I also teach Critical Thinking that Emily is taking, and the other class is Techniques and Writing Fiction, which is also upper-level."

Lisa waved her hand. "Oh, you're not busy then."

Celeste laughed. "No, not at all. I have so much free time I don't know what to do with myself." Celeste's words were dripping with sarcasm. "What about you? Do you teach any classes?"

Lisa took a drink from her water bottle then replaced the cap. "I do. I teach women's self-defense."

Celeste raised her left eyebrow, impressed with Lisa's answer. She thought if Lisa taught anything, it would be a basketball class. The fact that she taught self-defense for the women at the university in an effort to keep them safe was commendable and she said as much to Lisa.

"I took self-defense when I was in college, and I've been fortunate to not have had to use it, but that doesn't mean I shouldn't know. There are probably at least half a dozen guys on campus who probably feel entitled to help themselves to a woman if he buys her dinner or takes her on a date. If that's not what the woman wants, I try to teach them how to defend themselves and get away so she can call campus safety or the police."

"And then you started up the healthy classes too."

"Yes, well, I only have to do that about once every four to six weeks, depending on what's going on."

"Yes, but you're the one who organized it and got volunteers to run a class once a week. I'm just very impressed that you've brought so much good to our tiny school."

Lisa laughed and Celeste had decided that it was a very thrilling sound and Lisa looked sexy when she was laughing or smiling. Celeste wouldn't mind seeing more of that. Yet, Celeste wondered why Lisa had laughed.

"It's only because I never expected to be at a 'tiny school.'" Lisa used her fingers to air quote. "When I went to college, it was a large university, and my whole coaching career has been at large universities, so being here at GU is my first time being involved with a smaller school. I'm actually impressed with how progressive it is."

Celeste agreed. "I started out teaching at a large school and I hated all of the politics that went on there. I'm so glad I'm here now. I'll never go back to a large school."

Lisa checked her watch and was noticeably quiet. "Well, I better get back to my office. Thanks for letting me sit with you."

Celeste let Lisa's silence go, especially since Lisa didn't offer up any more.

"Yes, I had a nice time. I'll see you soon."

Lisa looked at Celeste, and that sexy smile returned. "Not if I see you first." Then she walked away. And Celeste watched. Good Lord, she was hot. Her view of Lisa was ruined when Jackie Stone stepped in her way. Dammit. Her day had been going so well up till now. Celeste sighed and went back to finishing her meal, but suddenly felt sick to her stomach. Jackie didn't even ask; she just sat in the chair that Lisa had just occupied.

Jackie picked a cherry tomato off Celeste's salad and popped it in her mouth. "Who is that?" Jackie tossed her thumb over her shoulder.

"Lisa Tobias. She's the coach of the women's basketball team."

"You two dating?"

"That's none of your business."

"It is since I want us to be together again. She's standing in the way."

Celeste let out a harsh laugh, wondering what she ever saw in Jackie in the first place. Okay, to be fair, Jackie didn't come off as the narcissist in the beginning that she truly was. When they first met, Jackie said all the pretty words and all the nice things to woo Celeste. Once she got Celeste in her bed, then Jackie's behavior changed. The nice words changed to insults, Jackie stopped opening the door for Celeste or scooting her chair in when Celeste sat at a table. And because Jackie was so handsome and had paid a lot of attention to Celeste in the beginning, Celeste kept waiting for the first Jackie to reappear. And maybe because her relationship with Jackie had been her first relationship with anyone, she'd wanted it to work out, she didn't want to give up. Celeste had finally come to her senses when, one night, she and Jackie were arguing and Jackie shoved her. She actually put her hands on Celeste and shoved her. It took only a moment for Celeste to overcome the shock of being physically abused before she grabbed her purse and left Jackie's house for the last time.

"Jackie, you're the one who got in the way of us being together. I learned my lesson and I won't make that same mistake twice. Now, please leave."

Jackie remained seated, looking intently at Celeste. Celeste let out a deep breath. She recognized the power play that Jackie was playing and Celeste didn't want to participate, especially not in the café where students were eating and studying. Celeste gathered her tray and left the table, throwing away the remnants of her food that she now had no appetite for.

Chapter Ten

L isa and Athena walked with the team through the casino to get to the hotel elevators. The clanging of the slot machines, the cheering from the gaming tables, and the music playing from the nearest lounge were overstimulating Lisa's senses. The cigarette smoke was burning her eyes and lungs, and she was sure the smell would never come out of her clothes. She was now regretting telling the athletic department's assistant to book them in the place cheapest and nearest to the arena they'd be playing their tournament. It would have been worth the extra money and miles to not have to deal with this chaos. However, it was a little worth it to see Athena in such awe of the noisy surroundings.

It was funny. Lisa and Athena had been best friends since they played together in college, but they couldn't have been more different. At this point in their lives, in their mid-forties, Lisa craved quiet and solitude outside of basketball, and Athena liked action. Not a lot of action, mind you. But she would rather be out and about, whereas Lisa would rather be home on the couch watching television or reading a book in the little free down time she had.

Lisa and Athena led the way to the elevators with the two volunteer coaches bringing up the rear, making sure the players didn't stray. The team looked sharp, wearing their matching tracksuits, maroon with a gray stripe and Glassell University embroidered on the back of the jacket. They were carrying university-issued duffel bags over their shoulders. This was a moment of pride Lisa had of her team. They looked good and were turning heads. Now all she needed was for them to put in a decent performance in the tournament.

When they got to their designated floor, Lisa and Athena handed out the key cards. The ladies had been given their room assignments before they left, and they all seemed pretty happy with their roommate situation.

"All right, Panthers. We're going to have dinner together in the main restaurant, then you're free to do what you want. Bed check is at eleven p.m. so make sure you're in your room. Anyone who misses curfew is suspended for the game. Got me?"

A chorus of "yes, Coach" was issued. "We'll see you at six in front of the restaurant." Lisa stood outside the door of the room she was sharing with Athena, waiting for all the ladies to get into their rooms. Once the hallway was clear, Lisa shut the door behind her and flopped onto her bed. She was exhausted from the four-and-a-half-hour drive through the Mojave Desert. She also hadn't been sleeping well lately, the past couple of weeks really, since she'd had dinner with Celeste. Well, not really dinner *with* Celeste, like a date, but when she ran into her and sat with her at the café on campus. Since then, it had been night after night filled with dreams starring Celeste Bouchard. Lisa had no business dreaming, or even thinking, about Celeste. For one, she had no time to think about starting anything with Celeste, especially during the basketball season. And two, she was hoping she wouldn't be at the small school much longer. If she'd had her way, she'd be offered a job at a Division I school and be out of GU by the end of the school year. The way this season had started, with only one loss in six games, advancing in her coaching career was looking promising. Making a good showing in the tournament would certainly help.

"Come on, let's go hit the tables. Blackjack is calling for me."

Lisa opened her eyes and looked at Athena. "Are you kidding? We just got here."

"I know, but we have three whole hours before we meet for dinner." Athena was practically bouncing up and down on the balls of her feet. She loved to gamble whereas Lisa could take it or leave it. She'd occasionally play blackjack or video poker when they were in a casino, but that didn't happen often. Lisa couldn't fathom spending too much money gambling when she could be spending it on other things. Athena, on the other hand, couldn't get enough of it, and Lisa was certain that if Athena had constant access to casinos, she'd be broke and she'd have to join Gamblers Anonymous.

"You go ahead and I'll meet you at the restaurant. I'm going to watch a little TV, maybe take a nap."

"Jesus, Lisa. How old are you? I didn't realize you'd become an old lady."

Lisa laughed and threw a pillow at Athena. "Fuck off, Chang. Go lose your money."

"Right. See you in a few hours."

Lisa fluffed her pillows against the headboard, turned on the TV, and set the alarm on her phone for five thirty. She flipped through the channels until she came across an episode of *Ellen*. Ellen was doing a bit where she had one of her staff members play a prank on her guest celebrity. When Ellen belly laughed, it made Lisa laugh hard too. The last thing Lisa thought of before she fell asleep was that she hoped she looked as good as Ellen when she was her age.

"Lisa, wake up!"

Lisa woke up discombobulated. Where was she? Strange bed, Athena hovering over her and shaking her. "What's wrong?" Right. Vegas. Hotel room. Basketball tournament. She rubbed her hands over her eyes. How long had she been asleep? She looked at her watch and noted it was five o'clock and she was upset that she could've slept for another thirty minutes. Suddenly, she had money raining down on her. "What the hell is that?"

"That, my friend, is called the progressive jackpot for a royal flush on video poker." Athena had a smile that practically went ear to ear, and she looked like she had just won the lottery. Lisa picked up the twenties, fifties, and hundred-dollar bills and looked up in amazement. "How much is here?"

"Almost twelve grand." Athena started laughing again. "I put one hundred dollars into a dollar machine, and I was just about out when I hit the ten, jack, queen, and ace of spades. I held those cards, then drew, and up came king of spades. I started screaming, people started gathering around, I was hugging strangers. Finally, an attendant showed up along with a supervisor and paid me my money. I came right back to the room to tell you."

Now Lisa was laughing along with Athena. "That's so exciting! I can't believe you won so much money. You want me to hold it so you don't spend it?"

"No!" Athena gathered her money and turned away from Lisa as if she was going to take it from her. "Okay, I'll give you ten grand and I'll keep the rest and play with it while we are here. Maybe we can go see a show."

"Uh, we're here for a basketball tournament, Athena, not to party."

"Duh! You said that already. I was thinking we could do it on our last night after basketball is done."

"We'll see. If we don't have a good showing, the last thing I'll want to do is have a night on the town. Now let's get ready to meet the team for dinner."

On the way to the restaurant, Athena pointed out an advertisement poster near the elevators. "Hey, check it out. There's a pole dancing competition this weekend in this casino. Is this lucky or what?" The eyebrows that Athena wiggled made Lisa give her a little shove.

"Remember. Basketball. Why we're here."

"I know, but I think it would be cool to check it out. Our game is at one o'clock tomorrow so we can go see it in the evening."

"Don't you think we should be studying game tape of our next day's opponent?"

"Jesus, Lisa. Loosen up a little, will ya? We're in Vegas. How often do we get here? We don't have to stay for the whole thing, but an hour isn't going to hurt."

"If I say yes, will you get off my back for the rest of the trip? I realize you're excited to be here, to be able to gamble and all, but we are the coaches of Glassell University and we are representing our school. We need to be responsible and focus on our team and the tournament."

"I get it. And if we go for just an hour, I promise it will be all basketball, all the time for me."

"Okay. We'll go."

"Yes." Athena did a fist pump and Lisa shook her head.

Celeste and Olivia pulled up to the valet and gave the attendant Celeste's name. He pulled their luggage out of the trunk and placed it on a cart that the porter took to the front desk for them. Ordinarily, the lights and sounds of a casino would fill Celeste's senses, maybe even overload them. But she was so nervous about her upcoming performance the following day that she was just concentrating on not throwing up before she got to the room. What the hell was she thinking, signing up for the pole competition? Maybe a case of temporary insanity? If Olivia hadn't signed up and wasn't there with her, Celeste would have packed her car back up and headed south on the I-15 freeway back home.

They got to the room, thanked the porter for bringing up their luggage, and Celeste started to unpack her suitcase. She needed to keep busy so she wouldn't think of the competition. She carefully hung up her costumes she brought—enough for three performances in case she got that far. She certainly didn't expect to get that far, but she could keep positive thoughts. That was part of her personal growth—keeping positivity in her life. But seeing how this was her first big performance, she just wanted to not embarrass herself. At least she had Olivia there with her, and a friendly face always helped.

"Ooh, I love that outfit, Celeste. Is it new?"

Celeste pulled the royal purple sequined outfit off the hanger and held it up to her body. "Yes, I did a little shopping last week. I got these shoes to go with it." She held up a pair of silver high-heeled platform shoes that gave her calves sexy definition and made the purple pop.

"I love them. Did you get those at the shop near our studio?"

"I did. They just got a new shipment in that morning so I practically had first choice."

They finished putting away their clothes and decided to go downstairs and check out the area that would be set up for the competition. There were three different ballrooms that had stages with poles and rows of chairs in front of the stages. There were lights in the back of the room that were multicolored and there was a sound check going on. Celeste was impressed with how professional this was looking to be.

"Are you nervous?"

Celeste swore she could feel her whole body shaking, but she tried to shake it off. "No, I'm okay."

Olivia put her arm around Celeste. "Liar. It's all right. I'm nervous too. But just think, we won't know anyone here so there's no need to be nervous. We'll be fine. We'll do our performances, and when we're not performing, we'll drink and play slot machines."

"That sounds like a great idea. Let's practice that part now."

They sat in a row of video poker machines and started playing, waiting for a cocktail waitress to come by and take their drink order. Soon after, there was a lot of screaming and hollering in the row on the other side of their machines. When the waitress brought their drinks, Celeste asked her if she knew why people were yelling, and she told them someone had just won a royal flush on a dollar machine. Celeste tipped her and took a sip of her vodka tonic. She'd tasted better, but it wasn't horrible, and she certainly wasn't going to complain about free drinks, even if she had to gamble to get those free drinks.

After having a couple of drinks and losing forty dollars, Celeste and Olivia decided to go have dinner then wander in and out of the shops. While they were waiting for their table, a group of young ladies walked by, some of them very tall, and she automatically thought of Lisa. She hadn't seen her since they ate together in the café and she'd been tempted many times to call her or walk over to her office. She couldn't even find an excuse since Emily Logan was performing much better in her class. The only excuse she'd been able to come up with was that she was attracted to Lisa and wanted to get to know her better. However, Celeste lacked the confidence to come out and tell Lisa she was attracted to her. Jackie had made the first move with her, and there'd been no other women.

Celeste wished she hadn't been such a late bloomer and had experience with dating at least a few women. She had never thought of herself as attractive or worthy of a relationship because of her obesity. A few kids in school, then some of the athletes and cheerleaders in high school never said anything to her face, but she'd overheard them and saw them stop their conversations as she would approach. Her parents kept telling her to ignore them, that she was beautiful and smart, and anyone would be lucky to be with her. But they were her parents. They had to say that. At least that's what she thought when she was a teenager. But even though her body image and self-confidence had improved, that didn't mean she was comfortable enough to make a first move with Lisa. That is, if she were to ignore her own rule of not dating anyone she worked with. Which she wouldn't. Well, she shouldn't. But, dang it, Lisa was so attractive.

Olivia nudged Celeste and leaned close. "There are a lot of tall women walking around here."

"I noticed that. I wonder if there's a basketball tournament going on. They look around college age."

"Speaking of basketball, any further developments with the coach?"

Celeste had told Olivia about her run-in with Lisa in the pool, then when she went to apologize, then finally running into her at the café. She thought she was being nonchalant when she was talking to Olivia about Lisa, but Olivia knew her too well and heard the giddy schoolgirl voice when she spoke of Lisa.

"No, I haven't seen her since the last time. I don't want to come off like I'm too anxious or like I'm interested."

"But you are interested."

"I think she's good looking. There's a difference. After the Jackie Stone fiasco, I'm not going to get involved with anyone I work with ever again. The campus is small enough that it's inevitable we'd run into each other if it didn't work out."

"But what if it did work out?"

"Liv." The way Celeste said her name was a warning to stop.

The hostess showed them to their table so their conversation was shelved for the time being. The rest of their dinner was spent discussing their routines and the songs they were going to perform to. All the talk about Lisa must've caused some hallucinations because she swore she saw Lisa walking toward the back of the restaurant. Well, she looked a little like Lisa, but she only caught the back of her head so she couldn't be sure. Celeste shook her head and chuckled. She was starting to lose it. For the remainder of dinner, she kept an eye out for the woman who looked like Lisa, but she didn't reappear.

"Come on, Olivia. Let's go gamble a little more before we go back to the room."

❖

Lisa returned to the private dining room area where the team was having dinner. She was grateful that the restaurant was able to accommodate their large group. Besides fifteen players and four coaches, they had three team managers to help with equipment and two trainers to take care of any minor injury or medical problem. The ladies on the team were well behaved so Lisa didn't worry about them getting into any trouble, but they were her responsibility. She promised the parents of her players that she would stand in as a surrogate parent while they were away from home.

They were all sitting around the table talking and laughing, and Lisa just stood observing them, admiring them. It was still early in the season, but Lisa knew this group was special. There was not only a basketball intelligence that many of the players possessed, but they were respectful, kind, and hard-working women. Even though it had been about twenty-five years since Lisa had been in college, the girls nowadays were a lot more mature than when Lisa and Athena were that age. She took a seat at the head of the table and joined in the conversation with a few of her players who were in close proximity.

Once dinner was done, Lisa went over a few business items. "Okay, ladies, listen up. Our game tomorrow is at two. We'll have an hour shootaround at ten to go through a few plays, then we'll grab an early lunch. Be in your practice gear and meet in my room at nine thirty a.m. If you're late, the vans will leave without you and you'll sit the bench for the game. It's now seven fifteen, and room check will be at eleven. You have free time until then, but anyone under twenty-one cannot hang out on the casino floor. They don't play around with underage gambling or drinking here, not that I believe my girls would do that." Lisa caught the eyes of a few players and got laughs out of most. "There's an arcade, bowling alley, and movie theater near the elevators to the hotel so that's a place for you to hang out if you want. Remember two things: you're here to win this tournament, and you're representing our school. See you all tonight at eleven."

Lisa held the coaches behind and waited for the others to leave. "I'm sure I don't need to say this, but I'm going to anyway.

Same goes for all of us. We're here for the tournament. Have fun, do a little gambling and drinking if you want to, but we also have a curfew. We'll do room checks, then we'll go to our own rooms. No drunkenness, no hangovers. Got it?"

They all nodded and walked out of the restaurant. The volunteer coaches, Chris and Joe, headed toward the casino while Lisa and Athena headed to their room to watch game tape on their first opponent and make notes for tomorrow's shootaround and game.

Chapter Eleven

The final buzzer went off, and Glassell University won by twelve points. Lisa walked the sideline, followed by her assistants and team to congratulate the other team on a game well played. They grabbed their gear and headed to the meeting room they had been assigned. Lisa waited for the players to be seated, and her coaching staff stood in the back.

"Off to a good start, ladies. We played sloppy a few times on offense but made up for it with tough defense. Go get your treatments, shower, then meet me back in the gym. One of the teams in the next game is who we're playing tomorrow. We'll leave at halftime, grab some dinner, then head back to the hotel. Everybody in a circle."

The team stood and gathered in a tight huddle with their arms in the air. They all shouted "Panthers," then left the room. Lisa asked one of the assistants to leave the video equipment up to record the first half of the game so she could review it later.

Lisa, Athena, Chris, and Joe sat together and discussed the plusses and minuses of the game. There were two players, Taylor and Kristina, her two post players, who Lisa was going to have to talk to about rebounding. Chris and Joe would work with them on boxing out tomorrow during shootaround. The team they were playing tomorrow had two post players who were three and four inches taller than Taylor and Kristina so they were going to have to work hard to get the rebounds.

Lisa noticed that most of her players paid close attention to the game rather than playing on their phones. She was pleased to see them studying the teams; it showed her they were serious about doing what they could to win the next game. Lisa saw a lot of herself in some of her players so she knew what she could likely expect out of them.

They arrived back at the hotel after having dinner at an Italian restaurant near the arena. Lisa wanted to go back to the room to come up with a game plan for tomorrow's game. Athena began disrobing the moment the door closed behind them, and she changed into a new outfit. She looked at Lisa impatiently.

"What?"

"Aren't you going to change?"

"To watch game tape?"

"No, crazy. To go to the pole competition."

"Oh, shit. I completely forgot. I'm gonna skip it tonight."

"No, you're not. You promised me an hour and I'm holding you to it. Come on, Ice. Just an hour. We'll just check it out for a bit, then we'll come back to the room and get to work."

Lisa tossed her clipboard onto her bed and let out a big sigh. "Fine. Just an hour though."

Lisa changed into jeans and a short-sleeved Henley shirt, and they went to the competition. As they got closer, they could hear the music come from the ballroom. They bought their tickets and stood in the back of the room. It was dark except for the lights highlighting the stage. A woman was performing, and Lisa didn't want to interrupt the people watching her to find a seat. Besides, they were only going to be there for an hour and it felt good to stand. She clapped politely when the performer finished. After a few more performers, Lisa started to get into the show. This wasn't what she'd expected when Athena told her about the competition. Truthfully, she didn't know what to expect. This type of thing was so far out of her universe, but she was really enjoying it. One thing that impressed her was that none of the women looked the same. There was one who was short and overweight, one tall and skinny, one who was flat-chested, and one who had large breasts. The thing they all seemed to have in common was that they all oozed sensuality, the way they moved their hips, stroked the pole, looked at the audience while they caressed their bodies, commanding attention. They got Lisa's attention, that was for sure. She was just mentioning to Athena how talented these women were when the MC announced the next competitor, Celeste B. Lisa's head whipped around to the stage just in time to see Celeste walk, no, not walk, saunter on stage. Her Celeste. Well, not her Celeste, but the Celeste she knew, that she worked with. Oh, God. How was she going to be able to have a platonic conversation with Celeste after seeing her dressed like…that?

Janet Jackson's "Velvet Rope" began to play, and Lisa felt her jaw drop. She'd always loved that song, always had fantasies about Janet tying her up and having her way with her like she did with some lucky guy during her concerts. Celeste was dressed in a deep purple outfit that looked like a bikini with lots of sequins and other bling that was barely covered up by a matching sheer robe. Celeste looked like she was wearing sexy lingerie, and Lisa was tempted to go up on stage and cover her so nobody else could see her practically naked. Not that Celeste didn't look good. That might have been the understatement of Lisa's lifetime. Celeste looked downright fucking sexy.

Celeste continued to move about the stage, touching, caressing herself. She looked different but the same. Her eyelashes were longer, she had more makeup on, she was sure of her movements and displayed a confidence that Lisa hadn't seen with her. Celeste grabbed the pole and held on while she squatted and displayed…well…everything to the audience. The "everything" was covered up, but that didn't matter to Lisa. Celeste stood upright and slowly made her way around the pole before she grabbed it and pulled herself up, impressing the audience as they clapped loudly. While holding on to the pole, she turned herself upside down and spread her legs apart then scissored her legs before sliding back down the pole. Once her feet were firmly on the floor, Celeste held on to the pole, hooked her leg around it, and swung around once more.

Lisa looked over to Athena who also let her jaw drop to the floor. Obviously, she'd recognized Celeste, as her eyes were wide with wonder and something else. Arousal? The thought enraged Lisa enough to smack Athena's arm, which broke the trance.

"What?" Athena looked at Lisa so innocently that Lisa smacked her again.

"Stop."

"But…" Athena pointed to the stage like that should've explained everything.

Lisa pointed at Athena to indicate she shouldn't say another word. Not. One. More. Word. Lisa wanted nothing more than to leave the room, pretend she never saw Celeste up on stage, looking sexier than Lisa could've ever imagined. From the very beginning, when Lisa had seen Celeste at the president's back-to-school gathering, Lisa had always thought Celeste was gorgeous and sexy, and it became more apparent once Lisa got to know Celeste better. But tonight put Celeste into a different stratosphere. Not because of the outfit she was wearing or the pole dancing she was doing, but because of the confidence she had in her body and herself. What had always attracted Lisa to other women was their self-confidence, and she was seeing it in spades now with Celeste.

Celeste had climbed the pole again, hung upside down with her legs apart, then crossed, and hung only by her legs wrapped around the pole. Holy Jesus! Not only was this performance provocative but was also extremely athletic. Celeste had told Lisa that she was always picked last in PE and on the playground, and that she'd never been coordinated, but seeing what was in front of her, Lisa didn't believe Celeste.

The things she was doing with the pole was something a person could do only with athleticism and coordination. Lisa had so many emotions running through her head and her lower regions. Her skin felt hot, she felt light-headed, and her clit throbbed as she fantasized sitting on a chair in front of Celeste as she danced for Lisa, giving her a lap dance. Lisa got dizzy and thought she might pass out, but then the music stopped and the audience erupted with applause. Lisa had to get out of there. She needed fresh air. She rushed out of the ballroom into the casino where she was engulfed with loud noises and cigarette smoke, but at least she felt free.

"Holy Mary, Mother of God, did you know she could do that?" Athena looked like she had just drunk three energy drinks; she was dancing and hopping around, talking as fast as an auctioneer, and it was driving Lisa crazy. Lisa, on the other hand, was in shock and speechless. When Celeste started working the pole, Lisa's brain short-circuited and hadn't fired back up yet. She started to make her way across the casino floor toward the hotel elevators.

"Hell, no, I didn't know that she did that. And now it's something I can't unsee."

"Yeah, me neither." Athena waggled her eyebrows.

Lisa arrived at the elevators and kept pressing the button as if that would make the car arrive faster. The bell dinged and the doors opened. Once the occupants got out, Lisa stepped in with Athena hot on her heels. Lisa turned on her and pinned her against the wall.

Lisa pointed at her and gave her a serious look. "Yes, you can. Don't ever mention seeing Celeste pole dancing. Not one word. Not one FUCKING word. You got me?"

Athena's eyes widened and she held her hands up. "Whatever you say, Ice."

They got into their room and Lisa sat on her bed and ran her fingers through her hair. What the hell did she just see? Up until Celeste appeared on stage, Lisa was actually having a good time and admiring all of the women and their performances. But a woman she knew, one she was getting to know and was secretly attracted to, was up on stage, looking sensuous, dancing seductively, and owning the audience. Lisa didn't know what to think or how to feel. She was turned on, that was for sure. She was embarrassed by seeing her colleague, her player's professor, dressed in a racy costume and having her way with a brass pole, bringing Lisa's fantasies to life. But most of all, she was proud that Celeste took ownership of her body and sexuality, and was making it work for her.

As turned on as she was, Lisa felt an overwhelming sense of pride for her friend. Was that what Celeste was? Probably not quite. They didn't socialize outside of school so that probably just made her a colleague. However, Lisa thought of Celeste as more than a colleague. Why was that? Maybe it was because Lisa was attracted to Celeste. But she couldn't let herself get carried away because she wasn't in a position to get involved with someone, even if that person was Celeste Bouchard.

"Geez, Lisa. When did you get so cranky? I'm not going to be a dick about it, but you have to admit that Celeste was incredible and looked really sexy. It must take a lot of strength, coordination, and stamina to be able to do the things she did. Like when she climbed up the pole and held on to it with her legs while she hung upside down. Then when she slid down the pole and went into splits. And remember when she was kind of writhing on the floor?"

"Stop! For the love of Pete, just stop." Lisa slammed her palms against her eyes as if that could erase everything athletic, erotic, exotic, and sexy. Everything that was Celeste. And not just when she performed. Lisa found her sexy all the time. This had been just another facet of Celeste.

"Ooh, this is serious."

"What are you talking about?" Lisa walked over to the window and looked out onto the Vegas Strip where the lights were always on and there were always people walking to the next casino looking for their next drink or next jackpot, sometimes both. The cold air couldn't keep the thousands of people off the Strip.

"You really like her."

Lisa didn't bother turning around because she knew Athena would see the lie in her eyes. "No, I don't. She's our colleague and the professor of our point guard. That's all."

"There's nothing wrong if you like her, Lisa. She's an equal, not a student or a player. What'll it hurt if you just maybe ask her to dinner or something?"

"I don't have time for a relationship, Athena. Not in the middle of the season."

"You're not planning a wedding. You're going on a date. Casual. No commitments. Geez, do I need to explain everything to you?"

That was easy for Athena to say. What Athena didn't know was that Lisa didn't think she'd be able to keep it casual with Celeste. She was unlike any other woman Lisa had ever known, and there was potential there for Lisa to fall hard for Celeste.

"Okay, look. We're not going to talk about this right now. We're here for basketball, and we need to get a game plan together for tomorrow. The team we're playing is really good."

Lisa went to get her laptop, then sat next to Athena on her bed. She inserted the DVD of the game, and they spent the rest of the evening watching the team they'd play tomorrow. Athena allowed Lisa to stay in their room and process what she'd seen that night while Athena, Chris, and Joe did bed checks. Lisa took a long, hot shower, allowing the extra time to clear her head, get refocused on her team and the tournament she was determined to win. Winning this tournament would get her closer to achieving her goal. Lisa needed to shelve her attraction for Celeste and get back to work.

Celeste came off the stage into the waiting arms of Olivia. She was feeling high from the audience reaction to her performance. She nailed it and she knew it. Celeste's performance was flawless in her mind, and it went exactly as she imagined it to go. She'd spent many nights practicing that routine, and a couple of others, in hopes of getting further than the first or second round. By the sound of the audience's applause, she'd hopefully be moving on to the second round tomorrow.

"You were amazing! I didn't know you had moves like that."

"I have moves you've never seen."

Olivia laughed and fanned her face. "Okay, sexy thing. You go on with your bad self."

Celeste was thankful Olivia was there to greet her coming off stage. Now that her adrenaline was coming down, her legs felt a little shaky. She took the towel Olivia offered her and wiped the perspiration off her arms and dabbed her face so as not to ruin her makeup. Celeste found the closest chair and sat before her legs gave out on her. She loved the way she felt after performing a pole routine in class because the ladies she took the class with were her friends and they encouraged one another. Tonight was a whole different feeling though. She didn't know anyone. It wasn't a studio with just eight or ten other people. There were probably at least two or three hundred people in the crowd, and they liked her. Celeste felt sexy and powerful and confident, and another sexy thrown in because, damn it, she did feel sexy and it took her a long time to own it.

She was unable to see the people in the crowd because of the lights, and that probably helped her perform. She was unable to see their faces or expressions. For some reason, Lisa popped into her head, and she wondered what Lisa would've thought of her routine. She'd never performed for Jackie because, even though they had a sexual relationship, Celeste didn't feel comfortable showing Jackie her vulnerability. She had it in her mind that Jackie wouldn't appreciate the hard work that Celeste put into her routines or would make some crude comment. While they were dating, Celeste didn't even tell Jackie that she was taking pole classes; she'd just tell her she had an exercise class. Jackie didn't ask what kind of exercise, and Celeste didn't offer up that information. Lisa, on the other hand, would probably appreciate Celeste's routine and be encouraging. She already knew that about her.

Once Celeste started getting feeling back into her legs, she and Olivia walked back to the dressing area so that Celeste could change out of her costume. Olivia had performed earlier so she was already dressed. There were only a few performers left, and then later she could check the website to see if she and Olivia made it to the next round. She really hoped so. As much as she loved the routine she just performed, the next one was choreographed to "Those Shoes" by the Eagles, and it was her favorite dance out of the three she put together.

Once she was dressed, Celeste and Olivia headed back to their room to shower and change. They had tickets to see Cirque de Solei's *O* later that night, and they still needed to eat dinner. It was nice that the competition ended in the early evening so they could catch some shows while they were in town.

Las Vegas was an interesting town, but along the Strip and Downtown Las Vegas, it was a tourist mecca. Olivia had informed Celeste that there was a zip line downtown where one could fly over Fremont Street, over all of the tourists and street performers. She wouldn't have time for it during this trip, and she didn't want to zip-line in fifty-degree weather, which it was predicted to be that weekend, but she would definitely try it on another trip out there. There was so much to see, from shows and concerts, to a museum of mobsters. There was shopping and high-end galleries. Heck, one could even visit New York in Las Vegas. Too many tourist things to do in one trip so this time, she'd stick to pole dancing, seeing a show, and eating delicious cuisine.

Chapter Twelve

Glassell University won the tournament, and Emily Logan made the All-Tournament team. She was certainly establishing herself as a premier player this season. Last year, when Emily entered GU as a freshman, she was so shy and quiet, Lisa didn't think she'd do much except play great defense and dish out assists, but toward the end of last season, more of her teammates were looking to her as the team's leader. Lisa and Emily had had some meetings throughout the season, and Emily's confidence had continued to grow. This season, Emily had continued to grow in that capacity, and she was voted captain by her teammates for this season.

Lisa wanted to get Celeste's feelings on Emily as well, but she wasn't sure how she'd react to seeing Celeste after watching her in her pole dance competition. Lisa had been tempted to go back to the competition the next day to watch Celeste again, but if she was going to be able to concentrate on coaching her team to the championship, she'd have to focus all her energy on basketball and tuck Celeste in a small box and in a small corner of her mind.

That strategy paid off, and it took her that much closer to her goal of returning to coaching at a higher level. Eyes on the prize. Still, it would be the responsible thing to check on her team's leader. Lisa could always call Celeste at her office, but to be perfectly honest, she really wanted to see her.

Athena checked out the competition's website and passed along that Celeste didn't make it past the second round. Lisa was secretly grateful for that information because Lisa really wanted to see how Celeste had faired, but she wouldn't have been able to ask Celeste. Lisa didn't want her to know that she saw her perform. Lisa felt like a voyeur while watching the competition and felt like she'd been doing something she didn't want to get caught doing. Silly, really, since it was a competition. It wasn't like she'd gone to a gentlemen's club and saw her with dollar bills hanging out of her G-string. Lisa just hoped she'd be able to be cool and look even cooler when she saw Celeste. Lisa also hoped that seeing Celeste in her business attire would help erase the image of Celeste in her pole costume.

Lisa grabbed her sunglasses, keys, and wallet, then locked her office door behind her. Even though it was approaching mid-December, the weather was beautiful in the midmorning, approaching seventy degrees. When coaching offers started coming in, Lisa hoped there would be a few from schools in Southern California. You really just couldn't beat the weather. She waved to a couple of her players and a professor on her way to Celeste's office and took in several deep breaths to calm her nerves.

Lisa knocked on Celeste's door and felt warm inside when Celeste smiled at her.

"Hey, I missed you at the pool this morning."

Lisa sat across from Celeste and crossed her legs. "Yeah, I got back from Vegas pretty late last night, and I decided to sleep in." Lisa noted that the color drained from Celeste's face, and she had a feeling she knew why.

"You were in Las Vegas this past weekend?"

Lisa quickly answered to try to put Celeste at ease and also to avoid an awkward conversation. "We had a tournament there, and guess what. We won and Emily made the All-Tournament team."

The color started returning to Celeste's face, and she noticeably relaxed a little bit. "That's fantastic news. Congratulations and I'll be sure to congratulate Emily in class later."

Celeste didn't mention that she was also in Las Vegas, so Lisa didn't bring it up. "I came by to see how Emily was doing in your class. Is she still keeping up?"

"Oh, yes, she's doing great. She's pulling an A-minus right now, and if she does well on her final next week, she should finish with an A or A-minus."

"That's great. I was worried there for a while, but she's a really hard worker so I'm proud of her for stepping it up."

A few moments of silence sat between them, and Lisa didn't know what else to say. All Lisa knew was that she wanted a little more time to be in Celeste's presence.

"Would you like to have dinner with me?" Lisa inwardly cringed. That wasn't supposed to happen. That's not what she wanted to say. She didn't need to be taking any time away from her coaching, but she panicked in an effort to stay for a few minutes longer and that was what she came up with. *Geez. Way to be cool, Tobias.*

"I'd like that, but would you mind if we kept it platonic? You see, I dated a woman I worked with and it didn't end well, but I like you and I'd like to be friends."

Lisa felt relief and disappointment all at once, and she didn't know how to react exactly so she just smiled. "Yes, of course. I'd like to be friends with you too. Who couldn't use more friends?" Now Lisa was just sounding like a dork. She tried to recover. "I don't have many friends here besides Athena. Not anyone I associate with. It'll be nice to have someone else to hang out with from time to time."

"Oh, good. I've wanted to ask you if you wanted to do something with me, but I didn't know how to ask without it sounding like a date or something." Celeste gave a small uncomfortable laugh. Now things were just starting to get weird. Time to shut it down.

"Great." Lisa stood to leave. "Is there any night that doesn't work? We have a game Thursday night, but every other night I'm free."

"How about Friday? I'm done with classes that day by four. Invite Athena. Since she's also a colleague, I'd like to get to know her too."

"Okay. I'll call you later this week with details."

"Wonderful. And, Coach? Congratulations on the tournament."

Lisa scuffed her shoe on the floor and thanked her in an aw-shucks sort of way.

When Lisa left her office, Celeste looked up to the ceiling and let out a deep breath. That was an interesting conversation. She'd been so happy to see Lisa when she'd arrived. But when Lisa said she'd been in Las Vegas at the same time Celeste had been there, she'd felt herself begin to panic. What if she'd seen Celeste perform? God, she would've been mortified if Lisa'd seen her dressed in her costume. It was one thing to dress like that and perform in front of strangers but quite another to do it in front of her colleagues. Now that she thought about it, maybe it was Lisa she saw in the restaurant the first night she was there. But Lisa didn't mention the pole competition so Celeste felt herself relax. Besides, Lisa was probably too busy with her team to do anything extracurricular.

She was looking forward to having dinner with Lisa and Athena, and getting to know them better. She'd felt like it was a safe idea to have an extra person as a buffer so she was glad that Lisa agreed to the idea. Maybe Olivia would like to go as well. Olivia had mentioned over the weekend that her husband would be on a business trip this coming week. She picked up the phone and dialed Olivia's extension.

"Hey, Carl is out of town this week, right? Would you like to have dinner with the coaches from the women's basketball team?"

"If you tell me how this came to be arranged."

"It's no big deal. Lisa asked me to dinner, we agreed to do it as friends, and I told her to invite her assistant coach. I thought it would be less awkward to have four of us instead of three."

"No, what would be less awkward is for the assistant coach and me not to be intruding on your date with the coach."

"It's not a date. How many times do I have to tell you that I won't date anyone I work with again?"

"Come on, Celeste. Lisa is nothing like Jackie, and I can tell just by the first time I saw her when she took us for a walk around campus. I never did like Jackie, and I could've told you from day one that she wouldn't be good for you."

"Well, why didn't you? You could've saved me from a lot of embarrassment."

"You didn't ask for my opinion. I try never to give my friends unsolicited advice."

"Now you tell me." Celeste chuckled to lighten things up and let Olivia know she was kidding. Sort of. "So, go with us to dinner, then you can give me an honest opinion of Lisa. Doesn't mean I'm going to date her, but I'll listen to your opinion."

"Whatever. Fine, I'll go to dinner with you."

"Great, I'll call Lisa and let her know, and I'll call you back with the when and where."

Celeste hung up and felt a little more relief creep into her. Having her best friend there with her would make her feel more comfortable. Olivia had always been great in social situations. Although Lisa and Celeste agreed to have this dinner as a platonic event, Celeste still had a small fluttering in her stomach. After all, Lisa was very handsome and Celeste was definitely attracted to her, but that didn't mean she would act on it.

Lisa was sitting at her desk drafting some recruiting letters when she looked up and saw Emily standing in the doorway fiddling with her backpack straps, not looking like her recently confident self.

"What's up, Logan?"

"Um, can I talk to you, Coach?"

"Always. Come in and close the door."

Emily took off her bulky backpack, and she flopped into the chair. She looked at Lisa and started crying. Lisa got up from behind her desk and took a seat in the chair next to Emily.

"What's going on, Logan? How can I help you?"

Emily wiped her eyes and took a couple of deep, shuddering breaths. "I'm gay."

Is that all? I thought she was in some sort of trouble, but given her background, I need to handle this carefully. "Thank you for telling me. That was very brave of you to come out to me."

"Are you mad, Coach? Do you hate me?"

"Just the opposite, kiddo. I'm so proud of you for having the courage to come out. I know how scary that is."

"You do?"

"Yes, Logan, I do. When did you realize you were a lesbian?"

"Last year." Emily went on to tell Lisa about the girl she dated last year.

That's why her grades were so bad last spring.

"It took me all summer to get over her, but I couldn't even talk to my parents or sister about it. It was the longest three months ever."

Emily came from a conservative religious family and Lisa could only imagine how they'd react to Emily's discovery.

"So, your family doesn't know?"

"No. You and Professor Bouchard are the only ones that know."

"You told Professor Bouchard? What did she say?" *This must be what Celeste was talking about when she referred to Emily's personal problems.*

"She was great. She said I could always talk to her if I needed to. She's the one who encouraged me to tell you. She said you'd be understanding, and she was right. I think she's the best professor or teacher I've ever had."

"I'm glad she's been there for you. Just so you know, Coach Chang and I will always be here for you too, Emily. Do any of your teammates know?"

Emily shook her head. "I haven't said anything, but they probably know or think it."

"Coming out is your decision, kiddo. Athena and I won't tell anyone so whenever you're comfortable, you can tell them when you want to. Are you doing okay?"

"Yeah, Coach. I'm a lot better now that you know and that you don't hate me."

Lisa smiled and put her arm around Emily's shoulders. "I could never hate you, Emily. I really appreciate you trusting me with this. Remember, you can talk to me about anything. My door is always open."

"Thanks, Coach." Emily gave Lisa a quick hug before putting on her backpack. "I'll see you in a few hours for the game."

Once Emily left, Lisa sat back in her chair and grinned at the thought that Celeste encouraged Emily to tell Lisa. She'd have to thank her for that.

Celeste walked down the bleachers just as the players were being announced. She took a seat on the hardwood bench about six rows up from the floor. That would give her a better view of the game, and if she was being honest, a better view of Lisa. A few students a little farther down said hello to her. When they said her name, Lisa turned around and looked pleased to see Celeste. She smiled and gave a little wave before returning her attention to the team.

The announcer welcomed the crowd to the game, and when he introduced each player, they did a cute greeting with a high-five, elbow bump, hand shake, and a little hop. Celeste had no idea why each player did that and had their own unique greeting, but it was certainly entertaining.

The game started and Glassell University quickly scored. The next time down the court, Emily passed it to a player who nearly missed it because she was pulling her hair tighter in her ponytail.

Lisa screamed out, "Novac, stop messing with your damn hair!" Probably everyone in the gym heard her because there was a lot of laughter.

The player yelled back, "Sorry, Coach," which brought on even more laughter. Lisa turned around and faced the crowd, running her fingers through her hair, looking frustrated and amused all at once.

Oh, no. Celeste could find herself in a little bit of trouble. Lisa looked adorable, and it gave Celeste a little tingle. *No, I'm not going there. Lisa and I are friends, and that's all we'll ever be.* She was able to put that thought in the back of her mind. And she was mostly successful. Every once in a while, Lisa would yell out to a player to run a certain play, yell at the referee for making a bad call, yell at a player for being careless and turning the ball over, and stomping her foot on the floor in frustration. Celeste was discovering that she liked the fired-up Lisa with her red face in a scowl and her hands on her hips. Something about that turned Celeste on, and a thought popped in her head, certainly uninvited, and she wondered if Lisa was that intense during sex. *Stop, Celeste. You're never going to find out.*

Celeste had been tempted to leave at halftime of the game so she wouldn't torture herself anymore by paying a little too close attention to Lisa, but she really did enjoy watching the team play. She felt like she was learning more about the game itself. She also liked supporting Emily. She'd realized that Glassell University was a lot different from her previous college and that the student-athletes did work hard in the classroom. Sure, their respective sports might have helped pay their way through college, but they needed to work hard in the classroom and get good grades in order to stay in school and continue to play. Celeste now felt ashamed that she assumed all college athletes were the same. In fact, she'd realized a very small percentage of the student-athlete population was looking for a free pass in school. She'd seen firsthand how hard Emily had worked to pull up her grade. It hadn't been right that she let a few dishonest coaches at her previous university ruin the whole lot.

Celeste waved back to Emily when the team came back into the gym to warm up before the start of the second half. Then Athena waved to her. Celeste laughed and wondered if the whole team would follow suit. They didn't, thankfully. The buzzer rang and the team and coaches transformed from a group that had looked light-hearted and goofy to a group that was on a mission to win.

The second half flew by. The opposing team had gotten to within five points toward the end of the third quarter, but the entire fourth quarter belonged to GU. Emily Logan had been especially impressive. Making a few steals, hitting four three-pointers, and commanding her team to a win. Celeste smiled to herself. That was Emily's team. Her teammates followed her into battle and listened to everything she said. Now that Celeste had gotten to know her a little more, she was impressed with her hard work and determination. She was going to be very successful in whatever she chose to do in life.

After the game finished and the teams congratulated each other, Lisa got Celeste's attention and called her down. Celeste took great care walking down the bleachers in her four-inch heels. She could do some serious damage if she fell down the steps.

"Hi. Thanks for coming to the game." Lisa leaned closer and lowered her voice. "And thanks for encouraging Emily to talk to me. She came to see me this afternoon and told me that she's a lesbian."

"My pleasure. Was she okay?"

"Yes. She was nervous, but we had a good talk and everything is good."

Celeste nodded and smiled. "I'm glad."

Athena came over and said hello. "I'm looking forward to dinner tomorrow night."

Celeste smiled at them both. "Yes, I am too. Did you decide on a place yet?"

Lisa nodded. "How about Rutabagorz near campus?"

"Perfect. I love that place."

Lisa looked pleased that Celeste liked their food and that she'd made the right choice. "Great. Athena and I will meet you and Olivia there around seven if that's okay. We could probably make it a little earlier, but practice is late tomorrow and doesn't end until six."

"Seven is fine. We'll see you both there. And again, great job tonight."

Lisa and Athena gathered their things and went to meet with the team.

"Are you sure you want me crashing your dinner tomorrow night? I feel a little weird."

"I told you, Athena, it's a friendly dinner amongst colleagues. It was Celeste's idea to invite you and her friend. It's totally fine."

"All right, pal. If you say so. It was nice of her to come to the game. What did she say when you told her we saw her in Las Vegas?"

"I didn't tell her and you're not going to either. I get the feeling she didn't want me to know, otherwise she would have told me when I told her we'd been in Vegas at the same time. She seems to keep things close to her vest. She's not very forthcoming about personal things, but she's starting to open up a little each time we see each other."

"Okay, I won't say anything, but I don't think it's anything for her to be embarrassed about. She did a great job."

"Agreed, buddy, but we're not going to bring it up."

They opened the door to the team's meeting room and found the ladies dancing and letting loose. They quieted down when they saw Lisa and gave her their attention.

"Great job, team. We're getting better with each game. Logan, great defense and shooting tonight." The team cheered and whooped it up. "Mac, outstanding rebounding." More cheers. "Novac, nice game when you weren't messing with your hair." The team busted out in laughter, including Novac.

"Sorry, Coach. Won't happen again."

"Okay, ladies, bring it in. Remember, practice starts at four tomorrow so be in the training room by three to get your ankles taped." They all reached in and put their hands together and shouted "team." They cheered then scattered to the training room and locker room.

Lisa loved how hard this team worked in practice, games, and in the classroom, but they also knew how to let loose and have a good time. Lisa felt this was one of the best teams she'd ever coached.

Chapter Thirteen

Celeste parked about a block away from the restaurant, and she and Olivia exited the car. The streets of Old Town had been decorated for the holidays for the past two weeks, but this was the first time Celeste had been able to appreciate them. There was red, green, silver, and gold garland wrapped around the street posts and different Happy Holiday signs on each side of the street. In the small park at the center of the traffic circle, there was a humongous Christmas tree decorated in lights and ornaments, and also giant decorative nutcrackers scattered about. Maybe after dinner, she could talk the ladies into taking a stroll over to the park to see the decorations up close.

They approached Lisa and Athena standing in front of the restaurant. Athena was dressed casually with jeans, a gray hoodie sweatshirt, and tennis shoes. She looked like she was dressed to have dinner with friends. Lisa, on the other hand, was dressed like she was going on a date, and Celeste couldn't help but feel a little thrill. Did Lisa dress that nice when she went out with friends, or did she dress up a little more for Celeste? Lisa was wearing nice dark blue jeans, a deep red button-down shirt, a black leather jacket, and black loafers. Celeste had seen Lisa dress nice before, but this was a different look from what Celeste was used to. Lisa looked gorgeous, and Celeste was disappointed once again that they worked together. If Lisa didn't work for Glassell University and Celeste had met Lisa at a random get-together or social function, she definitely would've loved dating Lisa.

Celeste and Olivia reached Lisa and Athena, and there was an awkward moment where she didn't know if she should hug or shake hands with Lisa, or just do nothing except say hello. Instead, she introduced Olivia to Lisa and Athena, they shook hands, then they all went inside. The restaurant was fairly busy since it was a Friday night, but they managed to get a back corner table away from the noise. Lisa, like a true gentlewoman, held out the chairs for Celeste and Olivia to be seated, then draped her jacket over her chair before sitting down. Celeste caught Olivia's side glance as Lisa was holding out their chairs, and she knew there would be a conversation about that later. If Celeste could read Olivia's mind, she would've said, "Are you kidding me? If you don't go out with her, I may leave Carl and go out with her myself."

Athena started off the conversation by asking if Olivia had been to this restaurant. She said she'd been just three or four times, then Athena told them that she and Lisa lived nearby and ate there at least once a week because of its healthier food choices, but she admitted indulging in a beer or two with dinner. Celeste idly wondered how Athena handled her alcohol, being as small as she was. She was shorter than Celeste and very trim. Olivia had said something humorous and Athena's laugh was loud, joyful, and infectious. So far, Celeste liked Athena. Halfway through dinner, Athena started focusing her questions on Celeste—how long she'd been at GU, where she'd taught before, where she'd gone to school. All innocent questions until Olivia started asking Lisa the same questions. Celeste thought she'd seen a look of plotting pass between Olivia and Athena, but she couldn't be sure. Lisa had been fairly quiet during the dinner, and Celeste wondered if she wasn't having a good time or if she was shy or if she just didn't know what to say. Celeste found that odd since she was so vocal during games, and she didn't have a problem talking when it was just the two of them.

After they finished dinner, Celeste asked if Lisa and Athena wanted to join them to go see the giant Christmas tree in the traffic circle park.

Athena answered without asking Lisa. "Yeah, that would be great. We were just talking about that earlier."

Lisa scrunched her eyebrows together. "We were?"

Athena elbowed Lisa in her ribs, causing Lisa to flinch. "Yes. Remember when I was telling you I'd like to go see the decorations and walk through the neighborhood to see the decorated houses?"

"No."

Athena's eyes grew wide and she spoke slowly. "Well, I did." Athena looked back to Celeste and Olivia. "She's usually not this forgetful." Athena laughed nervously.

Lisa shrugged and smiled. Celeste laughed and put her arm through Lisa's when Athena and Olivia walked ahead of them. Celeste leaned in close and quietly inhaled Lisa's scent. Whenever she smelled cedar wood or sage, she thought of Lisa. It was woodsy, slightly masculine, and Celeste could picture Lisa in a log cabin with her flannel sleeves rolled up, faded jeans, and boots, stoking a fire. Speaking of stoking a fire, Celeste was feeling very warm all of a sudden. She spoke softly into Lisa's ear. "I think our friends are up to something." Celeste could feel Lisa shiver when she spoke. She had an urge to evoke another shiver from Lisa.

"I have no idea why Athena is acting so strange tonight. I don't know what's gotten into her."

Celeste found Lisa adorably gullible. Did she really not see their friends conspiring to get Celeste and Lisa to spend more time talking to each other? Or wait. Maybe they weren't actually doing that and it was all in Celeste's head. Just then, Olivia and Athena turned to get a peek at Celeste and Lisa then quickly faced forward again. *Uh-huh. They're conspiring.*

"I really enjoyed dinner tonight."

Lisa turned her head slightly to look at Celeste. "I did too. I wanted to tell you that you look very pretty tonight."

Celeste blushed but was pleased with the compliment. She had stressed about what she was going to wear. She knew it wasn't a date, but she still wanted to look nice.

"Thank you. That's very sweet of you to say. You look pretty handsome yourself. I love this jacket." Celeste caressed the soft, supple leather that covered Lisa's arm, and she felt that shiver again.

Lisa stood a little taller and prouder after Celeste's compliment. Despite what others might think, Lisa didn't have a lot of experience with women. She'd had a girlfriend in college and in her early to mid-twenties, but once she started coaching, she started fully concentrating on that. Not to say she didn't date now and then, but never during a season. She hooked up with a woman occasionally when she was on vacation but hadn't met anyone she thought would want to be with a coach and all of the time it took up. Especially at the higher levels when there was more traveling for recruiting, trips, games, and tournaments.

To be honest, Lisa was extremely attracted to Celeste, but it wouldn't be fair to start something with her when she knew she wasn't planning to stay at GU for long. It might be this year or next, but she had her ear to the ground, listening for possible head coaching vacancies at the Division I level.

They arrived to the center of the traffic circle and wandered around with some other people looking at the decorations. When they got to the tree, Lisa pulled out her cell phone.

"Celeste, why don't you and Olivia stand in front of the tree and I'll take your picture?"

Lisa snapped a few, then Olivia offered to take a picture of Athena and Lisa. They threw their arms around each other's shoulders, and Athena made a goofy face in some of them.

"Okay, now Lisa and Celeste. I want a picture of you both."

Lisa looked at Celeste, who looked like she wasn't sure if it was a good idea. Finally, they stood next to each other with a respectable distance between them.

"For heaven's sake, act like you like each other."

Lisa and Celeste moved closer, and Lisa slid her arm behind Celeste's lower back and rested her hand on her hip. It felt intimate but natural to have her hand on Celeste's hip, and she pictured them walking down a street or the beach with her arm around Celeste, just as it was now.

Athena broke the daydream and the mood. "Hey, let's go to O'Hara's for a drink. My treat."

Lisa looked at Celeste. "We better take advantage of that. Athena's such a cheapskate, who knows when an offer like that might come around again."

Celeste laughed and hooked her arm through Lisa's again. "In that case, let's go have a drink."

They walked back toward the restaurant until they reached the pub. It was a dark hole in the wall joint that smelled like beer and decades-old cigarette smoke.

"Coach!" The greeting was so loud that Celeste startled.

"Hey, guys. How's it going?"

They walked up to the bar as the bartender was wiping it down with a white damp rag. "How did the game go last night?"

Athena piped in. "We won, of course." The bartender held up his hand and Athena gave him a high five.

"Still waiting to see you at a game, Connor."

"I know. You should schedule them on days I don't work."

Lisa winked at him and pointed. "Maybe you shouldn't schedule your work days on our game days."

"Ooh, Coach got you there, Connor."

"Anyways, what can I get ya?"

Olivia and Celeste ordered glasses of wine while Lisa and Athena ordered Guinness on tap. Since Connor was a true Irishman, he knew how to pour a proper pint. Athena handed over the money, and they took their drinks over to a table to continue their evening.

Athena set her drink down and asked Olivia if she wanted to dance, and she obliged. Celeste and Lisa watched them for a minute before they said anything.

"Is Olivia gay?"

Celeste stopped mid sip of her wine and set down her glass. "No, she's been married for twelve years to a great man named Carl. Why?"

"I'm worried that Athena may be barking up the wrong tree with her. She's been flirting with Olivia all night."

"No, she hasn't."

"Sure, she has. They're completely ignoring us."

Celeste laughed and placed her hand over Lisa's. "They're trying to give us time alone. I know that Olivia is very interested in you and I getting together, and I think she's hoping if they're not around, that we'll stare into each other's eyes and fall madly in love with each other."

Lisa rolled her eyes and shook her head. "Now that you mention it, Athena said we should get together, as well. She was pretty hesitant in coming tonight even though I told her we agreed to go out as friends."

"What a bunch of busybodies."

Lisa threw her head back and laughed. "To be honest, I am very attracted to you, but during basketball season, I don't have much time to go out. Besides, I don't know how much longer I'll be here."

"What do you mean?"

Lisa tried to downplay what she just said. She wanted to keep quiet about it because she didn't know what would happen, but now Celeste was curious. "Eh, I don't want to talk about it tonight, but I'll just say that other coaching opportunities at larger universities might come up."

"Oh, I see." Celeste picked up her wine and took a sip while she turned away from Lisa to watch Olivia and Athena dance. Lisa noticed Celeste got quiet after Lisa told her that, but what else was she supposed to say? At times like this, she'd wished she didn't feel so awkward with ladies in a social setting. Was that ever something she'd get over? Maybe she was destined to spend the rest of her life single, or married to basketball.

Olivia and Athena came over and asked them to dance. Athena took Celeste's hand and Olivia grabbed Lisa's. She reluctantly followed Olivia to the small dance floor, and the four of them danced together for two songs. When the next song was a ballad, Olivia and Athena gently pushed their respective partners together. Celeste was about to go back to the table when Lisa grabbed her hand.

"Dance with me." It wasn't a request.

❖

Damn it, Celeste felt good in Lisa's arms. A little too good. Lisa had her right hand on Celeste's left hip, and Celeste's right hand was in Lisa's left. Lisa pulled her closer into her body, and Celeste felt the heat immediately between them. She wondered if Lisa felt it too. God, she smelled good. The mixture of Lisa's cologne and her leather jacket was intoxicating. Celeste's left hand was on Lisa's right shoulder, and she could feel the hardness of Lisa's muscles under her hand.

Celeste had been taken aback when Lisa said she'd go to coach at another school if the opportunity came up. And why wouldn't it? She was great with her team and they were winning. Celeste would be sorry to see her go though. The more she got to know Lisa, the more she liked her. Celeste was sure they could've become better friends, and she'd miss her when Lisa left the school. Celeste didn't see the allure of working for a large university, especially now that she'd had a taste of working for a small private university. She liked being able to know her students, the faculty, and she liked feeling like she was part of the community. She wondered what drew Lisa to coaching for a large university. Celeste had to keep thinking about things like that because if she didn't, she'd think too much about how good she felt dancing with Lisa and being held so close to her body. She'd had an undeniable urge to get closer, to be like a second skin to Lisa, but she worried that Lisa would feel the pounding of her heart through her chest. Celeste also feared that Lisa would place her hand on her fat roll above her waist and would be grossed out. Celeste looked and felt better since she'd lost her weight, but with that weight loss came extra skin and stretch marks, as well as some leftover fat rolls. She already knew how Jackie felt about them; she'd told her the night they'd broken up.

The insults that Jackie had spewed had done some damage to Celeste's self-esteem. She'd felt that all of the counseling and lessons in self-love and self-respect gathered into a ball and rolled down hill. After she broke up with Jackie, Celeste went right back to work on having a positive body image, but she still had periods of doubt, like now that she was in a gorgeous, fit woman's arms. She felt herself grow warm and she was sure she was blushing. She was just thankful that it wasn't very light in the bar so that Lisa would notice.

Speaking of noticing (not), the song morphed into a faster tune, but she and Lisa were still dancing slowly. Lisa spoke into Celeste's ear, and she shivered throughout her body.

"The song is over." Lisa said it but she didn't back away in an effort to stop dancing so Celeste did.

"Thanks for the dance, Coach." Celeste and Lisa walked back to their table with Lisa's hand on the small of Celeste's back. Even though she knew better, that small gesture made Celeste feel protected, safe, and if she was being honest, a lot aroused. She had a vision of walking into an event on Lisa's arm and being the envy of the women in the room. Okay, it was time to call it an evening. Celeste's mind was a jumbled mess, and she didn't trust herself not to say or do something she'd regret.

"Well, everyone, I think it's time for us to go." Celeste gave Olivia a look that expressed she better not challenge her on that. "I had a really great time and I hope we can do it again." Celeste started to put on her jacket, but Lisa grabbed it and held it for Celeste to slip her arms through the sleeves. That awkward moment came again, and Celeste wasn't sure if she should shake Lisa's hand or give her a hug. She went for something completely different and a little bold for her—she took her hand then leaned in and kissed her on the cheek. She left a smudge of lipstick on Lisa's smooth skin, and Celeste wiped it off with the pad of her thumb. For someone who said they just wanted to be friends, Lisa was sending off mixed signals. While her words said "friends," the aroused look in her eyes said "lovers." Celeste caught one more shared look between Olivia and Athena before they left the bar.

As they were walking back to the car, Celeste nudged Olivia. "What's going on with you and Athena? Don't think I don't know what you two are up to."

Olivia opened her mouth and looked like she was going to deny it, then she just shrugged. "Look, Athena and I agreed that you and Lisa would make a striking couple. And Athena told me that she thinks Lisa is attracted to you."

"Athena thinks Lisa is attracted to me? Are we in the seventh grade now? Will she pass me a note asking me if I want to be her girlfriend? Come on, Olivia."

Olivia giggled. "Sarcastic much?"

"I told you before, and this will be the last time I say this. I don't want to date anyone I work with. Besides, she told me tonight that she's hoping to get a job offer from a bigger school, but keep that quiet. I don't know if Athena knows and I'm sure her team doesn't."

"Why would anyone want to leave Glassell University? This is the best place to be."

"I know, right? She said this is the first time she's been affiliated with a smaller school, and I think she wants to coach at a higher level. I mean, I can't blame her if that's what she wants, and she'd probably make more money, but if she does leave, I'm not going to follow because unlike her, I love being at a small school. Why should we get involved when her future is uncertain?"

"Well, now that I know that huge piece of information, I promise to leave you alone. But I stand by my opinion in that you two would make a great looking couple."

Celeste sighed. "I think so too."

❖

"That was fun."

"Uh-huh."

"And Olivia is a lot of fun."

Lisa and Athena were walking home from their night out with Celeste and Olivia, and although it was only a kiss on the cheek that Celeste gave her, Lisa was having a difficult time following Athena's simple comments. Her focus was on remembering how soft Celeste's lips felt on her skin. If she closed her eyes, she could almost feel them lingering on her cheek. But closing her eyes while walking was a good way for her to trip and do a face plant into the sidewalk. Also, she didn't want Athena to see how affected she'd been by a simple good-bye peck on the cheek. But really, how simple was it? There was a look in Celeste's eyes as she wiped her lipstick off Lisa's cheek. A look that said, "too bad you want to be just friends because you have no idea what you're missing." But Lisa already had a feeling what she'd be missing out on by the way Celeste moved her body and hips while pole dancing and while dancing in Lisa's arms earlier that night. Besides, Celeste was the one who wanted to have dinner as friends. She was being a tease, was what she was doing.

"Yeah, she seemed very nice." Lisa needed to stop daydreaming of Celeste or Athena was going to torture the hell out of her. The last thing she wanted was Athena telling her she told her so. "Celeste thought you and Olivia were pushing us together. How do you plead?"

"I plead the Fifth, Your Coach."

Lisa laughed and playfully shoved her. "You can be such an ass, you know that, Chang?"

"Yeah, so you've told me before. See? I'm not the only one that thinks you two would be good together. Olivia told me the same thing."

"And I told you to leave it alone. Why can't you just mind your own business?"

The night was dark, but there was enough light from the streetlamp to see Athena's frown. Lisa had seen that look more than a few times—she'd hurt Athena's feelings. "I'm sorry, buddy. That was a dick thing for me to say."

"Yeah, it was. I just want you to find someone for you to love and who loves you back. Is that so much for your best friend to ask?"

"No, and I appreciate your concern, but I'm not looking to start something with Celeste, okay? I don't see you going on any dates either, my friend."

"Well, Ms. Nosy, just so happens I have a coffee date next Sunday with a woman I met online."

"What? You didn't tell me you joined a dating site. When did this happen?"

"Just last week. I didn't want to tell you until I had a chance to see how it was."

"Wow. Good for you, buddy. Tell me about her."

"I will after I have coffee with her. I want to see if there's anything there before I get too involved."

"All right." Lisa slung her arm over Athena's shoulder and gave her a one-armed hug. "Hey, how do you feel about tomorrow's game?"

Athena laughed. "Why did you even schedule this game? Us against a Division I school? Are you crazy?"

"Come on. You know it'll be a good game for us. It's not like that team is a high-level school, but it helps build up our schedule strength in case we need that extra push to get into the post-season tournament. Besides, you never know, right? Can you imagine how our girls would react if they beat this team? And I honestly think we can win."

"I do too as long as they don't get intimidated."

They walked a little longer in silence, and before they reached the home they shared, Lisa stopped Athena. "I really am sorry for telling you to mind your business. You're my best friend and you know I love you, right? You're my sister from another mister."

"I know, buddy. We're cool. And I promise not to try to push you and Celeste together anymore."

Lisa knew Athena well enough to know she probably had her fingers crossed behind her back.

CHAPTER FOURTEEN

L isten up, ladies. Today's game is going to be a real test. We're having a great season so far with only one loss, but our opponents have a bit higher caliber of player than what we've faced so far. But I believe in you." Lisa looked around the room and was sure to meet every single one of her players' eyes to make sure they were hearing her. "I. Believe. In. You. We'll win this game if you give one hundred percent from opening tip to final buzzer. No letting up at all. Leave it all out on the floor and you'll win this game."

The team cheered and lined up to run out on to the court for warm-ups. The coaches followed and walked to the bench, then huddled together to talk once more about the game plan. Nobody would ever accuse Lisa of having her team unprepared. She looked up into the stands and saw Celeste and Olivia about six rows up from the bench. Lisa had been assaulted by the memory of Celeste kissing her cheek the night before and how her soft lips lingered just a smidge. She waved to both of them, then Athena looked up and waved a little more animatedly than Lisa did.

Okay, Lisa needed to focus which meant she couldn't continue to look at Celeste like she was the only woman in the gym. She called Logan over to give her some last-minute instructions. Emily had looked a little confused since Lisa had already given her that information, but Lisa needed to feel a little more game-minded.

The buzzer rang, and the team jogged over to the bench to get ready for introductions. Lisa took one more glance into the crowded stands to find Celeste looking—not looking—studying her, and she quickly turned away. Damn it. She needed to stop looking at her. There was something about Celeste that made Lisa forget about everything but her. Oh, good. The national anthem was beginning. Lisa placed her right hand over her heart and softly sang the words. She got so involved in the game from the opening tip, she didn't even glance into the stands for the duration of the game. She was happy she was able to regain her focus on her priorities.

Halftime came and GU was trailing the other team by fifteen points. Lisa got pretty colorful during her halftime speech. She criticized her players for being timid and letting their opponent do whatever they wanted. "I thought you ladies were better than this. The coaches and I have given you all the tools and knowledge to win this game. We can't go out and play it for you so you need to decide if you're ready to finally start playing like you're capable or just call it quits and hit the showers. Personally, I didn't think I was coaching a bunch of quitters, but hell, I've been wrong before. If you all don't start giving your all, and you keep playing like a bunch of scared little girls, you won't even see a basketball at the next practice. I'll toughen you up by running sprints. Is that what you want?" By that time, Lisa was yelling, and she was sure her face was red and her blood pressure was elevated. "Now, get your asses out there and stop embarrassing this team and this school." Lisa hated talking that way to her team, and she hardly ever did, but she only did it for shock value. Sometimes, a team needed tough love to get the fire started.

The way the girls hung their heads, Lisa was sure they were going to go out there and get their asses handed to them. They hadn't had much challenge with the teams they'd played so far, and in Lisa's opinion, her team was much better than the team they were playing. When Lisa and her assistants entered the gym, she saw her team huddled at midcourt and she could see Emily gesturing with her hands and pointing at different players. She was angry, Lisa could see it in her eyes, along with determination. At that moment, Lisa knew they were going to win.

For the remainder of the game, the Panthers were diving for loose balls, hitting three-point shots, blocking out on rebounds, taking care of the ball so as not to turn it over. This was the team she knew. She never did find out what Logan said to her teammates in the middle of the court before the second half started, but Lisa didn't need to know. Emily stepped up and took over the game. That's what Lisa had done when she was a player and captain of her team.

The game was tied with eighteen seconds, and GU had the ball. Lisa called a timeout and devised a play to get off the last shot. Logan had been making most of the shots in the second half, and Lisa knew the other team would be double-teaming her, but they'd be ready for it. The whistle blew and the ball was thrown to Emily. She stood facing the defender and the basket. When the clock got down to eight seconds, Emily faked a shot and dribbled closer to the basket. When another defender came out to help, Emily passed the ball to Novac and she made the short jump shot as time expired. Lisa tried to play it cool, like this was just another game, but she really wanted to jump in the air, pump her fist, scream out, and run up into the stands and hug Celeste. Wait. Back up. She'd revisit that later. She had basketball obligations first, and she led her team to congratulate the other team.

The opposing coach, a woman Lisa had known for over ten years in the coaching ranks, stopped Lisa and spoke softly into her ear.

"Great job tonight, Coach. If you're ever looking to get back to the big schools, let me know. I might have some leads for you by the end of the season."

"Thanks, Julie. I appreciate it. Good game." Lisa continued down the line until she'd shaken the last player's hand. She waved to some parents and other supporters in the stands on her way to the team's meeting room. The players and coaches celebrated what would now be the school's historic win. Never in Glassell University's women's basketball history had they beaten a Division I school.

"You guys had me going there for a while. Logan, I'm not sure what you said to the team before the second half started, and I don't need to know, but I am so damn proud of this team for not giving up, working harder than you've ever had to work on the court. The fact that you kept your cool and clawed back from fifteen points down says a lot about your character. You get tomorrow off from practice. You earned it."

Logan looked confused and raised her hand. "Um, Coach, tomorrow's Sunday. We don't normally practice on Sundays."

Lisa pointed at Logan and winked. "Exactly!"

The players laughed and groaned. "Not cool, Coach."

Lisa laughed and gave Angela Novac, who was standing next to her, a one-armed hug. "Get some rest tomorrow, ladies. It's back to work on Monday. You have finals next week so if any of you have conflicting schedules with practice, let me know. Conference games start in early January, just a few weeks from now, so we need to keep working hard and be ready. See you Monday."

Lisa walked back into the gym to greet some of the team's supporters. Not only were they there to physically and emotionally support the team, but they also financially helped out. Part of Lisa's job was soliciting donations to help pay for uniforms, travel funds, and the end of the season's awards ceremony. Some of the players' parents donated, but mostly they came from alumni, some former players, and some from alumni who just wanted to support GU athletics. Even though Lisa would like nothing more than to go grab a beer with Athena at the neighborhood pub, it was her job to talk with the people who'd been waiting around after the game.

The first two people she ran into when she came back into the gym were Celeste and Olivia. She gave them brief hugs—she'd wanted to give Celeste a better, longer hug, but she worried that it'd look strange so she refrained to a friendly one.

"Hey, thanks for coming, ladies. Olivia, I know this was the first game of ours you've seen. What did you think?"

"It was exciting. You must be so thrilled."

"I am. I'm so proud of my kids. Hey, I have to schmooze a bit, but would you two like to meet Athena and me at the pub for a beer?"

Without asking Celeste, Olivia answered for them. "That would be great. So, what? About thirty minutes?"

"Perfect. We'll see you soon." Lisa let her gaze linger with Celeste for a few seconds more, and she knew she was grinning like an idiot. At that point, Lisa felt like she was floating in the clouds. It was like breaking a powerful pull to look away and leave Celeste. Lisa spent the next fifteen minutes chatting with some of the older alumni, one couple that had graduated from the school in 1959. They were truly one of the most generous with donating their money, and they were in the stands for almost every home game. Lisa appreciated that more than the money. The couple had to be in their early eighties and still managed to sit on the hardwood bleachers. Okay, so they brought cushions to sit on but still.

Lisa moved to a group of parents that were standing together. That would be a quick greeting, just long enough to ease their minds about how well their daughters are doing, not only on the team but also in school. Besides checking in with Celeste for Emily Logan's schoolwork, she also checked on all of her players with the help of Athena. Her players wouldn't go on to play professional basketball, not that she'd encourage that anyway. It was a tough life to live in Europe part of the year, or some other continent playing basketball and being so far away from your family. They'd make a lot more money getting a job after graduation or post-grad studies. Lisa made sure to smile, shake hands, and look the parents in the eyes to let them know she was sincere, because she was, but she wanted to get out of there so they could go meet Celeste and Olivia.

She shook a few more hands and told them all to have a happy holiday. Finals were the following week, Christmas break started the week after, and Christmas was soon after that. Lisa didn't dare schedule games during finals week because she wanted her players to focus only on their schoolwork. And they had a few days off before and after Christmas so they could go home and be with their families. Come December twenty-eighth, the practices would resume, they'd have one more non-conference game shortly after New Year's, then their conference play began. All the games leading up to that point had been in order for the team to be ready. Their collective goal was to win their conference and move on to the national tournament.

Lisa spotted Athena talking to another set of parents so she walked over to say hello. She told Athena that she needed to speak to her privately in the office. They said good-bye to the parents and headed out.

"What's up?"

"We're meeting Olivia and Celeste at O'Hara's for drinks. We're due there in ten minutes."

"Cool."

They grabbed their wallets and keys then locked their office door behind them before they walked the two blocks to the pub. They walked through the door and applause erupted. Lisa and Athena were obviously surprised as they looked at each other with wide eyes.

"Congratulations, Coaches!"

"Thanks, Connor." Lisa walked over to the bar to place her order. "How did you know? I didn't see you at the game."

"I wasn't there, but they were." Connor nodded behind Lisa and Athena to Celeste and Olivia holding their glasses of wine up in salute. "First round is on the house, Coaches."

They had their beers poured and they went to sit with Celeste and Olivia.

"Hey there. Thanks for meeting us."

"Thanks for the invite. Did you get all your schmoozing in?"

Lisa laughed at the way Celeste said schmoozing. "We did. It's not so bad. In fact, I love that we have so many non-parents who are big supporters, including our esteemed professors."

Olivia spoke up. "Like I said, it was my first game I've been to, but it won't be my last. That was really exciting."

"I appreciate that. I think I can speak for Athena, given the finger marks she gave me from grabbing my arm," Lisa smirked at Athena, "that we found the game really exciting too. To be honest, I wasn't sure if we were going to have enough gas toward the end of the game to finish it off. When a team has to overcome a large deficit like we had, the players tend to expend a lot of energy, physically and mentally."

"Yeah," Athena said. "All that running we made them do during preseason conditioning and now during the season gave them the stamina to continue playing hard at the end."

Lisa laughed at Athena's maniacal look—wide eyes and mouth open.

Celeste raised her eyebrow. "It almost sounds like you enjoy torturing those poor kids."

Lisa and Athena answered together. "We do." They burst into laughter.

"We went through it when we played. It builds character." Lisa nodded her head matter-of-factly.

"Did you two play together?" Celeste looked to Athena, and Lisa felt like she was deliberately not looking her way. Lisa saw Celeste sneak some glances here and there but nothing lingering. Lisa wondered what that was about. Since Celeste continued looking at Athena, Lisa told her to tell them their story.

"Lisa and I played together in college, but when we graduated, Lisa went to Europe to play professionally for a few years. When she became a head coach for our alma mater, she called me up and asked me to join her. She got hired at GU a couple of years ago and asked if I wanted to come. I'd had enough of the East Coast winters, and California sounded like a good ticket."

The whole time Athena spoke, Lisa continued to glance over at Celeste. At one point, Celeste caught Lisa's gaze, and Lisa could swear there was a current that was passing between them. Celeste blushed and looked away. Damn, she was beautiful. And she made Lisa feel…things. She needed to put that thought in a little box and lock it up tight. The way the season was going so far, and especially after tonight, she would suspect coaching offers would start coming in toward the end of the season. That was another thing she didn't need to be thinking about right now. She was property of GU until the season was done, and she would continue molding her team while she was with them.

Athena finished her story and there was a blank space of silence so Lisa tried to fill it.

"Athena has been my best friend since college, and even though our paths went in different directions after we graduated, we always got together when I was in town in between seasons. We've been through a lot together, and when I became head coach, I couldn't think of anyone else I'd rather have by my side on the bench. We believe in the same basketball philosophy so there are rarely any coaching discrepancies between us."

Now Celeste's attention was on Lisa again, and Lisa couldn't pull her eyes away. Athena interrupted the moment.

"I'm going to get us another round."

Olivia jumped off her stool. "I'll come with you."

When Lisa and Celeste were alone, Lisa rolled her eyes. "I told Athena to stop trying to get us together."

Celeste nodded. "I told Olivia the same thing. Don't you love how they complied with our requests?"

Lisa shook her head. "I'm sorry, Celeste."

Celeste reached across the table and covered Lisa's hand with her own. "Don't be. They're harmless and they mean well. As long as you and I remain on the same page, then we'll be fine. I like you, Lisa, and I'm glad we've become friends. And I really like going to the games and learning about basketball."

"I like you too. You know, if you ever want to attend a practice, you're more than welcome."

Celeste thought about it, thought about what Emily would think about her being there. Or what the other players would think. Why would she be there? "I appreciate that, but I think I'll just let you tell me the mystique of women's college basketball."

"I'd be happy to."

Damn, why did everything that came out of Lisa's mouth sound like flirtation? They both were very good at flirting with one another. And why did Celeste feel the need to keep touching Lisa? She typically wasn't a touchy-feely person with people she didn't know well. True, she and Lisa were getting to know each other, as well as becoming friends, but it took Celeste a lot longer to be that way with Olivia and some of her other friends. There was something about Lisa that made Celeste want to touch her. Touch her a lot.

"So, no more games until after the first of the year?"

"No. With finals being next week and then Christmas, there really wasn't any time to squeeze in another game or two. Besides, the kids played really hard tonight. The break will be good for them. We'll continue with practices, but we'll have practice early on December twenty-third so the girls who are from out of town can travel that afternoon to spend Christmas with their families. We'll resume practice on the twenty-eighth."

"How about you, Lisa? Are you going home for Christmas?"

"No. Athena and I usually spend it together. Her parents are back in China, and my mom will go to my brother's to have it with his family. He has two kids under the age of ten so it's fun for her to be there on Christmas morning. Mom and my brother know that I don't have a lot of free time during the season so I usually take a week during spring break and two weeks toward the end of summer to go back home to Indiana and visit. How about you?"

"My parents live in France so I'll spend Christmas with Olivia and her husband. Is your father still alive? You only mentioned your mother and brother."

"No, he passed away almost ten years ago. He had a massive heart attack in his sleep."

Celeste reached out and grabbed Lisa's hand and squeezed it. "I'm so sorry." There she was, touching Lisa again, but this time it was for comfort.

Olivia and Athena were returning from the bar with their drinks so Celeste let go of Lisa's hand and sat back on her stool. She wanted to know more about Lisa's life, her family, but why? They were only going to be friends. She hadn't been this curious with Olivia. She also hadn't been attracted to Olivia like she was to Lisa.

"Hey, I have an idea. Why don't you all come to my house for dinner next Saturday night and celebrate the end of the semester? We'll have some drinks, listen to some music. What do you say?"

They all agreed that that sounded like fun, and they all exchanged phone numbers at that time since they were becoming friends. Once they'd finished their drinks, they said good-byes and agreed to see each other the following Saturday.

Later that night as Celeste was trying to fall asleep, she kept thinking about Lisa and Athena spending Christmas alone. Well, not exactly alone because they had each other, but she felt bad that they wouldn't see their families. Of course, neither would she, but at least her parents would be coming out to stay with her in February so she'd see them soon enough. She turned over in bed and fluffed her pillow. And she'd see Lisa on Saturday night. Correction. Lisa, Athena, Olivia, and Carl. She finally drifted off to sleep after thinking about what their night together would entail.

CHAPTER FIFTEEN

Lisa knocked on the door to a gorgeous one-story Craftsman home that was popular in Old Town. When she'd parked in front of the house with the screened-in front porch, she let out a small, low whistle. She loved the architecture that inhabited the tree-lined streets near the college, but the prices of these homes were way out of her league even if she wanted to stay at Glassell University and buy her own home. The house that she and Athena lived in was university-owned and provided free of charge except for utilities. The house had been included in Lisa's contract with the school, and it was a nice perk to have, especially since real estate was so high in this area. Her own place was only a little less than a mile away, four blocks south and six blocks east, but now that it was December, it was a little too chilly at night to walk. Besides, Lisa arrived with a nice bottle of wine and a bouquet of flowers she brought as a hostess gift.

Celeste answered the door, looking amazing in a burnt orange colored V-neck sweater and brown slacks. She looked more relaxed than Lisa had ever seen her, and she wondered if it was due to finals being over. Lisa didn't feel too underdressed—she was wearing black jeans, a white button-down shirt, and her black leather jacket. Athena would probably dress similarly to Lisa, and Olivia would probably dress similarly to Celeste. Lisa had noticed that they'd worn the same style of clothes. Lisa handed the flowers to Celeste who brought them to her nose and deeply inhaled.

"They're beautiful, Coach. Thank you."

Lisa checked her watch. She was a few minutes early, but she figured Olivia and her husband would be here by now. She didn't know how long it would take to grab the flowers so she'd left her house a little early so she wouldn't be late.

"Athena isn't with you?"

"No, she was in San Diego today scouting a team for us. She should be here soon."

"Well, I guess it'll just be us for a while then. Olivia called me this morning to say she woke with a fever and didn't want to get the rest of us sick."

"That's too bad. I hope she feels better soon."

"Come on in and make yourself comfortable."

Lisa handed over the bottle of wine that she'd brought for dinner. "I wasn't sure what we were having for dinner so if this doesn't go, you can save it for another time."

"I made a lasagna so this is perfect. Do you want a glass now or I have beer if you'd prefer?"

"A beer would be great." Lisa noticed Celeste pulled a bottle of her favorite beer out of the refrigerator and poured it in a glass she'd pulled out of the freezer. Lisa took a drink and set down her glass on the counter. "Perfect. My favorite."

"I know."

Lisa saw the blush that infused Celeste's cheeks before she opened the oven to check on dinner. She knew what Lisa's favorite beer was, huh? She'd been paying attention. Her phone buzzed in her front pocket and she pulled it out, seeing the name on the screen.

"Hey, Athena. What's your ETA? What? Are you serious? What about dinner? Okay. Be careful. Yeah, I'll tell her. See you later." Lisa put her phone back in her pocket and turned around to find Celeste staring at her. "Well, Athena is stuck in traffic. According to her traffic app, there was an overturned truck with a chemical spill. Freeway is shut down for the next few hours. She's going to pull off the freeway and grab a bite to eat. I guess it's just us tonight, or would you like to reschedule?"

"No, dinner is almost done and I'd like for you to stay. I guess we won't be playing any games tonight."

Lisa laughed and took another drink of her beer. "No, I guess not, but dinner smells terrific and I'm looking forward to tonight."

"I'm glad because I won't be able to eat all this food."

Lisa and Celeste decided to plate their food in the kitchen buffet-style rather than bring all of the dishes out to the dining table. They took their seats and Lisa poured wine for them both. She held up her glass to Celeste's. "To new friendship."

Celeste took a sip of her wine while holding Lisa's gaze. Lisa cleared her throat, placed her glass down, then cut into her lasagna with her fork. When she swallowed the piece she'd eaten, she shook her head.

"That's so good, Celeste. I'm glad Olivia and Athena aren't here. I'll probably end up eating their share." Lisa took another bite. "You know, I wonder if Athena and Olivia are in cahoots again to push us together." Lisa pulled her cell phone out and opened the traffic app. "Nope. Freeway is shut down."

Celeste answered back. "Olivia sounded awful on the phone this morning so I didn't have any doubt that she was truly sick."

"I'm sorry. It's awful for me to think that. I just found it suspicious that both of them weren't able to make it tonight."

"Yes, it would be easy to suspect those two, given their track record." Celeste laughed and Lisa joined in. "It'll give us a chance to know each other better." A vision of Celeste and Lisa in the throes of passion assaulted Celeste's mind, Lisa on top of her, exploring every inch of Celeste's body with her mouth, her tongue, her hands. That wasn't exactly what she meant when they could get to know each other, but maybe that wouldn't be such a bad thing. They could be friends with benefits. Leave the love and feelings out of it and just have sex once in a while to relieve stress or scratch an itch. Celeste wondered if Lisa might be a willing participant in that idea, but Celeste had no idea, or the courage to ask Lisa.

"What do you want to know?"

Celeste's musings came to a screeching stop. Did she say all of her thoughts out loud without knowing? "Pardon me?"

"You said we could get to know each other better. What would you like to know?"

"Oh, yes. Let me think." Celeste took a moment to take a sip of wine and gather her thoughts. "What got you involved in basketball and coaching?"

"Oh, so we're starting off easy." Lisa winked at Celeste and she nearly choked on her bite of food.

"Well, I started playing on the playground during elementary school. I was tall so the captain always picked me first during recess. It helped that I came from an athletic background. Parents, aunts, uncles, cousins, grandparents…nearly all of them played some kind of sport and were good at it. I kept at it. Practiced basketball all the time. I studied it. Watched games. There wasn't a lot of exposure to women playing basketball at that time, not like there is now. But my idols, Nancy Lieberman, Ann Donovan, Cheryl Miller, were the ones I wanted to be like. The early pioneers of the game. Am I boring you?"

"God, no. I wasn't really exposed to a lot of sports when I was growing up because my parents weren't athletes. I want to know more about basketball."

"Okay." Lisa took a bite of food and Celeste watched Lisa's mouth cover the fork. She looked down at her own plate so she wouldn't get worked up again.

"I got a scholarship to play basketball on the East Coast, and that's where I met Athena. We became good friends from the very beginning, which our teammates found amusing because we were so different from each other."

"Different how?"

"Well, I'm sure you've noticed by now that I'm a pretty laid-back person outside of basketball and Athena has a lot of energy. She's always on the go, always moving."

Celeste laughed and held her index finger and thumb close together.

"Right. But our work ethic was the same when we played, but I think we also balance each other out."

"Did you two ever get together?" Celeste wasn't sure she wanted to know the answer to that question, but her curiosity made her ask anyways.

"God, no. Neither one of us was attracted to the other. We've always been like sisters."

The relief Celeste felt was almost palpable, and she felt a small weight release from her body. She didn't think there'd been anything between them because they didn't act like lovers—or former lovers. They acted like buddies. That was the best word she could find to describe it. Celeste wouldn't exactly call Lisa and Athena butch. Well, maybe soft butches with athleticism thrown in. Lisa had medium length hair, and when she wore it down, it gave her a little more softness and that smidge of femininity. When it was up, her athletic butch side came out. Athena had short hair and always had her athletic butchness. She was nice and extremely funny, but there was nothing soft about her that Celeste had seen. Not that it wasn't there, but Celeste didn't know Athena that well yet.

Lisa continued with her basketball history. "After college, I played professionally in Europe for a few years, but I sustained a couple of serious injuries. My body started breaking down on me, and I wanted to come back to the United States. I called my college coach who had just been hired at a school in Chicago and she hired me on as an assistant. After five more years, she decided to retire and recommended me for the head coaching job. I had a few mediocre seasons, then a few winning seasons, and I was offered the head coaching job at a school that had a history of making the NCAA tournament every year, and they had standards they wanted to uphold after their coach left to coach in the WNBA. They hired me, I took Athena with me, and I had four years with them, but I failed to take the team to the national tournament the last two years so they fired me."

"How awful that they did that to you."

Lisa shrugged. "Eh, not really. Coaching is a business, and at that level, you either produce championships or they'll find somebody who will. Shortly after I got fired, I was approached for assistant jobs, but I only wanted to be head coach. I applied to Glassell University, and fortunately they hired me, so here I am."

"But you don't want to stay here." It was said as a comment, not a question. Lisa had already told Celeste that she was hoping to coach at a large university.

"Don't get me wrong, Celeste. I like GU. I like the campus, I like the friends I've made here, I love the community, but it can't give me what a Division I university can give me."

"And what's that?" Celeste was truly interested because she felt the exact opposite. She felt GU, being a small, private university, was able to give her what the larger universities couldn't—smaller class sizes; chancellors and deans who weren't completely driven by politics; a small gorgeous campus with grassy knolls, stone and metal sculptures, fountains, and mature trees that made it look more like a park rather than an academic institution. And despite it being such a small school, they were ranked in the top ten universities in the United States.

"More money, state-of-the-art facilities, better athletes," Lisa ticked each thing off her fingers, "and maybe an opportunity to coach at a professional level."

"Wow." Celeste shook her head and placed her fork on her plate, suddenly losing her appetite. "That sounds really…" What was the word she was looking for? "Selfish."

Lisa backed away from the table against the chair back like she'd been slapped. Celeste knew that might have been harsh, but Lisa basically disrespected GU, and Celeste wouldn't stand for it.

"Selfish? How is it selfish for me to want to pursue my dreams? To want to be the best coach I can be?"

"You don't think you can be the best coach here?"

"No, frankly, I don't. At my previous job, some of our games were televised. High school star athletes knew me, knew my name, and wanted to play for me. We traveled by our school's private plane, stayed in nice hotels, and the school paid for it. We didn't have to do fundraisers. Here, there isn't a lot of money to dish out to teams despite the fact that tuition costs over fifty thousand dollars a year. We fly on a cheap airline, stay in cheap motels, and eat at inexpensive restaurants. I've experienced it all, Celeste, and I don't think it's selfish at all to know what I want and how to get it. Thanks for dinner, but I've lost my appetite." Lisa set her fork down and placed her napkin on the table before standing and heading toward the door.

Celeste quickly followed, and when Lisa opened the door, Celeste closed it. Lisa turned around and looked so angry, so fired up, so *hot*. Celeste backed Lisa against it, grabbed her face, and kissed Lisa like there would be no tomorrow.

Lisa was stunned. Celeste had called her selfish a minute ago and now she was kissing her like she'd never see her again. Lisa didn't kiss her back. She broke her lips free from Celeste's then looked into her brown eyes that were dark with arousal. Celeste's face was flushed and her chest was heaving. Lust took over Lisa, and she turned them around until she had Celeste pinned up against the door, then kissed her hard.

Celeste parted her lips and Lisa pushed her tongue into Celeste's mouth, and Celeste moaned. Teeth clashed and lips pressed together. Lisa placed her hands on the door, on either side of Celeste's face, and leaned her body into Celeste. A whimper emanated from Celeste as she grabbed Lisa's hips and pulled her tight against her. God, how could Celeste drive Lisa so crazy one minute to the point where Lisa wanted to strangle her, to driving her so crazy the next where Lisa wanted to tear off Celeste's clothes and fuck her until she screamed? Lisa placed her hands on Celeste's sides and slid them up until she reached her full breasts and squeezed, feeling Celeste's nipples harden against her palms. Lisa played with her nipples and rolled them between her thumbs and index fingers. Celeste pulled her mouth away, grabbed Lisa's head, and pulled her hair.

"Oh, God, Lisa. That feels so good. I want your hands all over me."

Lisa's mouth moved to Celeste's exposed neck and she kissed, licked, nibbled, and bit the soft skin, feeling her pulse thrum against her lips. Lisa stopped just long enough to pull Celeste's sweater over her head and drop it to the floor. Celeste wore a cream-colored lacy bra that fully covered her breasts. Celeste reached behind her, unhooked her bra, and let it slide down her arms, where it joined her sweater on the floor. Lisa replaced her hands on Celeste's breasts and kneaded them then brought her mouth over one of Celeste's erect nipples and sucked on it hard. Celeste let go of Lisa's hair and clumsily unbuttoned and unzipped her pants, and took one of Lisa's hands and shoved it in her underwear. Lisa knew what to do from there, and she moved her fingers into Celeste's wetness and spread it over her swollen clit. Celeste's hips bucked and she screamed out.

"Right there." Celeste gasped and bucked her hips again.

Lisa stroked her fingers up and down over Celeste's clit until her breathing quickened, then she slid two fingers into her sex, pumped her fingers in and out, then used her thumb to stroke her clit simultaneously. Celeste's body started shaking and Lisa wrapped one arm around her waist to prevent her from falling. Three more strokes had Celeste screaming out Lisa's name followed by heavy breathing and panting.

Holy hell. Lisa just had sex with Celeste Bouchard. Up against her front door. They were both breathing hard, and Celeste was slumped forward as Lisa held her up. Lisa was in awe of how responsive and passionate Celeste was. Damn! What the hell just happened? Lisa had never thought for a second that that would happen. Not that she didn't wish or fantasize about it, but she really didn't have time to be in a relationship, and she didn't figure Celeste to sleep with someone just for the sex. She and Celeste were friends. Lisa couldn't think straight, and now that she'd caught her breath, she didn't know what to do. Was she supposed to go back and finish dinner? Was she supposed to leave like she was going to do before they'd had sex? Was she supposed to take Celeste to bed and have more sex with her? She'd prefer the latter, but she wanted to know how Celeste was feeling first.

"Are you okay?"

Celeste nodded, still breathing a little heavy. "Oh, yeah. Wow. That was... Wow."

Lisa felt like puffing out her chest with pride. She'd guessed Celeste was satisfied. To be honest, it had been so long since Lisa had had sex with another woman, she wasn't sure if she could satisfy Celeste, but it was like riding a bike.

"Uh, What now?"

Celeste looked at Lisa questioningly.

"I mean, we agreed to be friends. That was a little more than what most friends do."

"How about this?" Celeste began unbuttoning Lisa's shirt. "Why don't we enjoy the rest of the night—and each other— and we can figure all this out later?" Celeste took Lisa's hand and led her down the hall to her bedroom. Lisa barely had any time to look at the room before Celeste unbuttoned Lisa's jeans and slid them down her legs. Celeste's own pants were discarded near the front door where the night's wild antics had begun. Lisa enjoyed the view from behind a naked Celeste, one she would never forget. But now she was lying on her back on Celeste's bed, completely naked, watching Celeste crawl her way over to Lisa then straddling her hips. The view of this gorgeous woman straddling her nearly made Lisa's head explode.

"Come here." Lisa ran her hands up Celeste's back and pulled her down to kiss her. Celeste's lips met Lisa's and entered a slow, sensual kiss that might have lasted hours or seconds, but the only thing Lisa knew for sure was that was the best kiss she'd ever had. There was something—everything—about Celeste that Lisa could get lost in, and Celeste's kisses were number one on that list. The small whimpers that came from Celeste as her hips started moving back and forth, spreading her wetness over Lisa's mound drove her crazy with need.

"Oh, Lisa, I'm supposed to be making you feel good."

"You are. I love feeling you get excited. Keep going, baby. That's it."

With every word, every encouragement, Celeste moved her hips faster until the erratic movements stilled and she cried out once again. Lisa was so close to coming herself from feeling Celeste rub her clit on her. She put her fingers on her own clit to finish herself off, but Celeste intercepted and quickly rubbed Lisa's hardened bundle of nerves until Lisa cried out and came all over Celeste's hand. Lisa's body jerked a few more times against Celeste's hand, and she grunted with each jerk. Fuck. It'd been so long. So long since Lisa had been able to let herself go at the hands of another woman. She didn't realize how much she'd missed being with a woman. She thought she'd been satisfied just being a coach, but it was Celeste's touch that brought her to orgasm and now she wanted to do it again. She wanted more. She needed more.

Lisa flipped Celeste over onto her back and poised herself over her. She dipped down and caught Celeste's lips with hers, and kissed her passionately. She was just buying time until Celeste recovered from her last orgasm to have another one. But this time, Lisa wanted to make Celeste come with her mouth. Lisa's saliva built up with just the thought of tasting her. Lisa worked her way down Celeste's body, inch by inch. She kissed her neck, tasted the skin over her collarbone, snaked her tongue around Celeste's nipple, and lightly bit it. Lisa decided to stay there a while to ramp up Celeste's excitement. The harder she bit, the sharper Celeste's intake of breath became. Lisa continued kissing her way down Celeste's stomach until she reached her sex. The smell of Celeste's arousal made Lisa's mouth water even more. The first taste was like nirvana on her tongue, and Lisa wanted to stay there for hours. And the benefit of Celeste already having two orgasms, Lisa would have time to indulge in that deliciousness.

She used her tongue to circle Celeste's clit languidly then flicked it back and forth before sucking it into her mouth. She kept going, taking her time, trying to draw out everything Celeste had to give her. When Celeste started shaking, Lisa applied more pressure until Celeste came in her mouth. She felt a soft tap to the top of her head and Lisa started chuckling.

"Enough. I can't take anymore."

Lisa looked up to find Celeste's arm draped across her eyes.

"Are you sure?"

"Come up here."

Lisa slid her body along Celeste's and finished her journey with a long, slow kiss. The room was quiet with the exception of their breathing. Celeste framed Lisa's face with her hands and gazed into her eyes.

"You were amazing."

"You're pretty amazing yourself."

"But we're supposed to be just friends."

Lisa rolled off Celeste and sat up with her back against the headboard. "You started it." Lisa smiled to take the sting out of her words.

"Yes, I did. So, what do we do now?"

"Well, I suppose we can go back to being friends. Unless you want to be friendly friends." Lisa waggled her eyebrows and Celeste laughed.

"Friendly friends? You'd be okay with that? Because I really like you, Lisa, but I got hurt by someone I worked with, and I promised myself I wouldn't do that again."

"I know, and I'm busy with basketball, and I don't have the time to put into a relationship. Also, I don't know where coaching will take me." Lisa grabbed Celeste's hand and intertwined their fingers. "But I like you too, and I don't want us to stop being friends just because we had sex. Amazing sex."

"Yes, it was." Celeste sat next to Lisa, leaned over, and kissed her. "I'm glad we're on the same page about this. So, to clarify, we are going to have sex again?" Celeste trailed her finger around Lisa's nipple and it sent a jolt straight to her clit.

Lisa could feel the flood of wetness. "If the mood strikes, I don't see why not. In fact, I'm ready to go again."

"Is that right?" Celeste crawled down to the foot of the bed and instructed Lisa to do the same. Celeste spread Lisa's legs apart and licked her lips. "My turn to taste you."

Lisa closed her eyes and hummed her approval when Celeste took her into her mouth. *Oh, yeah. I'm going to enjoy this friendly friend thing.*

❖

Lisa quietly closed the door behind her and locked it before tiptoeing down the hall to her room, not wanting to wake Athena. Hopefully, she didn't notice Lisa didn't come home last night. It was only five thirty a.m., still dark out, and Lisa figured Athena would still be asleep. The door to their shared bathroom opened, and Athena looked surprised to see her fully clothed. In fact, they probably had mutual surprised looks on their faces.

"Well, well, where have you been, young lady?" Athena sounded awfully awake—and loud—for it being so early in the morning.

"What are you doing awake?"

"I had to pee. Are you going to tell me what happened?"

Lisa tried to slide around her to go to her room, but Athena grabbed her arm and stopped her in her tracks.

"Wait. Did you sleep at Celeste's? Did you sleep *with* Celeste?"

"Not exactly." Lisa tried to dislodge her arm from Athena's grasp, to no avail.

"Wait. What does 'not exactly' mean?"

"It means we didn't get any sleep." That comment must have shocked Athena enough for her to loosen her grip. Lisa went into her room and kicked off her shoes.

"You slept with Celeste? I thought you said you just wanted to be friends."

"I did. We are. We decided to be friendly friends." Lisa laughed and started unbuttoning her shirt. She wanted to change into a T-shirt and boxers so she could sleep for a few hours. Luckily, they didn't have practice today, otherwise she would've been a complete zombie. They did have practice over the next two days before having four days off for Christmas. Lisa had planned to take it a little easy on them since they didn't have a game for another ten days. They would run through some drills, scrimmage a little bit, then have contests where the winning team would decide the loser's fate. Wait. Why was she thinking about basketball practice after spending all night having awesome crazy sex with Celeste?

"What the hell is a friendly friend? A friend with benefits?"

"Exactly. Now get out of here. I need sleep."

"Forget it. I want details."

Lisa continued to undress. She and Athena had seen each other naked a thousand times and it wasn't a big deal to them. She got into her sleep clothes, pulled back the covers on her bed, and climbed in.

"Athena, I need to sleep. I promise to tell you all about it when I wake up."

"Okay, Ice. Just tell me one thing. Was it good?"

Lisa threw a pillow at Athena and told her to get out. Lisa had settled into bed, and she could still catch a little hint of Celeste's perfume. She smiled. *Oh, yeah. It was definitely more than good.* Lisa slept hard for the next few hours, too exhausted to move.

Chapter Sixteen

It was Christmas Eve, and Celeste hadn't talked to Lisa since the night they had dinner together. Correction. They didn't eat a lot of dinner before the argument that turned into the night of the best sex she'd ever had. Granted, she only had her experience with Jackie to compare to. She thought Jackie was good, especially in the beginning when she was still courting Celeste. But her night with Lisa? Wow! Celeste had no idea a woman could have so many orgasms in one night. Once they'd talked and decided they'd still be able to stay friends, they were able to let their inhibitions go. Even though Celeste had hardly any experience with women, she felt totally at ease with Lisa. She felt emboldened and free and safe.

She couldn't explain what it was about Lisa that made Celeste feel so comfortable. Initially, when they were first starting to become friends, and before, Celeste didn't have the most positive body image, but Lisa worshiped her body like a goddess that night. It was like she praised every stretch mark, scar, and skin roll. Lisa didn't give any indication that she thought Celeste was anything but gorgeous. She kept telling Celeste over and over how beautiful and sexy she was. If it was just Lisa's words, Celeste might have had trouble believing her, but the way Lisa touched her, looked at her, kissed her, made love to her, it was easy to believe her. Celeste sincerely hoped that they would have sex again, but if they didn't, at least she still had Lisa's friendship and the memory of one of the best nights of her life.

Celeste had been busy all week finishing up her Christmas shopping and getting the gifts for her family sent off in the mail. She didn't know why she'd waited so long to do that. The line at the post office would've been a lot shorter if she'd just done it two weeks earlier. She also baked some cookies to take over to Olivia and Carl's on Christmas day. Maybe she'd call Lisa and see if she and Athena wanted some cookies. Yes, she was using that as an excuse to call Lisa. They hadn't made any plans to talk or get together this past week, so she didn't want to be *that* person who appeared needy or head over heels and wanted to talk to the other person once, or multiple times during the day. Even though Celeste had thought of Lisa, she refrained from calling or texting.

Celeste picked up her phone and looked at Lisa's contact page. She almost pushed the home button, then got the courage to finally call her. Lisa answered after three rings, and Celeste took a deep breath to calm her nerves. "Hi. How's your week been?"

"Pretty good. I've been doing a little research on our next few opponents."

"Don't you ever take a day off, Coach?"

"Well, as a matter of fact, I took last Sunday off so I could sleep. Someone kept me up the night before."

Celeste could feel her face get hot, but she heard the flirtatious tone in Lisa's voice so she decided to play along. "Is that right? How rude of that someone to not let you sleep. I hope it was worth it at least and that you had fun."

"It was completely worth it. How was your week?"

"Busy. I finished up my shopping and sent the presents off to my family, and I baked some cookies to take over to Olivia's tomorrow."

"What kind of cookies did you bake?"

"Sugar, chocolate peanut butter balls, and pecan balls."

"Ooh, all of my favorites."

"I'm glad you said that because I wanted to bring you some. Would it be okay if I stop by today to drop them off?"

"Actually, how would you like to have dinner and hang out with us tonight? We're just having a boring dinner of chicken and vegetables then watching Christmas movies. What do you say?"

"That sounds nice. Are we watching *It's a Wonderful Life* or *Miracle on 34th Street*?"

"Uh, not exactly. We always watch *Rudolph the Red Nosed Reindeer*, *The Year Without Santa Claus*, and *Frosty the Snowman*. You know, the classics."

"Yes, the classics." Celeste chuckled. "That will be fun. What can I bring?"

"The cookies, of course." Lisa laughed and was joined by Celeste. "I'll text you our address. Come over around four, okay?"

"Will do. See you then."

Celeste hung up and immediately started thinking of what she was going to wear. She had six hours to kill and needed to find something to keep her busy, otherwise she'd go out of her mind. She went into her room and changed into her workout clothes then went into her exercise room where she had a pole installed shortly after she bought her house. Whenever she worked out at home, she was able to empty her thoughts and just be in the moment. Pole dancing was her release. It allowed her to relax and work out at the same time, much like yoga did for some people. She tied up her hair and started performing some stretches. When she was warmed up, she turned on her satellite radio, found a smooth jazz station, and she started dancing.

She spent the good part of an hour doing back hook spins, back slides, arches, releases, floor work. She always started with beginner moves then transferred into intermediate, and finished with advanced moves. She still needed a lot of work on the advanced moves, but she was improving. By the time she was done, she was sweating and breathing hard, but more importantly, her nerves had calmed down and she was feeling much better about tonight. She wasn't sure why she was so nervous. Lisa was her friend. They were just having dinner and watching Christmas movies. Besides, Athena would be there. Oh, shit. Athena would be there. Did she know that she and Lisa slept together? It wasn't like they'd laid any ground rules, but Celeste had hoped Lisa would be discreet and keep it between them. She didn't understand why it bothered her if Athena knew, other than it sort of felt like Lisa was betraying their secret.

When Celeste and Jackie had broken up, Jackie talked about her behind her back and spread rumors about her that just weren't true. She still got an occasional glare from Jackie's colleagues on campus. She wanted to keep her private life private, which was one of the reasons she didn't want to date someone she worked with.

Fantastic. She just spent an hour getting relaxed and now she'd managed to get herself all worked up again. She paced her house, trying to calm down. She stopped in her living room and closed her eyes. Even if Lisa told Athena, Celeste didn't think Athena was the type to spread rumors. The one thing she didn't want though was for Olivia to find out from Athena. Celeste hadn't told her yet because she wasn't sure she wanted to tell her. Celeste would never hear the end of it since she'd pleaded with Olivia to stop trying to get Celeste and Lisa together. Besides, it might have just been a mutual one-night stand. Lisa and Celeste had not made any promises of sleeping together again, but it would be a shame if they didn't. They seemed to be extremely compatible in bed if the total amount of orgasms between them was any indication.

Celeste needed to stop thinking about the sex. All it was doing was getting her worked up. Until last weekend, she'd been celibate for eight months following the breakup with Jackie. Now that she'd had sex with Lisa, she realized the sex with Jackie had been mediocre at best. In just one night, Lisa learned all of Celeste's erogenous zones, learned what she liked, what drove her crazy. Lisa paid attention. And Lisa was focused on pleasuring Celeste, not in it just for herself. Oh, yes, Lisa was a very giving lover, but that really didn't surprise Celeste for some reason. Okay, that was enough.

Celeste went into the kitchen and packed up Lisa and Athena's cookies in a Christmas tin then went to her closet to figure out what she was going to wear.

❖

Lisa was in her closet trying to figure out what she was going to wear. She kept flipping through her shirts, unsure of whether to dress up or stay casual. It was Christmas Eve, so there was that excuse to dress up, but they were just staying home so really not needing to dress up. Geez, she'd never had this much trouble choosing her clothes. Lisa knew it was only because of Celeste. She wanted to look nice. She wanted appreciative looks from Celeste. Lisa's head was all mixed up when it came to Celeste, a completely new experience for her. Even in her baby lesbian days, when she was discovering her attraction to girls, she couldn't remember putting so much thought or effort into what she wore. She decided to go with white jeans and a green sweater.

She mentally went over her checklist for dinner. She had the chicken and vegetables marinating in the fridge, table set. Shit. She only had beer to drink. She grabbed her keys and wallet and headed to the store for wine. She knew nothing about wine. She drank only beer, maybe an occasional whiskey. She slowly walked to the wine aisle, trying to figure out what kind to buy. White? Red? Chardonnay? Pinot grigio? Pinot noir? Merlot? Lisa ran her fingers through her hair and felt her heart race. Celeste would be at her house in fifteen minutes. She needed to find wine. Thankfully, someone came down the aisle who looked like they were a wine drinker. They gave suggestions for two different whites and reds, so she walked out of the store with four bottles of wine. Thankfully, the store was only a couple of miles from her house because she was a bundle of nerves. Tonight was going to be Celeste's first time at her house, and she wanted everything to be perfect.

She pulled into the driveway, and as she was getting her bag of wine out of the back seat, she felt a tap on her shoulder and jumped. She heard giggling behind her and she looked. Celeste was standing there with her hand over her mouth, presumably to hide her smile.

"You scared the crap out of me."

Celeste couldn't hide her smile any longer and burst out laughing. "I'm sorry. I was sitting in my car because I got here so early, I didn't want to intrude."

"You could have cleared your throat or something to let me know you were there."

"You're right." Celeste put her hand on Lisa's arm. "I'm sorry."

"It's okay." Lisa seemed to forget all things when Celeste touched her.

"Where were you?"

Lisa held up the bag and the clink of glass could have answered the question. "I went to the store to get you wine."

"Oh, Lisa, you didn't have to. I could've had water with dinner."

"Are you kidding? I know you drink wine so I wanted to have it for you. I have to be honest though. I know nothing about wine, and I asked a complete stranger to help me pick out a bottle. Instead, I picked out four different types." Lisa felt like a complete amateur, which she was when it came to wine, but Celeste placed her hand on her chest and appeared touched.

"That was so sweet of you, Coach. Thank you. I think you deserve some homemade cookies for your trouble." Celeste pulled the lid off the tin that held three different types of cookies. They all looked delicious, and Lisa grabbed a sugar cookie. Lisa's mom always made sugar cookies at Christmas time. She used cookie cutters in the shapes of stars, trees, and angels, and then she frosted them and poured sprinkles on top. She always thought her mom made the best sugar cookies, but Lisa had to admit that Celeste's were the best she'd ever tasted. There was a hint of citrus in either the frosting or cookie itself, and it gave a unique flavor to the cookie.

"I think I'm just going to eat these for dinner." Lisa went to grab the tin, and Celeste turned away from her and replaced the lid.

"You will not. You are to share these with Athena after dinner."

"Ooh, bossy. I like it." Lisa raised an eyebrow.

Celeste took a step closer to Lisa, not much space between them. "I can do bossy if that's what you like."

Lisa whimpered. Actually whimpered. She could be in real trouble with this one. She better watch her step. "Come on in. Dinner should almost be ready." Lisa opened the door and allowed Celeste to enter before her. "Hey, Athena. I'm back."

Athena called out from the kitchen. "Have you calmed down yet? I don't understand why you just don't ask her out. You two obviously like each other."

"I'm sorry," Lisa whispered to Celeste as they walked into the kitchen. "Are you going to need some help pulling your foot out of your mouth, Chang?"

Athena turned around and saw Lisa and Celeste standing there with smiles on their faces. "Shit, I'm sorry."

"Oh, yeah? Who are you apologizing to?"

Athena hugged Celeste hello. "Celeste, of course. I don't care if I embarrass you."

Lisa uncorked the wine Celeste said she liked and poured her a glass. She grabbed a couple of beers out of the fridge for her and Athena and raised a toast. "Happy Christmas Eve."

"If you guys want to go have a seat, I'm almost done with dinner, just another five minutes."

"Come on, Celeste, I'll give you a tour of the house."

The tour was quick because the house was fairly small. Just two bedrooms and one bath, a little over a thousand square feet, but Lisa wasn't complaining. It was nice to be in university housing and having to pay only utilities. By the time they were done with the tour, Athena had the food on the table and they were ready to eat. Once they finished dinner, Lisa cleared the table and started dishes while Athena and Celeste sat at the table and talked. The table was just out of the kitchen so Lisa was able to be a part of the conversation.

"Athena, your name is beautiful. I've never met anyone with that name, and I think I've only heard it before in Greek mythology. She was the goddess of wisdom and war, right?"

"Yes. It's believed that she'd been born from the head of her father, Zeus. The story goes that he had a terrible headache, he took a sword and cut his own head in half, and Athena popped out fully grown and armored."

Lisa shook her head and wiped her hands on the towel. "Mr. Chang named her that because he had a huge headache when Athena was born. Now she's my headache."

Celeste and Athena laughed, but Lisa caught Athena slyly giving her the middle finger. Lisa had the tin of cookies in her hand and three small paper plates.

"Come on, let's go sit in the living room and watch the movies."

Athena chose to sit in the recliner, leaving the couch to Lisa and Celeste. They put a few cookies on their plates and settled back to watch the movies. Lisa and Athena sang along to the cold/heat miser song from *The Year Without a Santa Claus*. Celeste clapped her approval when they were done.

"Just how many times have you two seen this movie?"

"I think almost every year since I was about five years old." Lisa grabbed another cookie and ate half of it.

"Same," replied Athena.

"That's unreal. This is the first time I've seen this movie."

Lisa saw Athena's wide-eyed expression and was sure it was identical to her own. "How is that possible? I mean, it's a Christmas classic."

"I don't know. My parents and I always watched *It's a Wonderful Life* and *Miracle on 34th Street.* In fact, I never watched any type of cartoon when I was growing up."

"What? No Bugs Bunny?"

"No Tom and Jerry?"

"No Scooby Doo?"

"No, none of them."

Lisa grabbed her head like she was trying to stop it from exploding. She reached over and patted Celeste's leg. "I'm so sorry you had such a deprived childhood. Your parents should have been arrested for neglect."

Celeste covered Lisa's hand and Lisa felt the warmth envelop her. "I assure you, I had a wonderful childhood, but I am realizing that I did miss out on some essentials."

Lisa jumped up from the couch and started rooting around in the cabinet below the television. "Ah, here it is." Lisa held up a DVD case and came back over to the couch. "I'm loaning this to you. Don't lose it."

"Looney Tunes Golden Collection." Celeste turned the case over and read the back.

"It's all of the best Looney Tunes cartoon shorts. No kid should ever go through their childhood without watching these. The funny thing is, they're even better as an adult."

"Okay, I'll be sure and watch it during winter break. Thank you."

They'd finished watching the movies then Athena announced she was heading to bed. She hugged Celeste and said good night to Lisa. Lisa and Celeste remained seated and with the remote, Lisa turned the radio on to Christmas music. They sat silently looking at the lit Christmas tree in the corner adorned with decorations Lisa's mom had given them a few years back when Lisa and Athena started being roommates. They tended not to overdo it with decorating since it was just them. There were two decorative stockings hanging from the fireplace mantle and some wrapped presents under the tree.

"Would you like another glass of wine or some hot cocoa?"

"Oh, no. I should be going. Let you get to bed so Santa Claus can come down the chimney and deliver your presents." Celeste stood, then Lisa stood and faced her. She took a step closer and began playing with the hem of Celeste's sweater.

"You know, your perfume has been driving me nuts all night." Lisa leaned in and started kissing Celeste's neck and inhaling the sweet citrus smell on her skin. She tasted Celeste's neck with the tip of her tongue and Celeste quietly moaned.

"Oh, you're driving me a little nuts, too."

"Yeah?" Lisa continued her assault on Celeste's neck then sucked her earlobe into her mouth. "You like that?"

Celeste wrapped her arms around Lisa's neck and rubbed her breasts against Lisa's. "Yeah, I love it."

Lisa moved her mouth to capture Celeste in a frenzied, passionate kiss. "Come to bed with me?" Lisa was breathless and had difficulty getting the words out.

"What about Athena?" Celeste asked as she ground her pelvis into Lisa's. There wasn't any space between them, and Lisa liked that just fine.

"Athena's in her own bed." Lisa grinned to let Celeste know she was kidding. "Come on, she won't know if that's what you're worried about. Come on, Celeste. I want to feel your naked body under mine."

Lisa started making her way toward her bedroom, and Celeste hesitated at first then went willingly. Lisa closed the door behind them and leaned back against it. There was a little light that came in through the blinds, just enough for Lisa to see Celeste's heaving chest. Lisa closed the distance and they removed each other's clothing before lying down.

Lisa laid her body over a naked Celeste and kissed her while grinding her sex against Celeste's. Their make out session in the living room got Lisa hard and wet, and she couldn't hold back. She didn't want to. She slid her hand between them and discovered how wet Celeste was. She easily slid two fingers deep inside her and thrust in and out while grinding against Celeste. It wouldn't take long for either to come.

"Oh, God, Lisa. Harder. You're going to make me come."

Lisa did as Celeste commanded and she dug her nails into Lisa's ass, pulling her in tighter. Celeste cried out and Lisa came right after, nearly collapsing on top of Celeste. They lay there breathing hard until Lisa rolled off and they started laughing softly.

"That was incredible."

"It sure was. God, Celeste, you're so incredibly sexy."

Celeste scooted closer to Lisa and kissed her. "You're pretty sexy yourself, Coach."

After about twenty minutes of basking in the afterglow, Celeste got up.

"Hey, where you going? Come back to bed."

Celeste pulled her sweater over her head and brushed her fingers through her hair. "I'm not spending the night and risk running into Athena in the morning. Did you tell her about us?"

"Sort of. She caught me coming in the morning after I left your house, and she asked if we had slept together. I told her we did, but I didn't give her any details and I told her not to tell anyone."

Celeste looked at her with raised eyebrows. "That surprises me. Why didn't you tell her? I know she's your best friend."

"Yes, she is, but what happened between us is our business. I'm not the type of person to kiss and tell."

"How about Athena? Does she have loose lips?"

"Nope. If I tell her to keep something private, she'll take it to the grave."

Celeste finished dressing and sat on the bed next to Lisa. "If you want to tell her, you can. But please ask her not to tell anyone. Not that you or Athena would do it, but my last girlfriend spread rumors about me after I broke up with her and a few of her friends told some stories as well. I'm not ashamed of what we're doing, but I do like to keep my life private, especially on campus."

ICHARDSON

"I completely understand. I feel the same way. If it comes up again, I'll tell her, but I won't volunteer anything." Lisa lightly rubbed Celeste's back. "Are you sure you don't want to stay?"

Celeste smiled. "No, I should get going. I'm going to Olivia's tomorrow, and I still have a few things to do in the morning."

"Okay. Let me get dressed and I'll walk you out." Lisa threw on a sweatshirt and sweatpants, as well as her slippers and walked Celeste to her car. Before she opened the door, she put her arms around Celeste and kissed her again. "Drive carefully and I'll talk to you later."

"Good night. Merry Christmas, Coach."

Lisa waved as Celeste drove away. "A merry Christmas, indeed."

CHAPTER SEVENTEEN

Celeste had never done this before, had a friend with benefits. And because she'd only had one girlfriend in her life, she didn't know how to act or what to expect. Was it okay for her to call Lisa and ask her to do something? That sounded an awful lot like a date. But it had been four days since she'd seen her and talked to her, and Celeste found she was missing Lisa. Was it actually Lisa Celeste was missing or the sex? Because sex with Lisa was off the hook as the kids would put it. Being a college professor made her privy to the latest "hip" lingo. Maybe a little of both? Or a lot of both. She was trying not to get emotionally involved because they'd both agreed they'd stay just friends. She also didn't want to come off as needy or like she was attaching herself to Lisa. It wasn't like Celeste didn't have any other friends, but to be honest, they weren't Lisa. Her musings were interrupted by her phone ringing. She was pleasantly surprised to see Lisa's name on the screen.

"Hi, Coach. I was just thinking about you."

"Good thoughts, I hope."

"Good, sexy thoughts, actually."

"Oh, my."

Celeste found she enjoyed teasing and flirting with Lisa.

"I just pulled into a Thai place to pick up dinner, and I was wondering if you'd like to have dinner with me? I can bring it to your house."

"That would be great."

Celeste gave Lisa her order and rushed through her house to straighten it up. She opened the door to her "pole room" and threw some of her shoes in there before Lisa knocked on the door. She brushed her hands down her body to straighten her clothes. She opened the door to find Lisa standing there holding a large paper bag containing their food, and Celeste thought she was going to faint. Lisa stood there looking amazing. She'd cut her hair short. Like, really short.

"Oh, good God."

"What?" Lisa looked concerned.

"You cut your hair." Celeste loved the look. She didn't know how it was possible, but Lisa looked even more amazing, more butch, and Celeste felt her heart rate increase. She had an urge to run her fingers through her now two-inch-long hair. "It looks fantastic. When did you get it cut?"

"Just this morning. My players gave me all kinds of crap about it at practice today."

"Why would they do that?" Celeste thought it was mean-spirited for the young women to tease their coach, and she felt very protective of her.

Lisa placed her hand on Celeste's shoulder and kissed her cheek. "It's okay. It's what we do as athletes—we tease each other. But I am their coach, an authority figure, so I made them run some sprints for disrespecting me." Lisa laughed.

"Ooh, you're so mean."

"It's good to be the coach," Lisa said while smiling and slowly nodding.

"Come on in." Celeste led Lisa into the kitchen and pulled down two plates from the cupboard, and Lisa scooped out the food from the containers while they discussed what they'd been up to for the past four days. Celeste didn't care what they talked about, she just liked that Lisa was there. Celeste was miraculously able to hold some sort of conversation with Lisa, but she felt herself often just staring at her. She couldn't find words of how good Lisa looked with short hair, how sexy she looked. She had some sort of gel that gave it some volume and some areas a little spiky. Lisa now looked like the type of women Celeste fantasized about. Celeste thought about Lisa getting out of the pool with her short hair wet and slicked back. Whew. That image was almost more than she could take.

"Come on, I'm starving." And not necessarily for food.

Lisa set her plate on the table "I'm going to wash my hands first."

Lisa headed down the hall, and Celeste sat patiently waiting for her to come back. The house was quiet and Celeste was able to hear the water turn off in the bathroom. Another two minutes went by, and Celeste got up to see if Lisa needed anything. She knew Lisa wasn't still washing her hands since she heard the water turn off. She saw the door to her pole room open. Celeste became upset that Lisa was snooping around.

"What are you doing in here?" Celeste was a combination of mad that Lisa was in the room without permission and embarrassed that Lisa had her hand on the brass pole that was bolted into the ceiling and floor.

"You have a pole?"

Celeste grabbed Lisa by her upper arm and dragged her out of the room. "You shouldn't be in there. Why are you snooping?" Celeste felt her face grow hot and tears start to sting her eyes.

"I wasn't snooping. I mean, not really. I was walking back from the bathroom and I saw the pole in the room. I was curious."

"Like I said. Snooping. And that door was closed."

"No, it wasn't, Celeste. I'd never open a closed door in your house."

Celeste calmed down enough to think that maybe she didn't close the door all the way. The hinges were a little off balance so if the door didn't latch, it would open all the way on its own.

"Why are you so mad? I think it's a cool place to work out."

Celeste wiped a tear from her eye and willed the other tears to stop. "I didn't want you to see the pole."

"Why not?"

"I don't know. I thought maybe you'd judge me."

"Because you pole dance?"

Celeste felt her pulse race. How would Lisa know that just by seeing the pole?

"Celeste, I didn't say anything because you didn't mention it first and I wanted to respect your privacy, but I saw you compete in Las Vegas."

"You what? You saw me and you didn't say anything?" Celeste turned away from Lisa, embarrassed to know Lisa saw her dressed in a scantily clad costume.

Lisa moved closer and placed her hands on Celeste's shoulders, causing her to jump. She was torn between wanting to be held by Lisa and shooing her out of her house. How did this happen? How did Lisa happen to be in Las Vegas at the same time as Celeste and see her perform? When did Celeste start caring what Lisa thought? Sure, they were friends, but they weren't girlfriends. And they'd only known each other a little more than a few months, so why was Celeste getting all worked up? Celeste took a deep breath and willed herself to calm down. She needed to start owning who she was and the things she was good at, and she was really good at pole dancing. She was almost at expert level. She'd worked hard to get to where she was in pole dancing, it gave her joy, it empowered her, and she'd made good friends in her class. She turned around and squared her shoulders. She didn't have to justify herself to anyone. Pole dancing was nothing to be ashamed of, and it was becoming a very popular form of exercise.

"What I was going to say was that you were amazing up on that stage. I don't know if I could find the words to describe what I saw, but I'm going to try."

Celeste felt herself relax a little as Lisa took her hands and looked into her eyes.

"When Athena and I arrived—"

"Athena was there too?" Celeste's voice was high and loud and she closed her eyes before taking in another deep breath and letting it out slowly.

"As I was saying, when we arrived, I didn't know what to expect. Well, what I thought it would be, I'm ashamed to say. Anyway, with each performance, I got more and more into it. Then they announced your name and you came out looking all hot and sexy. I almost left because I thought it would be inappropriate to watch you dance like that, but you were so fluid and athletic. I was so damned impressed with your performance and so proud of you that I wanted to find you and give you a humongous hug. What you did up there on stage was beautiful and strong and amazing. So, if you're embarrassed about me knowing you pole dance, don't be. There's no way in hell I could do anything like that and I've been an athlete most of my life."

Now Celeste was experiencing a mixture of pride and embarrassment. Lisa liked her performance and was impressed with Celeste's routine.

"Thank you. I appreciate your sentiment."

"Are you still mad at me?"

Celeste smiled and shook her head.

"Good. Let's eat. I'd like to ask you questions about pole dancing if that would be okay."

"Sure, I guess so."

They sat at the table with their plates full of now lukewarm food. Celeste took both plates back into the kitchen and put them in the microwave for a minute to warm them back up. Once they'd taken their first bite, Lisa started with her questions, and for some reason, Celeste had no qualms about answering them. Maybe because Lisa seemed to treat pole dancing as some sort of art form. Maybe it was because there had been no judgment from her. Celeste was willing to answer all of Lisa's questions because she knew Lisa wouldn't use it against her or use it to embarrass her.

"What made you start pole dancing?"

Ah, that was an easy one. "I grew up overweight. I never got asked out on dates when I was a teenager and never got picked for teams at recess. I was a book nerd, fat, and nearly friendless. When I got into college, I took some nutrition and exercise classes. I had lost a lot of weight, but I still had poor self-esteem. When I was in my late twenties, one of my colleagues at the previous university I worked at suggested pole classes. I thought she was crazy to suggest I try a class, but she dared me, so I took a beginner class."

"So, if I want you to try something, all I have to do is dare you?"

Celeste shook her finger at Lisa and raised an eyebrow. "Don't get any bright ideas, Coach."

Lisa held her hands up in surrender. "Go on."

"I took a beginner class and I was so timid, but a few of the ladies in the class were in similar situations so we formed sort of a sisterhood. When we finished the class, we decided to keep doing it so we signed up for a membership at the studio we were going to. It all became baby steps but cheering each other on, it was therapeutic for some of us. When our instructor started talking to us about dressing up, we all looked at each other like she was crazy. I was still overweight. I wasn't going to get a skimpy costume to wear. But she was so encouraging and understanding. So, a few of us plus-sized gals went to a store our instructor recommended. The ladies there were helpful, encouraging, and made us feel like we should own our bodies and sex appeal. It really opened my eyes to acceptance."

They took another bite of food and Celeste decided to add some music to the conversation. She used the remote to put on the sixties soul station. When an Aretha Franklin song came on, Lisa closed her eyes and started moving her head to the beat of the music. So, they liked the same music. Good to know.

"When I got the job at Glassell University, and I had to move, I was worried I wouldn't be able to find another studio like the one I belonged to. I talked Olivia into going with me."

Lisa's eyes widened at the mention of Olivia's name. Okay, obviously she didn't know Olivia did pole either.

"The one we belong to now is also great. The ladies are welcoming, nonjudgmental, and fun."

"That's so wonderful, Celeste. I'm really happy that you've found something that you really enjoy and get a lot out of. For the record, I thought you were amazing during your performance."

"Thanks. That was the first showcase I performed in, and I didn't make it past the second round."

"I know, and I'm sorry about that."

"You know?"

Lisa cleared her throat. "Athena may have checked on the results."

"Wow. Thank you for following up on the competition. For what it's worth, I appreciate that you appreciate my pole dancing. I never know how anyone will react to that information so I just don't tell people."

"I completely respect your privacy, so Athena and I won't tell anyone. If you enter another competition, I'd like to come watch if that would be okay with you. I'd like to cheer you on."

"All right. If I enter another one, I will tell you."

They finished dinner while talking about the basketball team—practices, upcoming conference games. The team had only lost one game thus far, and prior to the season starting, they were expected to finish in the top four teams in conference standings. Now, Lisa thought they might actually win the conference. That would certainly help her cause about moving to a bigger school. Celeste felt the sadness overcome her, thinking about Lisa leaving GU, moving away. Maybe not necessarily moving away as there were a few larger universities in the Orange County area, but not having her on campus would be bad enough. They didn't interact often while on campus, but they could. The potential was there.

"Hey, are you okay? You got quiet on me."

"I'm fine. I was just thinking of you getting a better coaching offer and you moving away. I like having you as my friend."

Lisa reached over and placed her hand over Celeste's. "I like having you as my friend, too. Even if I leave to coach somewhere else, we can still stay friends."

"I know. I'm just being silly. I always get a little melancholy around the holidays. I had a great time with Olivia and Carl on Christmas day, but I do miss my parents. I'm looking forward to them coming to see me in February."

"I bet you are. How often do you see each other?"

"About once a year. We take turns going to see each other since we live in different countries. I flew to see them last Christmas."

"I hope I get a chance to meet them. You should bring them to a game."

"They're not really into sports, but maybe they'll make an exception."

Lisa helped Celeste put the food away and clean the dishes, then donned her jacket. "I'm going to get going. I have some things to do at home to get ready for next week's games."

"More game film to watch?" Celeste smirked to let Lisa know she was joking.

"Actually, yes. It's never-ending during season. Thanks for having dinner with me, and for trusting me to tell me about your past."

"No, thank you. For everything. Next time, you can tell me more about your past."

Lisa hugged Celeste and told her she'd talk to her later. Celeste leaned against the door and wondered how she was going to get her heart to listen to her head.

CHAPTER EIGHTEEN

Celeste arrived to the university's pool bright and early Monday morning. It was the first day of the spring semester, and it was time for her to get disciplined again in her eating and exercising. She hadn't exercised much and overindulged in sinful food over the holidays. She'd begun to feel sluggish physically and mentally. She always felt better when she regularly exercised, and she had the pool to herself that morning. She was disappointed that Lisa wasn't there, but it wasn't like Celeste came to swim just because Lisa did. Not entirely. Seeing Lisa in her one-piece racing suit didn't hurt matters.

Celeste hung her towel on the hook and walked over to the edge of the pool to dip her toe in to check the temperature. That was nice. What else was nice was that the pool was indoors. Forty-eight-degree weather at six in the morning in mid-January wasn't ideal to be swimming, but the pool water was nice enough and it wasn't too cold in the pool area. She pulled her goggles over her eyes and jumped into the water. She started out with easy freestyle strokes for a couple of laps before picking up her pace. By the time she'd finished ten laps, she was out of breath. Swimming was a lot harder than pole, that was for sure.

She'd managed to be in the pool for almost an hour when Lisa came out, looking sexy in her black racing suit and her wet hair slicked back. Celeste was grateful to still be in the pool as she knew her legs wouldn't hold her if she was on land. She also had the pool to blame for her hardened nipples even though she knew differently.

"Good morning, Coach." When did Celeste's voice become sultry?

"Good morning to you, Professor Bouchard."

Oh. She loved the way Lisa just said her name. Lisa made the butterflies take off in Celeste's stomach. "Late start this morning?"

Lisa jumped in the water and treaded over until she was in Celeste's space.

"Mmm-hmm. I didn't want to wake up from the sexy dream I was having about some English professor."

Celeste's insides caught fire and her breathing rate picked up again. "Just *some* English professor? Do I know her?"

Lisa didn't move any closer; she just nodded. Lisa stared into Celeste's eyes, and Celeste could feel herself being pulled further and deeper into Lisa's eyes. She was just about to close the distance and kiss her when an older man she didn't recognize came walking out to the pool. Celeste stammered. "I was just about to get out of the water."

"Would you like to meet for coffee later? What is your schedule like this semester?"

Celeste knew the answer to the latter question, but for the life of her couldn't quite remember at that moment. She knew she didn't have a class at eleven so she told Lisa that would be a good time to meet.

"I'll meet you in the café at eleven then, Professor. Enjoy your shower." Lisa pulled the goggles over her eyes and kicked off the end of the pool to begin her laps. She had wonderful form and looked so sleek and hot. Celeste ducked her head under the water to try to cool herself down. Even when she and Jackie were starting to date, she never had this type of reaction to her, and she and Lisa were only friends. Maybe a smidge more. She climbed up the stairs, went to her towel, and started drying off. She turned toward the pool to find Lisa hanging on the edge watching her intently. Celeste shooed her away with her hand and Lisa smiled at her before continuing with her laps. Sure. Only friends.

❖

Lisa was just getting ready to meet Celeste for coffee when Athena came in the office. She'd had a dentist appointment earlier that morning so she was coming to work a little later. Not that they had anything pressing to do. They'd gone over everything they knew about their next two opponents and they had their practice plan in place. All Lisa had planned to do until practice was send out a few emails and find out what was going on in the world of women's college basketball.

"Hey, I was just going to meet Celeste for coffee. You want to join us?"

"Uh, no thanks. I have some things I want to take care of, but tell her I said hello."

"Will do. See you later."

Lisa made the short walk across campus to the café. The sun was shining, but the air was crisp and Lisa inhaled deeply. Today was the start of a new semester. All her players got really good grades in the fall semester and were eligible to play. The team had a fantastic pre-conference season; they were a cohesive unit that worked hard and understood each other. They were probably the best group of kids Lisa had ever coached. She felt really positive about her life, she thought as she walked through the doors of the café to see Celeste wave and point to two coffee cups. To add to Lisa's good mood was the friendship she'd developed with Celeste. Sure, they'd had incredible sex a couple of times, but there wasn't the pressure of starting a new romantic relationship. Everything between them was easy and fun and flirty. Lisa felt they reached a new threshold after their dinner the other night. Celeste had opened up about her pole dancing and what she went through with her body image issues. Lisa had lain in bed that night thinking about everything Celeste had told her. She was sure there was more, but just the fact that Celeste had trusted her enough to tell her what she'd felt like a mark in the win column.

"I took it upon myself to get your coffee. I hope you don't mind."

"Not at all. Thank you for this." Lisa sat across the table, picked up a pack of sugar that was on the table, and stirred it in. She took a sip of the hot liquid and closed her eyes in appreciation. "So, hi." Lisa smiled at Celeste, who smiled back.

"Hi, yourself. How was your swim?"

"It might have been better if you had remained in the pool, although I probably wouldn't have swum many laps."

"Oh, yeah? Why is that?" Celeste raised an eyebrow and looked over the edge of her cup as she took a sip of her coffee.

"Are you kidding? You in the pool, in a bathing suit, with me?" Lisa rested her forearms on the table and leaned closer to Celeste, anticipating her comeback.

"Damn it."

Celeste looked disappointed, then a little angry. Well, that wasn't what Lisa was anticipating.

"Hello, Celeste. You look beautiful today."

The female voice came from behind Lisa, and she turned her head to find a sharply dressed butch woman with short platinum blond hair full of hair product and parted to the side. She didn't even spare a look at Lisa, and she immediately disliked whoever this woman was.

"What do you want, Jackie? I'm busy right now."

Lisa stood and tried to be a little intimidating, standing about five inches taller. "Can I help you with something?"

Jackie slowly looked Lisa up and down, then turned her attention back to Celeste, not even acknowledging Lisa. Lisa wasn't a violent person, in fact she was usually pretty laid-back, but she really wanted to throat punch that chick.

Jackie spoke without even looking at Lisa. "Maybe you could excuse us. Celeste and I have things to discuss."

"Jackie, I have nothing to discuss with you. Lisa and I are having a conversation about one of her players so you need to leave."

Jackie looked at Lisa again and squinted. "Oh, right. You're the basketball coach. Isn't that...nice?" Jackie sneered and Lisa had never wanted so much to smack a look off someone's face. She took a step closer to Jackie but saw some students looking their way so she shoved her hands in her front pockets and rocked back on her heels.

Jackie turned back to Celeste. "Call me, baby. We have things to talk about." She left without giving Lisa another look.

"Well, she seems like a gem."

Celeste's face was so red and tight with anger that Lisa was actually concerned. She went to the counter and got a cup of water to give to Celeste, set it in front of her, then sat back down. "Are you all right? Who was that?"

"That was my ex, and yes, I'm all right. I'm actually getting used to her harassment. She just can't take no for an answer."

"You mean this is a regular thing? Celeste, why don't you tell someone?"

Celeste waved her hand like she was shooing away a fly. "It's not that big of a deal, really. It's not like she's a stalker or dangerous, or anything. She's just mad that I broke up with her. Apparently, nobody has ever broken up with Jackie Stone before, and she's having a hard time accepting it. I broke up with her last year."

"Does she work here? I don't think I've noticed her before."

"Yes, she's a professor in the business and finance school."

Lisa was silent for a moment before the light bulb above her head lit up. "Wait. I think I saw her talking to you at the president's back-to-school party."

"Wow, that was over four months ago. How did you remember that?"

"It was the first time I saw you."

Celeste blinked and her mouth made an O shape. "Well, Coach. You sure can say the pretty words."

Lisa chuckled and took a swallow of her now cold coffee. Yuck. She slid the cup away from her. "Now, if you want to talk about your ex, I'm a good listener."

"I think we are going to need more coffee for this." Lisa stood and started to walk toward the counter. "And pastries," Celeste yelled out.

Lisa returned with a tray containing two more fresh coffees and even fresher croissants. She removed the contents then returned the tray to the counter.

"Okay, I'm ready when you are."

Celeste took a deep breath as she cradled her coffee cup in both hands. "Jackie was the first woman I'd ever dated."

"So, you dated men before?"

Celeste shook her head. "I'd never dated anyone before Jackie."

Lisa was speechless. She sat there staring at Celeste, not knowing what to say. How was that even possible given that she was in her late forties? Celeste seemed to have read Lisa's mind.

"Remember I told you I was overweight? Well, that was a large part in me not dating. I never got asked out and I didn't have the confidence to do the asking. It took me a long time, a slow and steady process, to lose the weight."

"How much weight are you talking?"

"One hundred and eighty pounds. I'm five foot five so you can imagine how big I was. Like I said, it took a long time."

"Dang, Celeste. That's amazing!"

"What? That I weighed that much?" Celeste let out a nervous laugh

"No, that you were so persistent and dedicated to losing all that weight. Good for you for being so determined."

"Thank you." Celeste's face turned red, and Lisa reached out to hold her hand. Celeste squeezed it then took her hand away.

Apparently, she was more aware they were in an on-campus café that was filled with students. Lisa sat back and asked her to continue her story.

"I lost the weight, but I didn't have any confidence in my new body or my sensuality and sexuality. That's when I tried pole. It's really helped my self-esteem even though I still get insecure at times. It also helped tone my body a little."

Lisa nodded and stayed quiet. She wanted to give Celeste the freedom and the power to tell her story.

"I guess my self-confidence started to show. Jackie asked me out while we were attending a school faculty function. She wore a sharp looking suit, had her hair styled, and she had this cocky swagger to her when she walked over to me and introduced herself. She was so charming and gorgeous, I would've said yes to almost anything she asked of me."

Lisa shrugged, feigning nonchalance. "I guess she's not bad looking."

Lisa saw Celeste smirk and wink at her. "She said all the right things to me that night, seemed very interested in me and getting to know me, so I agreed to go to dinner with her. She did all the right things in the beginning—held the door open, pulled my chair out, complimented me—and I started to believe her. I was flattered that she gave me so much attention, but I never felt completely comfortable with her, didn't fully trust her. One night, we were having dinner and she was in a foul mood. I asked her if there was anything I could do to help, and she said something like I could start by making her a better meal, that I was a terrible cook. I chalked it up to her being in a bad mood, but the insults continued to come. One night, while we were being intimate, she told me that I should work on losing some weight because there were some flabby areas on my body. She said she wanted a girlfriend who was hot and in shape."

Lisa sat there with her eyes wide and her mouth agape. She couldn't believe what a bitch that Jackie was. "Celeste, you are one of the most beautiful women I've ever seen and extremely sexy. I hope you didn't listen to her."

"No, in fact I got dressed and left her house. The next day, I broke up with her. But I'd be lying if I didn't say she put doubt in my head. I'd worked so hard to love myself and she tried to destroy it. When I told her I didn't want to see her anymore, she called me some nasty names. It took some sessions with my therapist to get over what Jackie had unraveled of my self-esteem. She spread rumors about me in her department and I was thoroughly embarrassed. Since then, she's been trying to talk to me, asking me to take her back. Even if I never have a date with another woman or another romance, I'll never regret ending it with her."

Lisa placed her hand on top of Celeste's and gently squeezed. "Thank you for telling me. For what it's worth, I'm proud of you for not staying with her. You are an incredible woman who has so much to offer, and any woman would be lucky to be loved by you."

Celeste had a look on her face that Lisa couldn't quite decipher. Embarrassment? Appreciation? Hope? Maybe all three?

"Jackie is why you don't want to date anyone you work with. Because she spread those rumors." Lisa posed that as a statement, not a question.

"Yes."

Lisa let go of Celeste's hand and leaned back in her chair, aware again that they were in a public place. She didn't want anyone in the café speculating and possibly spreading rumors of Celeste. "I hope you know that I'd never do that to you or treat you the way Jackie did."

"To be honest, Coach, I didn't know you well enough in the beginning to know that. Now I'm pretty sure you wouldn't."

The fact that Celeste still couldn't fully trust Lisa hurt, but Lisa knew it had nothing to do with her. Jackie had done a number on Celeste, but in time, Lisa hoped Celeste would be able to trust again. She vowed never to give Celeste a reason not to trust her, even though they were just friends.

"Okay, then. I better get going. Conference play starts this week and I have to get my team prepared. I'll walk you out."

They stood and threw their trash in the bin on their way out. When they reached the bottom of the steps, they turned to face each other, and Celeste placed her hand on Lisa's forearm and let it trail down until she held onto Lisa's finger.

"Thank you for listening, Lisa. It means a lot."

"I'm here for you, Professor. If you want to talk, or if you want me to kick Jackie's ass, just let me know."

That got the desired laugh from Celeste, and Lisa felt some tension leave her body. "I'll talk with you later." Lisa slowly stepped back and released her fingers from Celeste's loose grasp then walked back to her office, enjoying the sunshine and slight breeze. Celeste was opening her life more and more to Lisa, and for that, she was grateful.

CHAPTER NINETEEN

Celeste was enjoying a Sunday morning by herself. It was quiet outside. It was a little breezy, but the sun was shining and not a cloud in the sky. It was a gorgeous day, she was feeling grateful, and she wanted to reward her mind and body. She tied her hair up in a bun, put on her booty shorts, a snug camisole, and went into her pole room. She put on some sensual, soft music and spent twenty minutes performing some stretches and yoga poses then went to work on the pole. She wasn't following any sort of routine; she was just doing whatever came to her. It was fluid and organic, and she got lost in her own mind. She almost didn't hear the knock on her door and she was tempted to ignore it, but her inner voice told her to at least see who it was. She looked through the peephole and saw Lisa standing on her front porch with a tray containing two cups and a paper bag.

Shit. There was no time to get cleaned up. But why should it matter? They were just friends, after all. *Yeah, right, Celeste, you know there would be more if Lisa was on the same page.* She took a deep breath, then let it out before opening the door.

"Good morning."

Lisa held up the tray as an offering. "Good morning. I wanted to know if you're interested in breakfast? I'm sorry I didn't call first, but I went for a walk this morning and I found myself getting closer to your neighborhood." Lisa looked at Celeste and how she was dressed, and she blushed. "I'm sorry. I should have called first." She turned to go, but Celeste stopped her.

"No, come in. I was just doing a little workout on the pole."

Lisa's face lit up and lust filled her eyes. "Oh, yeah?"

"Why, Coach, you look interested in staying for breakfast."

Lisa stammered and Celeste felt the desire radiate between them. "Would you like to watch?"

Celeste felt emboldened by the wanton look in Lisa's eyes, and she wanted to do anything to keep it there. This could be fun and who knew what it would lead to. Actually, Celeste knew exactly what it would lead to if she did it right. She took the tray from Lisa and placed it on her coffee table, then took Lisa's hand and led her to the pole room, neither saying a word. Celeste unfolded a chair and gently pushed Lisa down onto it. She walked over to her music player and quickly scrolled through the songs she downloaded for pole performances. She picked out Paula Cole's "Feeling Love" and got her inspiration just from looking at Lisa.

She walked seductively toward Lisa and trailed her fingers on Lisa's shoulder, across her neck, and to her other shoulder as she moved behind her. Celeste moved toward the pole, placed her back against it, and squatted and spread her legs open. Lisa's face was slack, and she almost looked like her brain had short-circuited. Celeste stood and grabbed the pole before turning and throwing her head back. She swayed her hips, thrust her chest out, and squatted again. She glanced a look over at Lisa who looked mesmerized by what Celeste was doing, which spurred Celeste on to continue her seduction. She climbed the pole, hooked her leg around it, grabbed it below her body with her opposite hand, and spun slowly around in a clockwise direction while her free leg stuck straight out. She then lowered herself to the floor and did a belly slide toward Lisa.

Celeste knelt in front of Lisa, placed her hands on her knees, and spread her legs, easing her body upward against Lisa's chest until she was upright. She straddled Lisa's thighs and moved her pelvis against Lisa's, then stood again and sat back in her lap, this time with her back to Lisa. Celeste grabbed Lisa's hands that were grasping her hips and moved them up her body and over her breasts. Celeste squeezed Lisa's hands, prompting Lisa to squeeze her breasts. Celeste arched her back again, thrusting her hard nipples into Lisa's palms. Celeste felt her clit grow hard and her sex get drenched. Even if she wanted to, there was no way her legs would allow her to continue her private show. She was way too turned on. She turned around once more to face Lisa and ground her pelvis again into Lisa's lap. She grabbed the back of Lisa's head and brought her face into her chest.

"Did you like the show, Coach?"

Lisa said nothing, but the fire in her eyes and the flare of her nostrils said everything. Celeste had no idea how Lisa did it, but she stood with Celeste's legs wrapped around her and kissed her hard while Celeste's back was against the wall. Celeste dropped one leg so her foot was on the floor but kept the other leg wrapped around Lisa's waist. The only sound that came from Lisa was groaning and low growling as she slid her hand into Celeste's booty shorts and easily slid two fingers inside her. Celeste cried out her pleasure. She didn't know Lisa had this aggression in her, and it turned her on. She allowed Lisa to take what she wanted. She gripped her fingers into Lisa's contracted back muscles, urging Lisa to take her harder. Lisa slid a third finger inside and filled her up. It didn't take much longer before Celeste cried out her release and held tight to Lisa so she wouldn't fall.

Lisa pulled out and Celeste dropped her other leg from around Lisa's waist. They stood, hugging each other close, breathing hard. Finally, Lisa spoke.

"That was the sexiest fucking thing I've ever seen."

Celeste laughed and it sounded deep and sultry to her own ears. "I'm glad you enjoyed it. I bet you didn't expect that when you brought over coffee."

Lisa laughed and kissed Celeste deep and slow. She broke the kiss and looked into Celeste's eyes. "No, I did not. But I'll bring you coffee and bagels every Sunday if you want to perform for me. If you don't though, I'll still bring you coffee and bagels just to hang out."

Celeste kissed Lisa, took her hand, and led her down the hall to her bedroom. She stripped out of her clothes while Lisa stripped out of hers.

"We'll heat up the breakfast later. Right now, I'm in the mood for an appetizer."

Lisa lay back on the bed and Celeste decided to skip the foreplay and go right for the feast.

Lisa had gone home later that afternoon and Celeste lounged on her sofa in front of her living room window, sipping a glass of wine, contemplating if she was going to fix dinner for herself or just nibble on some cheese and crackers. Just the thought of getting up from the couch to slice some cheese didn't appeal to her. She was basking in the afterglow of a day full of sex— touching, kissing, licking, caressing, moaning, laughing, teasing, crying out commands.

In the grand scheme of sexual experience, Celeste had very little, but when she was with Lisa, she felt experienced, uninhibited, experimental. Primal. She felt primal, and it was a marvelous feeling. She felt at ease with Lisa, like she could say or try anything and not be or feel judged. She felt free to sexually explore, and in the few times they'd been together, Celeste now felt like an experienced lover.

When she'd been with Jackie, she'd been completely submissive. She let Jackie rule the bed, letting her tell Celeste how to do things to her, and it always made Celeste feel like she was being judged or graded on her performance. Celeste never let go and experimented with Jackie. Jackie had pleased her, always made Celeste come, but she never really allowed Celeste to do her own thing, to see what she was good doing or learning to do new things. Sex was always in bed, always lying down, always one woman on top of the other.

That afternoon, there was standing up against the wall, on all fours, on her stomach, on her back, on her knees. Celeste felt like they had covered so many positions already, she didn't know if there were many more.

When Celeste had first started dating Jackie, because of her lack of experience, she ordered the book *Lesbian Sex* and studied it until she felt she knew every word and every illustration. She wanted to be ready for Jackie. She didn't want to reveal to Jackie that she'd be her first sexual partner. Because that whole judgment thing? Not something Celeste wanted to experience with her first girlfriend. She wanted to fake it till she made it, but she never was really given the chance because of Jackie's dominance. Lisa, on the other hand, seemed willing to let Celeste take control some of the time. And just because Celeste hadn't had a lot of experience with a sex partner didn't mean she hadn't had fantasies of how she wanted to take and be taken. That whole friendly friend thing was a really good thing for Celeste and Lisa.

There was a problem though.

Celeste was starting to have feelings for Lisa. More feelings. She was thinking about Lisa. A lot. She often wondered how Lisa's day was going, how the team did in practice, how Lisa was spending her limited downtime. Celeste wondered if she was getting enough sleep, getting enough to eat, getting enough exercise. She sort of sounded like a mother, but she certainly didn't think of Lisa as her child. No, she definitely thought of Lisa like more than a friend. She thought of her as her lover. Celeste wondered if Lisa thought of her during the day. Hopefully, after this morning's pole and lap dance, Lisa was thinking about Celeste, thinking sexy thoughts about Celeste.

Lisa sat on her couch, drinking a beer, staring at the television but not seeing the college basketball game that was playing.

Her mind was occupied by sexy flashbacks of earlier in the day. While she'd been on her walk, she'd only had pure and innocent thoughts of sharing coffee and bagels with Celeste for breakfast. She'd been completely upended when Celeste took her to the pole room, sat her in a chair, and gave her a private performance. It had been obvious that Lisa had interrupted Celeste's workout routine by the way Celeste had been dressed and had her hair pulled into a messy ponytail, but that didn't diminish how hot Celeste had looked in her tight shorts and shirt.

When Celeste practically pushed Lisa into the chair then turned on the music, Lisa grew instantly aroused. She had fantasized about Celeste doing a private pole dance for her, but she never would've asked for one. She wasn't sure if Celeste would've taken the request the wrong way or if she'd even be comfortable doing it. Oh, she'd seemed comfortable, all right. Right at home as she twirled around the pole, moved her hips, prowled toward her, and gave her a lap dance. Never in Lisa's wildest dreams did she think she'd get a lap dance from Celeste— and how much it turned her on. Celeste had asked Lisa if she liked what she was doing and Lisa felt animalistic. She might have growled when she picked up Celeste and carried her over to the wall and kissed her then fucked her hard and fast. Lisa had never done that with anyone, but Celeste made her wild with lust and Lisa just had to have her right then and there. The rest of the day was spent pleasing each other in different positions, with fingers, lips, and tongues. Lisa was exhilaratingly exhausted.

She was having feelings though. Feelings she wasn't supposed to be having because Celeste wasn't interested in a relationship. No, that wasn't fair. Neither one of them was interested in a relationship for their own specific reasons. They'd agreed to be friends with benefits. The only problem was that Lisa was thinking of Celeste as more than a friend now. She thought about her nearly all day unless she was thinking about her team's next practice or game. Celeste and basketball. That's what Lisa's thoughts were all about now. And sex. She couldn't forget sex with Celeste. So, sex, Celeste, and basketball, and not necessarily in that order. Maybe sex with Celeste was getting in the way of Lisa's coaching plans.

No. Not entirely. Even if they weren't having sex, Lisa would still be thinking about Celeste all the time. When Lisa first saw Celeste, she thought she was beautiful, elegant, and sophisticated. When Lisa first met Celeste, she thought all of those things, then added pain in the ass and stubborn, and someone who jumped to conclusions. Now that she'd gotten to know her, she could add funny, kind, assertive, and determined. Add all of those traits together, and without knowing what she was looking for in a woman, Lisa had found her perfect woman in Celeste. Lisa wasn't the kind of person to kiss and tell, but she wished Athena was home so she had someone to talk to about that. She had other friends, but she trusted Athena to listen, give Lisa her thoughts, and never say a word to anyone else. That was especially important since Jackie had spread rumors about Celeste after they broke up. That Jackie was a real asshole. No wonder she didn't like her before she even knew her. She was a real smarmy type—Lisa would definitely keep an eye out for her, make sure she didn't cause any more grief for Celeste.

Lisa laughed. She had an image of Celeste dressed in a hoop skirt and her hair in large ringlets like Scarlett O'Hara, and Lisa and Jackie with swords out, ready for a duel, the winner getting the love of Celeste.

She looked at her watch and figured Athena wouldn't be home for some time. She was out on a date with the woman she'd met online. Stephanie was her name and this was their third date. Athena had been mostly tight-lipped about it so far, not wanting to jinx it, she claimed. Because Athena had her own dating life to think about, she wasn't too involved in what was going on between Lisa and Celeste. She knew that they'd had sex a few times because there was no way she could keep that quiet from her. At first, Athena seemed shocked, but then she playfully punched Lisa and told her it was about damn time.

Lisa was keeping her fingers crossed that Athena and Stephanie would work out because she really wanted Athena to find a love she could cherish and spend the rest of her life with. If Lisa got a head coaching job at another school, Athena would probably stay at Glassell University if they decided to hire her as head coach. It would make Lisa feel less guilty about taking another job out of town, or likely, out of state. It would make Lisa feel better knowing Athena would have someone to look after her. Of course, Celeste and Olivia would look after her as well, since they'd all become friends. But damn it, she really wished Athena would come home so she could talk to her about her growing feelings for Celeste.

Lisa turned off the television, threw her beer bottle in the recycle bin, and got ready for bed. Whatever she was feeling for Celeste could wait another day for Lisa to discuss with Athena.

Chapter Twenty

Olivia, can we have lunch today? I want to get your opinion and advice on something." Celeste sat in her office grading papers, but she had a difficult time concentrating. Ever since Lisa had left her house two days ago, Celeste had only thought of Lisa and her growing feelings for her. That wasn't supposed to happen. They were only supposed to be colleagues. It started out simple enough. Lisa showed up to her office wanting help for one of her players. Simple, right? But then they kept running into each other, and Celeste kept saying crazy things that required apologizing. Okay, fine. They could be friendly, maybe even friends. Celeste started going to the games, Lisa seemed to stop by her office more, occasionally sharing a conversation over coffee. Great. Celeste could always use a new friend. Two, actually, because it seemed Lisa and Athena were a package deal, and Celeste really liked Athena. She wasn't attracted to her like she was to Lisa, but Athena was funny and she enjoyed the banter between them.

Celeste grabbed her purse, locked her door, and she ran into Jackie as she turned around.

"Where's the fire, doll?"

"Excuse me? Did you just call me 'doll'?"

Jackie leered at Celeste, and she'd had it.

"I'm serious, Jackie. If you don't start leaving me alone, I'll take this to Gerald Prescott and let him take care of you."

Jackie snorted. "For what? For trying to win you back? For calling you terms of endearment?"

"No, for sexually harassing me. For making unwanted advances. For making me uncomfortable in my place of employment. For the last time, leave me alone."

Celeste nudged her out of the way and went to pick up Olivia at her office. She wouldn't tell Olivia about her encounter with Jackie. More important matters were at hand. They walked to a nearby restaurant and found a table near the back that was free. After they'd ordered their iced tea, Celeste got to the point.

"I think I'm starting to have feelings for Lisa."

Olivia stared at Celeste and didn't say a word.

"Stop rolling your eyes at me."

"I did no such thing."

"Mentally, you did."

"What do you want me to say? At the risk of sounding like a thirteen-year-old…duh."

If Celeste was thirteen, she would've thrown something at Olivia and called her a smart-ass.

"This is serious. I need you to give me reasons why I shouldn't have feelings for her."

Olivia thought for a moment, then Celeste could almost see the light bulb go off.

"I know. She's single. She's really good-looking." Olivia started ticking off her fingers. "According to you, she's great in bed…and against the wall. She treats you with kindness and respect. She forgives you when you've acted like an ass. She has a great job, great best friend. She seems normal. Shall I go on?"

"I think you misheard me. I said reasons not to fall for her."

Olivia placed her finger under her chin like she was considering what Celeste said.

"Huh. I guess you're right. Let me think for a moment." Olivia picked up her iced tea and sipped it, keeping Celeste waiting. "No, I can't think of anything."

"Are you serious? What about when she takes another coaching job, leaving me and GU behind?"

"What if she takes another coaching job in Southern California? Are you aware of how many universities there are in Orange and Los Angeles Counties? You'd be willing to deny a possible relationship based on *if* she gets another coaching job? Have you considered that you might be a game-changer for her? That she might want something more with you than an occasional night of sex?"

"Well, there's also the problem that she works at the same university."

"I'll admit you had a good reason when you implemented that rule."

Finally. Celeste felt like she was finally getting somewhere with Olivia.

"But Lisa is not Jackie, and she wouldn't betray you like that."

Their food came and Olivia doctored her salad while Celeste sat there looking like someone kicked her puppy. Olivia pointed her fork at her.

"Stop pouting and eat your salad. You know I'm right."

"You'd certainly like to think so." Celeste had to get in one last jab to make her feel this lunch wasn't a total loss. Despite her diminished appetite from Olivia's dressing down, Celeste managed to eat most of her lunch. Every once in a while, Olivia would mention another wonderful thing about Lisa, just to drive her point further in. It appeared that Celeste would have a lot to think about when it came to Lisa.

If she decided to take a chance on a relationship with Lisa, how would she even bring it up with her? That is, if Lisa was even interested in the same thing. God, she'd wished she had more experience with women. She'd felt so out of her element with that whole dating thing. And, honestly, she still couldn't believe that a woman as good-looking as Lisa would be interested in Celeste. She guessed the saying "Beauty is in the eye of the beholder" might be true.

❖

"Hey, let me ask you a question."

"Shoot, Ice."

Lisa and Athena were sitting in their office, both quiet as they did some work on their computers. They still had a couple of hours before practice started, and Lisa needed to voice some things she'd been thinking about.

"I might be in trouble."

Athena looked up from her computer and over at Lisa. "What did you do now?"

"You say that like I get into a lot of trouble," Lisa said as she threw a paper clip at Athena.

They laughed at the absurdity of that statement.

"Shut up so I can ask you a question. I think I might be having some feelings for Celeste."

"You don't say." Athena pretended to yawn and placed her hand over her open mouth.

"I'm serious."

"Oh, I know. I just find it funny that you took this long to realize it."

"You're right. Actually, my question is, what do I do about it? Celeste and I already decided we'd be just friends and the whole benefit thing is working well for us, but I find myself thinking about her all the time. How do I get over that?"

"Why would you want to? Why not take it to the next level?"

"A couple of reasons. One is because of the possibility of me leaving the school, and two, she doesn't want to date anyone she works with. I met her ex the other day and she's a real piece of work. I won't tell you Celeste's story with her, but the ex spread some rumors about Celeste when she broke things off."

"Wait. She has an ex that works here?"

"Yeah, some butch chick who teaches in the business school She looks kind of like Jane Lynch."

Athena laughed. "How do you do that?"

"Do what?" Lisa played dumb because she knew exactly what Athena was talking about. She'd always had this uncanny ability to assign a regular person to a celebrity—either in the way they looked, their mannerisms, or the way they spoke. "If we're ever together when I see her again, I'll point her out, but you'll already know."

"I'm almost tempted to walk over to that building and look around until I find her."

"Believe me when I say you don't want to waste your time. She's a piece of work that'll make you frustrated and you'll want to throat punch her."

"Did you want to throat punch her?"

"So many times, you have no idea. Celeste and I were having coffee the other day and she interrupted us, didn't even acknowledge me, and told Celeste they could work things out. When she finally did acknowledge me, she basically told me to stay out of it, that it wasn't my business. After she finally left, Celeste told me their history. I have a feeling, though, that that isn't the last time I see her."

"We should go have a talk with her."

"Athena, I appreciate you wanting us to protect Celeste, but she held her own and gave it to Jackie. Besides, we're not in our teens. We're almost fifty and we have to act mature, even if we don't want to. At least in public."

"I know, but I can't stand bullies. And being butches, we want to help save the damsel in distress."

"Yes, except when the damsel isn't in distress and can take care of herself. I saw the way Celeste talked to Jackie, and she can definitely handle things on her end. Anyways, back to my question. What do I do about it? I'm really starting to care for her a lot and I don't want to lose her, especially as a friend."

"I think you're just going to have to buck up and tell her how you feel. She might feel the same. Or maybe you two can stop having sex and go back to being just friends without benefits."

That last idea sounded awful. The few times Lisa and Celeste had had sex were amazing. Lisa couldn't get enough of her. Celeste liked to explore Lisa sexually, and Lisa certainly didn't have a problem letting Celeste explore until her heart was content. But Athena was right. Lisa needed to talk to Celeste about her feelings to see where she was and what she thought about possibly dating. If Celeste wasn't down for it, they could always just stop having sex.

"You're right. This should be something we both have a say in. I'll talk to her later about it."

After practice, Lisa texted Celeste to see if she was still on campus.

Yes. Are you all right?

Yeah. Just wondering if I could come by and talk to you about something. Can I come to your office in about thirty minutes?

Sure. I'll see you then.

Lisa paced her office for the next twenty-five minutes, talking to herself and planning what she was going to say to Celeste. She wanted to be cool, not let Celeste think they couldn't be friends if she didn't want to date. Keeping Celeste as a friend was important to Lisa if that was all she could have. She didn't want any awkwardness between them. She looked at her watch and decided to leave a little early. She spent the walk across campus mentally going over her planned speech. She didn't even see Emily Logan walking toward her until she almost ran into her.

"Hey, Coach. What's going on?"

"Oh, hi, Logan. I'm just…" What was she doing? She didn't want her players to know she was trying to get Celeste to be her girlfriend, or whatever. "I'm just taking a walk to get some fresh air and grab a snack. Are you okay? You need anything?"

"No, I actually just stopped by Professor Bouchard's office to thank her for believing in me and helping me understand her class. It meant a lot to me that she gave me extra time."

"That was really sweet of you. You're right, that was nice of her." *Whew. Close call, missing Emily in Celeste's office.*

"Yeah, and I like that she comes to our games. I've seen her look at you, Coach. You should ask her out."

What? She'd never discussed her personal life, especially her sex life, with any of her players. It wasn't any of their business and it would be inappropriate. She didn't hide the fact that she was a lesbian, but she didn't flaunt it either.

"What are you talking about?"

"I think she likes you, Coach. She's fantastic. I think you're fantastic. I think you two would be great together."

"You do, huh?" Even though it was none of Emily's business, Lisa did appreciate that she was on her side and looking out for her.

"Yep." Emily looked pleased with herself that she was playing matchmaker for Lisa and Celeste, not knowing what was already going on between them.

Lisa squinted and stared at Emily. She clapped her hand on the side of Emily's shoulder before she started past her. "Mind your business, Logan." The sound of Emily laughing followed her a little while longer.

She got to Celeste's office and knocked on the door. When Celeste looked up and smiled, Lisa's breath caught. Damn, she was gorgeous and she had no idea how turned out Lisa's insides got when she smiled like that.

"Come in and have a seat."

Lisa shut the door, took a deep breath in, and sat down before letting it out. She rocked back and forth a little, getting up her nerve to say what she wanted.

"I need to tell you something and I don't want you to feel obligated to do something you don't want to do, and if you don't want to do it, we'll still be friends." Lisa took a breath and waited for Celeste's reaction, but she stayed silent. Why wasn't she saying anything? Lisa realized *she* hadn't said anything yet.

"Right. So, here's the thing. I like you. A lot. I think you're beautiful, sexy, smart, kind, funny. I've realized lately that I'm having stronger feelings for you and I'd really like for us to be more than friends."

"Wow. That's interesting."

"In a good way or bad way?"

Celeste chuckled. "Good. I had been thinking the same thing, actually."

"You have?"

"Yes, but I'm not sure that would be a good idea. You see, I vowed I would never date anyone I work with and you fall into that category. You're also looking to leave the school and go to a larger university. What happens when you leave? Do we carry on a long-distance relationship?"

"I don't know, Celeste. All I know is that I like you. I want to be more than just your friend. I want to take you out on dates, and I'm not interested in seeing other women. And if you think about it, we're already sleeping together. If I was an asshole like Jackie, I could've already spread rumors, but that's not who I am, and I think you know that about me. I don't like drama. I just want to do my job, take care of my team, and see where we can take this thing going on between us." Lisa waved her finger between them.

"You make a good argument, Coach. I actually talked to Olivia about this. I'm having feelings for you, too. More than friends feelings."

Lisa walked slowly over to Celeste, reached for her hands, and helped her up so that they were standing face-to-face.

"Oh, yeah? What did she say?"

"In a nutshell?" Celeste smirked and Lisa nodded. "Duh."

Lisa burst out in laughter. "Athena basically said the same." She took another step closer so that there was only a sliver of space between them.

"Maybe we should've listened to them that first night we all had dinner together."

"Mmm, I'm not so sure. I don't think either one of us was in the right mindset to consider it. Besides, I liked being your friend and getting to know you." Lisa slid her arms around Celeste's waist and Celeste wrapped her arms around Lisa's neck.

"Are you going to kiss me, Coach?"

"You better believe it, Professor," Lisa whispered before capturing Celeste's lips with her own. Lisa's entire body felt on fire and she had no control over her pulse. The longer they kissed, sliding their tongues against each other's, Lisa's libido grew out of control. She broke free and quickly locked the office door and turned out the overhead lights. She hastily moved a stack of papers to the other side of Celeste's desk to clear a space. She moved her hands under Celeste's skirt and pulled her panties down around her ankles, and lifted her skirt above her hips. Celeste had high-heeled shoes on, and the heels dug into Lisa's ass when she lifted Celeste onto the desk and she wrapped her legs around Lisa's waist.

Lisa kissed Celeste's neck, moving her way down to her chest as she slid two fingers into Celeste's hot and wet sex. She slid easily in and out, pumping her fingers faster and deeper. She felt Celeste grab her hair and pulled it hard, causing Lisa to gasp. Her own clit grew hard and Celeste's walls clenched around Lisa's thrusting fingers.

"Oh, God, Lisa. You're going to make me come."

"Come on, baby. You're so close. Come for me."

Celeste turned her face into Lisa's shoulder and bit down while she cried out her release. Lisa slowed her fingers and gently withdrew. She kissed Celeste and held her tight against her body.

"That was amazing and so damned sexy."

Celeste chuckled. "I'll never be able to work at my desk without thinking about this night. You wouldn't know this, but this had been one of my fantasies."

"What? Having sex on your desk?"

"No." Celeste trailed her finger down Lisa's neck into the vee of her polo shirt. "You. Taking me on my desk. Owning me like you just did."

"Jesus." Lisa's head spun and she had to brace her hands on the desk to steady herself.

"Now, I'm going to fulfill another fantasy of mine." Celeste untied the drawstring to Lisa's track pants and slid them down to her ankles. "Sit." Celeste pointed to her office chair and Lisa obeyed. "Don't move. Don't make a sound. You wouldn't want anyone coming in here before I finish with you."

Lisa shook her head and said nothing. Celeste folded up her sweater that was hanging on the back of her chair and placed it on the floor in front of Lisa before getting down on her knees. Sweet baby Jesus. Lisa couldn't believe what Celeste was about to do to her. In her office. On a school night. Celeste placed her hands on Lisa's knees and unabashedly spread them as wide as they would go.

Lisa's scent wafted to Celeste's nose and her mouth immediately watered. Since Celeste had met Lisa, she'd fantasized about this moment. Celeste had always been proper and reserved at school. She typically only let her wild side out while she was pole dancing. Something about Lisa made Celeste uninhibited, and she wanted to do all the sex things in all the places with her.

She looked at Lisa, looked at her glistening sex, and she licked her lips. At first taste, Celeste closed her eyes in rhapsody and took a moment to feel her mouth on Lisa, to taste her, to smell her. She was in heaven. Lisa smelled clean, tasted a little salty, and Celeste started to feast. She took her time, kissed her labia, slowly ran her tongue from the base of Lisa's clit to the very tip, then she pulled it into her mouth. It grew against her tongue and she felt increased wetness against her chin. Celeste released Lisa's tight bundle of nerves and used her tongue to clean up the excessive wetness from Lisa's opening, and Lisa's hips bucked up toward Celeste's mouth.

Lisa's breathing was loud, but to her credit, she was keeping the volume of her moans on low. Lisa's knuckles turned white with the death grip she had on the arms of the chair. Celeste used her own hands to spread Lisa's lips apart and blew cool air on Lisa's clit. She used the tip of her tongue to quickly flick it, then she moved her tongue slowly around the growing bud. Celeste looked up at Lisa with her mouth open, allowing Lisa to see what

Celeste's tongue was doing to her. Oops, there was more wetness against her chin. She'd better clean that up. Without breaking eye contact with Lisa, she used her tongue to lap up Lisa's juices before thrusting her tongue in and out a few times. Lisa's eyes slammed shut and she begged through clenched teeth.

"Please, Celeste. Let me come. I want to come in your mouth."

Celeste felt herself grow hard again and she sucked Lisa's engorged clit back into her mouth, stroked it with her tongue, and reached down with her hand to stroke her own clit. She wanted them to come together. She felt Lisa swell even more into her mouth, against her lips, and Celeste whimpered when her own hips started to buck back and forth quickly.

"Fuck. Fuck. Fuck. I'm coming so hard."

Lisa's abdomen tightened, she stilled, then cried out when Celeste moaned her own climax while Lisa's clit was still in her mouth. Lisa grabbed the back of Celeste's head and held her there. Celeste kept Lisa's clit in her mouth until it stopped throbbing and softened.

Celeste rested her cheek on Lisa's bare thigh until their breathing slowed down.

"Wow, Professor."

"Indeed, Coach."

"For a couple of academic types, we sure are having a tough time coming up with words, aren't we?"

Lisa ran her fingers through Celeste's hair, the intimate act made Celeste want to snuggle closer.

"Celeste, please go out with me."

Celeste got off the floor and sat in Lisa's lap. She kissed her softly. "Okay, Coach. I'll go out with you."

CHAPTER TWENTY-ONE

L isa and Celeste had been busy the remainder of the week with classes, practices, and games so they hadn't had time to have a proper date yet, but they'd texted each other numerous times, and they'd managed to meet for coffee on campus once too. Lisa had warned Celeste that for the next couple of months, she wouldn't have much free time because of games and practices. That was one of the main reasons for not wanting to get involved with anyone during basketball season, but she couldn't not ask Celeste to be her…what? Girlfriend? Was she too mature (old) to call Celeste her girlfriend? Maybe lady friend? Lisa smiled trying to think of a term that was appropriate for two women in their mid to late forties just starting out in a relationship. Maybe she'd talk to Celeste about it and figure out what they would call each other.

Glassell University won their game that night against a team that was in the top three teams in their conference. Lisa had changed her clothes in her office, told Athena not to wait up, and met Celeste at her office so they could go on their first real date as a couple. They had reservations for a late dinner at a small Italian restaurant near the campus but not too close. They actually had to drive, which would work out better since the rare rain shower in Southern California happened to be occurring that night. They were seated in a quiet corner, their table lit by candle, and they laughed together when they pulled out their cell phones to use their flashlight app to read the menu. The ambience was certainly romantic but not conducive to reading the menu. Once they'd ordered, they put away their phones and concentrated on each other.

"You look gorgeous tonight, Celeste. That dress looks really good on you."

"Thank you. You clean up well yourself. I love that shirt on you. You wore it to the faculty reception at the start of the school year."

"I did. I'm surprised you knew that."

"What? Did you think I didn't notice you that night? I saw you looking my way during Gerald's speech."

"I couldn't help it. You were the most interesting thing about that night. And I was just working up my nerve to go talk to you when someone else intervened and took your attention."

"That would be Jackie. After I told her to buzz off, Olivia and I left the party. I hate being anywhere she is."

"If I knew then what I know now, I would've gone over there and interrupted."

"Well, we're here now, hopefully with no interruptions."

Lisa took Celeste's hand and rubbed her thumb across her knuckles, looking at the flicker of the candle flame reflected in her deep brown eyes.

Their food was brought out, and after a couple of bites, then praise for the food, Celeste mentioned her parents would be arriving in two weeks, staying two weeks, and then traveling around the western United States for a month before returning to France.

"Would you like to meet them? I know it's not what couples just starting out usually do, and if you're not comfortable with that, it's okay."

"No, that would be great. Maybe they would want to come to a game. We have to have at least one home game while they're here. I know you don't get to see them often, so as long as you're all right with it."

The rest of dinner was spent eating, gazing at each other, reaching across the table to caress the other's hand. For this being their first honest-to-goodness date, it was going very well. They'd always been able to hold a conversation, and now that they were no longer walking on the proverbial eggshells of not owning up to their feelings, things were a lot more relaxed. Lisa couldn't remember being this relaxed at this point in the season. They had about four weeks of league play left, and as of now, they were in first place. Being with Celeste made Lisa almost forget about basketball, and if it wasn't so ingrained into her life, she might have. Celeste appeared to be understanding of the time basketball took up in Lisa's life, but her willingness to learn more about the game incorporated Lisa's basketball and personal time.

Lisa tried to remember that it wasn't all about her and basketball. She wanted to know more about Celeste's interest too. Celeste had already told her about the struggle with self-esteem and pole dancing. Lisa thought Celeste was beautiful just the way she was. In fact, even more so considering her determination to be healthy and live her best life. That's all Lisa wanted for Celeste. That and to be happy and content in her life. She was really looking forward to meeting Celeste's parents. Lisa felt that it would give her more insight into who Celeste was.

"I'm really glad we met, Lisa. I've really enjoyed watching your team play and getting to know Athena. You've taught me so many new things in the short time we've known each other, but I especially like how kind you are and how supportive you are to me."

"I'm glad we met too, Celeste. I look forward to getting to know you better."

When they got in the car, Celeste asked Lisa to go home with her, and Lisa happily obliged.

❖

Celeste and Lisa had been officially dating for two weeks, and it was going well. Celeste would watch Lisa's home games,

Lisa would meet Celeste for coffee or a little break during their day, and thankfully, Celeste hadn't had any more run-ins with Jackie. Celeste's parents were arriving that day, and Lisa had agreed to meet them for dinner the following night. Since her parents were jetlagged, Celeste decided to cook dinner herself rather than going out to a restaurant. Celeste's insides were churning and her palms were sweaty. She couldn't remember ever being this nervous. Of course, she'd never had to introduce her parents to anyone she was dating. It wasn't like Celeste and Lisa were getting engaged or anything, and she never would have introduced Jackie to her parents. But it just felt like the right thing to do with Lisa. Sure, she could have continued to see Lisa only at school while her parents were in town, but that didn't seem like enough time to spend with her.

Lisa didn't seem uncomfortable when Celeste asked her if she wanted to meet them. She wondered if Lisa had met any girlfriends' parents before. Come to think of it, Lisa had never mentioned any of her previous dating life. Maybe during a quiet evening, she could ask Lisa about that. She didn't see her as a promiscuous type, but she also didn't see her as a nun, either. Especially if Celeste was judging by how great Lisa was in bed. Okay, enough of that. Celeste didn't want to be dealing with a heightened libido while her parents were there.

Celeste waited at the baggage claim, anticipating the arrival of her parents. She spotted them descending the escalator. Her father was still a handsome, healthy looking man in his late seventies, with a head full of thick, silver hair, as well as a matching silver full mustache. He was dressed casually in khaki trousers and a blue button-down shirt that Celeste knew would match his eyes. Her mother also wore trousers and a flowing tunic blouse. Unlike her father, her mother continued to dye her long hair jet-black, claiming she didn't have to look like she was seventy. Celeste knew if she could have the stunning silver hair her father had, she wouldn't spend so much money on highlights, but she wasn't that lucky. She thought that once she reached a certain age, she'd stop coloring her hair. She had compromised and had highlights instead.

They spotted her halfway down the escalator and waved to Celeste who returned the gesture. She reached the bottom of the escalator as they did, and they hugged each other once they'd moved out of the way of the other passengers.

"Mama, Papa, you look fantastic. Retirement is treating you well." Her father had retired a year ago, and her mother three years ago from a museum in Paris. Her father worked as an archivist and her mother as a curator, which helped Celeste develop a love for art. She'd considered following in her parents' footsteps, but English and teaching became her love.

"Oui, chéri. Your mother and I have been keeping busy touring all of the museums in France. We have seen some amazing displays."

Celeste loved the accent that was so thick in her father's speech. Her mother, who was American, spoke fluent French, as did Celeste, but they never developed the accent.

"Well, I'm so happy you're here. I'm just sorry that I'll have to teach while you're in town."

"Ah, no worries, chéri. You know how much we love your quaint little town with antique shops and eccentric stores. We'll have plenty to do while you're positively influencing today's generation."

They grabbed their luggage and walked with Celeste to her car. Once they got on the freeway, Celeste told them her news.

"Mama, Papa, I have something to tell you. Actually, someone for you to meet."

Celeste's father turned to face her. "Oh?"

"I have started seeing someone recently. Her name is Lisa Tobias, and she's the women's basketball coach at the university I work for."

"Well, I hope she's nothing like that terrible woman you dated last year."

Celeste looked in the rearview mirror to see her mother looking out the side window and her arms crossed over her chest.

"No, Mama. Lisa is nothing like Jackie. She's kind and funny, and she's considerate. But you can form your own opinion because she's coming for dinner tomorrow."

"Well, she better be worthy of you, chéri, or your father will have to have a talk with her." The twinkle in his eye let Celeste know he was kidding. Kind of.

"Oh, Papa, I'm almost fifty years old. You can't treat me like a little girl anymore."

"Chéri, as long as your mother and I are alive, you will always be our little girl."

"I promise, you will like her. She asked if maybe you would be interested in seeing one of her games. Her team is really good and a lot of fun to watch."

"How did you meet, honey?" Her mother was now leaning forward to get involved in the conversation. Celeste guessed that once she said Lisa was nothing like Jackie, her mother became more interested.

"One of her players was in my class and she wasn't doing very well. Lisa came to talk to me about getting her some help. I initially thought she was asking me to boost her grade."

"Yes," her father said. "I remember that happened to you a few times before. Did you set her straight?"

"Turns out, I jumped to conclusions. She was looking for a tutor or someone to help her learn what I was trying to say in lecture. Lisa was very offended that I questioned her integrity."

Her father laughed. "I think I might like this lady."

"I have no doubt, Papa. There were many times I accused her of things and she called me out on it every single time."

"Looks like my baby has finally met her match," her mother said from the back seat.

"Indeed. She's opened my eyes to new things. I love going to watch her team play. Those young ladies are so athletic and talented. What I love most is that away from basketball, Lisa is very relaxed, laid-back, and quiet. But when she's coaching, she's intense, loud, and aggressive." Celeste saw out of the corner of her eye her mama and papa look at each other. She briefly looked at her father before returning her eyes to the road. "What's that look for?"

"Nothing. It sounds like you're smitten with her."

Celeste laughed. She was nearing fifty years old, and she never thought the word smitten would be used to describe her. "I suppose I am. It's hard not to be. She's an incredible lady."

Celeste pulled into her driveway and helped her parents with their luggage. They spent another hour catching up, then her parents went to their room to take a little nap before dinner. Celeste decided to send Lisa a quick text.

Hey there. My parents arrived safely and are taking a nap. They're looking forward to meeting you tomorrow night.

A few minutes later, Lisa texted back.

I wish you and I could take a nap. I'm looking forward to meeting them, as well. On my way to practice. Talk soon.

Celeste wished her a good practice then she set her phone down to start preparing dinner. She felt good. Really good. Her parents were there, things with Lisa were going well, and she was in a place in her life that made her feel good. She finally felt at peace.

CHAPTER TWENTY-TWO

Immediately after practice, Lisa hustled home and got ready to meet Celeste's parents. Now that she had short hair, getting ready took a lot less time, which she was grateful for tonight. As she was getting dressed, Athena came into Lisa's room and sat on her bed.

"Ready to meet the parents?"

Lisa huffed. "I'm actually a little nervous. It's been a long time since I've met the parents of a woman I'm dating. But since they live in Paris and are here for only a couple of weeks, it's now or much, much later."

"You'll be fine, Ice. Just be your normal charming self and they'll love you."

Lisa was waiting for a smartass comment to come from Athena, but she actually looked sincere. "Thanks, Athena." Lisa finished dressing then put on her lucky one-carat diamond stud earrings. She had bought them when she got her first bonus check as a professional basketball player.

"Ooh, your lucky earrings. Lisa, all kidding aside, how serious are you about Celeste?"

"I don't know what you're talking about. I just want to look nice when I meet Celeste's parents."

Athena remained silent but didn't break her glare from Lisa.

"Okay, fine. Yes, I like her. A lot. But we don't know what the future holds for us. We're both aware that I might leave for another coaching job, but we agreed to deal with it when the time comes."

Athena stayed quiet.

"Yes! Okay? Yes, I really like her and in case it goes further, I want her parents to like me. Damn, Chang. Give me a break."

Athena held her hands up in surrender. "I didn't say a thing. This is all on you, buddy."

"Do I look okay?" Lisa's voice was a little shaky, and Athena took pity on her.

"You look great. They're going to love you, buddy. Don't worry. Now, get going, and don't forget to bring flowers. Show Celeste's parents you're not a Neanderthal and that you care about her."

"Right, flowers. I'll see you later. Oh, what do you have going on tonight?"

Lisa had been so deep in her head about meeting Celeste's parents, she'd almost forgotten about her best friend.

"Stephanie and I are having dinner tonight. If things go well, we'll end up either back here or at her place. But if we end up back here, don't knock on my bedroom door when you come home. We've been taking it slow, but she has me so wound up I'm about to explode like a pressure cooker. I'm hoping tonight will be the night."

"That's great, buddy. So, you really like this gal?"

"Yes, I like her a lot."

"Well, I can't wait to meet her." Lisa looked at her watch. "I gotta get going. Good luck tonight."

"You too, Ice. Go get 'em, tiger."

Lisa stopped for some flowers, then she arrived at Celeste's. Once she was on the front porch, she took a deep breath to calm her nerves before she knocked on the door. Although Celeste and Lisa were new in this relationship, she felt this was a really big step in getting to know Celeste. Meeting the parents was normally a really big deal, so the significance of tonight didn't escape Lisa. If she was being honest with herself and had the free time to examine this further, Lisa could see Celeste and herself living a long life together. They got along really well, the sex was unbelievable, and Lisa loved that Celeste was intelligent and classy, and she had a great sense of humor. Her musings were interrupted when Celeste opened the front door. She looked beautiful, maybe a little nervous. Maybe they were in the same boat tonight.

"Hello, Coach."

"Professor, these are for you." Lisa handed over the flowers and kissed her briefly on the lips.

"Thank you. Are you okay?"

"I'm a little nervous," Lisa whispered.

Celeste cupped her cheek. "No need. They'll love you. Now come in and meet my parents."

Lisa wiped her sweaty palms on her slacks as Celeste led her into the living room to meet the firing squad.

"Papa, Mama, this is Lisa Tobias. Lisa, these are my parents, Claude and Marie Bouchard."

Lisa shook their hands and greeted them with her best smile. She'd been practicing all afternoon in front of the mirror until she had it right.

"Mr. Bouchard, Mrs. Bouchard, I'm so pleased to meet you."

"Please, call us Claude and Marie. It is so nice to meet you. Celeste has been telling us all about you." Claude took her hand in his and covered it, making her feel welcomed by him. Marie, on the other hand, seemed like she'd be a tougher egg to crack. By her body language, standing stiffly with her hands clasped together in front of her, Marie didn't seem as welcoming. Although Marie was a little standoffish, she was an elegant, beautiful woman, and Lisa knew where Celeste got her looks from. Lisa had some work to do to get Marie to loosen up toward her. The thaw started when Celeste showed her parents the flowers Lisa gave her. Ah, Marie was making sure Lisa was respectful of her daughter. Thankfully, her father raised Lisa and her brother to respect women, hold open the door, pull out the chair. Lisa definitely knew how to be a gentlewoman, and it looked like she would be tested.

"It smells amazing in here. Is there anything I can help with?"

"No, sweetie, the sauce is on simmer and will be ready in a little while. Why don't we go sit for a while and we can all get to know each other? We all have something to drink. What can I get you?"

"I'm fine for now, but thank you."

Once they were seated, Lisa started the conversation by asking how their flight was. After Claude answered, Marie's interrogation began. Lisa had been sitting relaxed in an armchair but moved to the edge when Marie started her questioning.

"My Celeste told me you work at the same university. What kind of education do you have?"

"Well, I have my undergraduate degree in psychology and my master's in education."

"But you are a coach, yes?"

"Yes, ma'am. I played basketball in college and at the professional level in Europe, but I was forced to give up that level of playing due to some serious injuries. My college coach hired me as an assistant, at which time I got my master's degree. I've been coaching ever since then."

"Do you teach, as well?"

"Yes, sir. I teach self-defense at the university." Lisa felt Claude might ask her the easy questions.

Celeste spoke up. "Lisa felt it was important for students, particularly women, to know how to defend themselves. It seems there are so many reports of campus attacks and rapes, it really is a great class to offer. She also started a healthy living initiative that is free for students and faculty. Once a week, we have a different exercise class or nutrition class. It seems the classes grow a little more each week."

"We? Are you involved, Celeste?" Her mother's look of surprise almost made Lisa laugh.

"No, I take the classes, Mama. I'm not always able to make it, but I try."

"I thought it would be a good idea to offer ideas for a healthy lifestyle. Our university's president was very excited about it, and we have coaches and nutrition professors volunteer each week so there's a good variety." Lisa could see Marie's ice begin to melt.

"Dinner should be ready. Lisa, would you help me, please? Mama, Papa, you can take a seat at the table."

Lisa was grateful for the short reprieve and followed Celeste into the kitchen. She was taken by surprise when Celeste turned on her, pushed Lisa up against the counter, and kissed her breathless. Lisa welcomed Celeste's tongue into her mouth and sucked on the tip. She felt her body heat up until she remembered Celeste's parents were in the other room. She placed her hands on Celeste's shoulders and gently pushed her away.

"Are you crazy? Your parents are in the other room."

Celeste wiped the edge of her lips with her fingertip to erase any smudge of lipstick. "It was your fault. You didn't even kiss me when you arrived." Celeste pouted her lips and Lisa tapped them with her finger.

"I did too kiss you."

"It was barely a peck."

"Because I didn't know if your parents would be all right with it. I was trying to be respectful."

"You're so cute. And sweet. Thanks for thinking of them." Celeste rewarded her with another kiss with a little less heat. They carried out the food to the dining table and Lisa held out the chair for Celeste to sit down. Wait. Was that a small smile that Marie gave Lisa? She did a little mental fist pump. She took her seat and waited for Celeste to take the lead.

Once everyone had their plates filled, they continued their conversation. Lisa asked the Bouchards about art and museums. She didn't know a lot about art so her questions were about finding out more about certain artists and periods. Lisa had a feeling that Marie might have thought of her as just a dumb jock and unworthy of dating her sophisticated daughter. Lisa was holding her own though, and every once in a while, she would catch an affectionate glance from Celeste. All in all, Lisa felt the meeting of the parents was an overall success. Marie's ice had melted, and she even laughed at a few things Lisa had said. Lisa could honestly say that she liked the Bouchards. When it came time to say good night, she got hugs and cheek kisses from both Claude and Marie, and it nearly brought tears to her eyes. They liked her. They really liked her.

"I'm going to walk Lisa to her car."

"Good night, Claude and Marie. I really enjoyed talking with you tonight."

"The pleasure was ours, chéri. We will see you at the game next week." Marie kissed Lisa on the cheek once more before letting her go.

Celeste walked Lisa to her car and wrapped her arms around her neck. "My parents like you."

Lisa placed her hands on Celeste's hips and pulled her closer.

"Yeah? Good. I like them too. You look just like your mom, you know."

"That's a wonderful compliment. Thank you."

"No, thank you. I had a really great time tonight getting to know your folks. And dinner was delicious."

Lisa leaned in to kiss Celeste and wrapped her arms tight around her. She was really falling for Glassell University's most popular and prettiest English professor. She hoped Celeste was falling for her too.

"Sweet dreams, baby." That was the first time she called Celeste "baby" since they'd started dating, but it felt so natural.

"Good night, sweetheart."

Lisa stayed put until Celeste walked through her front door. She finally drove away, but instead of leaving, she felt her life was finally coming home.

CHAPTER TWENTY-THREE

The whole school started rallying around the women's basketball team. They had finished the conference undefeated, they had cruised through their conference tournament, and they were getting ready to leave for the national tournament in Chicago. Getting this far was beyond what Lisa was expecting. Hoping for? Sure. But not expecting. It was nearly unheard of for a coach to turn around a team that used to be so bad into a title contender in a short amount of time. It was a little more difficult to prepare her team for their first opponent. First, there would be nerves. It didn't matter how good a player someone was, when they got on a stage of this caliber, the jitters kicked in. Also, Lisa didn't know anything about the team they would face first so she had to work her magic to find some game film to study.

It was pretty impressive to see the rally put on in the center of campus. The quad had cement benches all around and a huge fountain in the center. There was a podium set up on the steps of the library, the school's band was playing, and the cheerleaders were waving their pom-poms. Her players were all matching in their GU travel sweats. The president gave a good luck speech, followed by Lisa thanking the students and faculty for their support over the season. She reminded them they could watch the games on the GU athletics website since the games would be streamed.

The crowd dispersed after Lisa introduced the team and thanked them once again. She saw Olivia and Celeste off to the side and waved. They waved back, then turned to head to their respective classes. Lisa and Celeste already had plans to meet later that night for a private farewell. Athena and Lisa were standing around and collecting congratulations and good lucks from students and faculty. Her day had been so awesome until Jackie Stone came walking up.

"So, you're off to Chicago for your little basketball tournament. That's great, Coach. That's really great."

Lisa remained quiet, not trusting herself to say anything civil to Celeste's ex.

"Will Celeste be joining you?"

"How is that your business?"

"Well, I was thinking I could use the time you two are apart to convince her that we should get back together. After all, she's too high class for a jock. She's rooting around the gutter with you."

"Who the hell do you think you are?" Athena started to come at Jackie until Lisa held her back.

"Stay out of it, little girl."

Lisa saw the vein pop out on Athena's temple and knew that if she let go, Athena would attack Jackie in front of all of these people and quite possibly put Jackie in the hospital, and most likely get arrested herself. Lisa really needed Athena on the bench with her so she told Athena to stand down.

"Well, you could try, but I think you already know how Celeste feels about you." Lisa remained quiet after that comment, but she kept looking into Jackie's eyes, silently letting her know she wasn't going to get her way. Lisa grinned, then she winked at Jackie.

Lisa didn't expect the closed fist to connect with her face, but her cheek felt like it caught fire before exploding. She covered the area with her hand as tears welled in her eyes. *Motherfucker, that hurt!* She looked up to find campus police restraining Jackie and a male faculty member holding back Athena.

"Officer, I'd like to press charges against that woman for assault."

The campus police took Jackie Stone away while most of the students had their cell phones out and recording what was going to be the next video sensation on YouTube. *Just great. I better text Celeste to let her know what happened.* Gerald came over to Lisa and Athena.

"Coach Tobias, Coach Chang. What the hell just happened?"

Lisa could feel the pressure building in her cheek and winced when she lightly touched it. One of the campus officers was standing next to Gerald, taking notes for his report.

"I'm sorry, Gerald. Jackie Stone said some nasty things about a fellow colleague, and I felt I should defend her honor."

"Who are you talking about?"

Shit. There was no getting out of this one. She looked at Athena who looked like she pitied Lisa for getting caught up in this. She didn't want to betray Celeste, but she didn't see any other way.

"I'd appreciate it if you could keep this as quiet as possible for my colleague's sake. She'd already had rumors spread about her because of Jackie."

Gerald stayed quiet and waited for Lisa to continue. She took a deep breath.

"Celeste Bouchard is my colleague. Apparently, Jackie has been harassing Professor Bouchard despite her telling her to leave her alone. I don't feel right saying any more because it's not my story to tell. If you want to know the whole story, you'll have to talk to Professor Bouchard. For the record, she doesn't know about this confrontation."

"I see."

"Are you going to fire me?"

"No. I witnessed the whole thing and Ms. Stone was the one who assaulted you. But there will be an investigation. We'll see what the outcome brings." He pointed at Lisa's eye. "You better get some ice on that." He walked away, and Lisa turned to Athena. "I need to get to Celeste before she hears this from anyone else."

"Right. I'll meet you back at the office. I'll run over to the training room and get you a bag of ice."

"Thanks, buddy. Oh, and, hey. Thanks for having my back with Jackie."

"Always, buddy. And you're right—she makes you want to throat punch her."

Lisa laughed and slapped Athena on the back. "No lie. See you soon."

Lisa started to run, but the pounding made her eye feel like it would pop out of the socket. Instead, she walked quickly to Celeste's office to find the door locked. Lisa forgot she was in class. She went to the desk of the administrative assistant to the English department.

"Hi, I'm Coach Tobias. I'm looking for Celeste Bouchard."

"Yes, Coach. Professor Bouchard is teaching a class right now."

Lisa could feel her patience wearing thin, but it wasn't the assistant's fault. She wasn't aware of the urgency Lisa felt.

"Could you tell me what room that's in?"

"Certainly, let me pull it up. Here we are. Reeves Hall, room 204."

"Thanks." Lisa resumed her speed walking to the west side of campus. It *would* have to be the building farthest from her office. She quietly opened the door and all heads turned to her, including Celeste's. So much for trying to be discreet. Celeste excused herself from class, telling the students she would be back in a minute. She stepped outside and closed the door behind her.

"Baby! What on earth happened to your face?"

"Jackie Stone happened."

"Jackie? What?"

"After the rally, she came up to me and indicated that she would use my time away from you to win you back. We had some words. She threw a punch. I had her arrested." Lisa shrugged like it was no big deal.

The flabbergasted look on Celeste's face indicated it might be a little bit of a big deal.

"Hey, Jackie is just lucky I held Athena back. Athena was ready to cut her at her knees."

Celeste stood there speechless, just staring at Lisa in disbelief.

"The thing is, Gerald was there and asked what happened. I didn't want to tell him, but I felt I had to."

"Tell him what, exactly?"

Lisa still couldn't tell if Celeste was angry with her or not. Her next statement might seal the angry deal.

"That she'd been harassing you, and I was defending your honor."

Celeste looked at her classroom door then back to Lisa. "I have to get back to my class. We'll talk about this tonight."

"Okay. Just one more thing. A lot of people had their cell phones out recording it. It might make it to YouTube."

Celeste rolled her eyes and went back into her classroom. Lisa headed back to her office. *Well, that went well.*

"Come in and tell me what happened."

Celeste had been reeling all day since Lisa told her about the confrontation between her and Jackie. It was all she could do to put it in the back of her mind so she could finish her lecture. By the time she got back to her office, she had an email waiting for her from Gerald. She was scheduled to meet with him the next morning. She probably could have greeted Lisa a little nicer at her door, but she was off-kilter from her relationship with Jackie coming back to haunt her.

Lisa sat on the couch with her hands folded in her lap, looking like she was about to be reprimanded. Celeste was torn between sitting in a chair away from Lisa and sitting next to her on the couch. Celeste realized that she tended to jump to conclusions with Lisa and she was trying to change her behavior. She chose sitting next to Lisa on the couch.

"Baby, your eye looks terrible. Does it hurt?"

"Only when I have facial expressions." Lisa tried to smile but winced instead. "I know you're probably mad, but I can really explain."

"Lisa, I am angry, but not with you. I just don't understand what she wants from me and why she won't leave me alone."

"I didn't want to tell Gerald that you were involved with Jackie, and I was very vague about it. I told him to talk to you about it."

"I got an email from him and I'm meeting with him in the morning."

"What time? Maybe I could drive myself to the airport and meet the team there."

"No, you need to be with the team and concentrate on your game. Now, tell me what happened."

Lisa went through the whole story of her confrontation with Jackie from her first words to speaking with Gerald. Celeste actually laughed when Lisa told her how fired up Athena was and that she'd defended both her and Celeste.

"I was proud of myself for not saying what I really wanted to say, but I thought better of it when I noticed how many people were watching."

"What did you want to say to Jackie?"

"I wanted to ask her what made her think you wanted her back because she was apparently awful in bed and needed to do some research on how to please a woman."

Celeste covered her mouth with her hand to stop the laughter from bubbling out.

"Instead, I kept quiet and let her anger build up. When I winked at her, she came unglued and hit me."

"I'm glad you didn't say anything. Now it's all on her."

"Well, Gerald said there would be an investigation, and if I happen to get in trouble, it'll be worth it if Jackie gets what's coming to her." Lisa took Celeste's hand and held it in her lap. "Are you sure you're not upset with me?"

Celeste scooted closer and cupped her non-injured cheek. "I'm sure. Now, let's not talk about this anymore and just enjoy our night. I won't see you for five whole days."

They spent the rest of the night cuddling on the couch rather than having sex. Celeste needed a different type of intimacy from Lisa that night and Lisa gave it to her. Celeste felt really good about the direction the relationship was heading.

CHAPTER TWENTY-FOUR

The team arrived in Chicago two days before the tournament started, and they spent the first night in a ballroom at the hotel walking through plays against the type of defenses and offenses their opponent tended to play. After a long flight and changing two time zones, this idea was what Lisa and Athena came up with to shake off the travel fatigue and keep their minds focused on basketball instead of Lisa's black eye or their nerves. Early in the morning, when the team met at Lisa's office before their trip to the airport, her players showed genuine concern for her. A couple of them started speculating a little too loudly about why the black eye happened, but Lisa and Athena both shut them down quickly by saying Professor Stone, for some reason, had an ax to grind with Lisa but now it was over. Once those players had their tails tucked between their legs, a few of the other players who were starters, including Emily Logan, started teasing Lisa good-naturedly about it.

After their impromptu practice, they all had dinner together and went back to their rooms to do their homework or watch television. The bed check was at ten, reminding the players that breakfast would be at nine a.m., practice at the arena at eleven thirty for a couple of hours, then back to the hotel after treatment for any injuries the players had. None of the ladies had expressed any interest in sightseeing; they knew why they were there and what their focus should be on.

Lisa took her cell phone to the lobby and called Celeste. Since it was two hours earlier in California, Lisa didn't worry she would be disrupting bedtime.

"Hi, Coach. I was hoping I'd hear from you."

"I just got the kids to bed so I thought I'd call you. Are you busy?"

"Yes, as a matter of fact. I'm busy thinking about you. I miss you."

"I miss you too, baby."

Celeste chuckled. "You do not. You're too busy going over game tape and coming up with a game plan to miss me."

Lisa mock-scolded Celeste. "You don't know me."

"Oh, I think I do know you, handsome." Lisa shivered when Celeste lowered her voice. She sounded so sexy when she did that.

"What are you wearing, Professor?"

There was a pause, and Lisa thought she might've pushed too far. She was about to apologize when Celeste answered.

"I'm wearing the black lacy nightgown you like so much."

"Ooh, I do like that one. It looks really good on you. Shows off your luscious cleavage and delectable hips." Lisa had to be careful to keep her voice low so no one else would hear.

"I like the roughness of the lace on my nipples when I pinch them." Celeste gasped. Lisa grew hard. She squeezed her legs together to apply pressure to her swollen clit.

"Are you squeezing them now?"

"Yes, but I'm imagining they're your hands squeezing them. God, Lisa, you have the best hands."

"Are you wet, baby?"

"Yes," Celeste whispered. "So wet and hard for you."

Jesus Christ. "Baby, I'm not alone, so can you tell me what you're doing and feeling? I want to hear you come for me."

"It won't take long, stud. Just the thought of you makes me so hot."

"Let me hear you, baby."

"Well, I'm not wearing panties, so I have no confinement of my hand. I can easily stroke my clit or slide two fingers deep into my pussy. Would you like that?"

"Yes. Jesus, yes." Lisa wiped the bead of sweat from her forehead and looked around the lobby, making sure nobody she knew was around. She'd never heard Celeste use that word before and her body sizzled.

"Oh, God, your fingers feel so good in me. Stroke in and out of me nice and slow."

Lisa could feel her face grow hot and she stuck her fingers under her nose, across her upper lip, and imagined Celeste's scent on her. She wished she had some privacy so she could actively participate. Better yet, she wished Celeste was here so she could use her own fingers and mouth to bring her pleasure.

"Lisa, I'm going to come all over your hand. I'm almost there, baby." Celeste sounded out of breath and her voice got higher. Lisa felt her own breath and pulse quicken. It was a good possibility that Lisa would come just from hearing Celeste come. She squeezed her knees harder together when Celeste squealed, her sure sign that she'd been completely satisfied. Lisa was content to sit and listen to Celeste come down from her release, to hear her breathing return to normal, then the slow chuckle Celeste always did after she came, like it was a wonder why they didn't do that more often. To be honest, the only thing that prevented them from having sex more often was work. Lisa whispered into the phone so that only Celeste could hear her words.

"You're so beautiful when you come for me. So responsive, so damn sexy."

"You make me feel so good, baby. I can't wait till you come back and do that to me for real."

"I have no idea how I'm supposed to walk through this lobby and back to my room in the state I'm in."

Celeste chuckled again. "And I'm assuming you're sharing a room with Athena so you won't be able to take care of it yourself."

"You got it. I guess I'm going to have to take a cold shower instead."

"How are you feeling about tomorrow?"

The abrupt change in topic had Lisa confused. "Huh?"

"The game tomorrow. How are you feeling about it?"

Geez, Lisa almost forgot about the game, she was so caught up in Celeste. "Good. We're as prepared as we're going to be."

"I wish I could be there, sweetheart, but Olivia and I are going to watch it online. We'll be cheering you on."

"Thank you, baby. I appreciate it."

"Okay, Coach. Get to sleep. You have a big day tomorrow."

"I'll call you tomorrow after the game. Sweet dreams."

"Good night." The softness in Celeste's voice reminded Lisa of when she was thoroughly satisfied and on the brink of slumber.

She hung up and held the phone against her cheek. That wasn't the first time she'd had phone sex, but it was definitely the best. She looked once more around the lobby before standing. She wanted to make sure nobody was paying any kind of attention to her. Her clit was still hard and her underwear was soaked. It was going to be an uncomfortable walk back to her room.

Glassell University won the first game by a pretty good margin. Lisa's team came out owning the court. They played effective defense, shutting down their opponent's best player, and had an amazing offensive showing. The team had spent their day off pretty much resting. They did go to the gym to shoot around and run through the plays their next opponent would be running. The players were in good spirits but still focused on the next game. This was the furthest any GU women's basketball team had gotten in the post-season. Until this year, they'd never made it out of the conference tournament. Finally, in this historic position, they found that it wasn't enough for them and they weren't quite ready to call it quits on the season just yet.

After the game, Lisa returned to the hotel with the team, got them situated, and then gave Celeste a call. Celeste had told her they watched the game, the team looked great, and Celeste threw in that Lisa looked extremely hot in the suit that she wore. Lisa didn't readily respond this time because if she were being honest, the nerves were getting to her. She kept her conversation short with Celeste that night but called her the next night and hoped Celeste could talk her down.

"Hi, baby. I wasn't sure I'd hear from you before the game."

"I need you, babe."

"What's wrong?"

"I'm almost sick to my stomach with nerves for tomorrow. I really want my girls to keep winning."

Celeste was quiet for a moment. "Of course, you do, baby. Is there any reason to think you won't win tomorrow's game?"

"No, I just have a bad feeling."

"Coach, listen to me. You're great at what you do. The girls have worked their asses off to get this far. You and Athena have done everything in your power to get them ready for this moment. I wish I could be there with you, but I have the utmost faith in your ability to lead your team to victory."

"I don't know, Celeste. What if I call a wrong play that loses the game?"

"Honey, where is this coming from? Do you think if you lose, it will hinder your chances of advancing your coaching career?"

Lisa was quiet. Was that it? Was she so worried about getting back to Division I coaching that she was making herself sick over this tournament and in particular the next game? She mumbled into the phone, upset and grateful that Celeste seemed to know her so well.

"Maybe."

"All right. Listen to me. If by chance you don't get an offer at a higher level, at least you still have a job at GU. Gerald loves you and you've made quite a name for yourself around campus. Your team loves you. I...I love you."

Huh?

"I'm sorry. I didn't mean to say that."

"You didn't mean to say that? Or you didn't mean to say it this way?"

Lisa could hear Celeste blow out a deep breath.

"I didn't mean to say it this way. I wanted to say it, but I didn't expect it to come out of my mouth so soon, and I especially didn't picture myself telling you over the phone. It doesn't change how I feel though. I am absolutely falling for you."

Lisa felt her heart swell. Celeste loved her. Those three tiny words that held so much meaning made her momentarily forget the angst she'd been feeling about the next game. She'd been wanting to tell Celeste that she loved her, but it never felt like the right time, and it also frightened her that she would say it too soon. This wasn't how she wanted to tell her either, on the phone, but she wanted Celeste to know that she loved her too.

"Celeste, I..." Lisa saw Athena waving to her frantically, walking quickly across the tile floor in the lobby.

"I have to go." Lisa hung up without saying good-bye, starting to panic from the look on Athena's face.

"What's wrong?"

"Emily and Kristina have food poisoning. Apparently, they both had the shrimp for dinner and they've been puking for the past thirty minutes."

"Shit!" They both ran to the stairwell and took the stairs two at a time until they got to the third floor. The team had congregated in the hallway outside of Emily and Kristina's room.

"Coach, they're really sick."

"Okay, ladies, go back to your rooms. Coach Chang and I will take care of this."

Lisa and Athena walked into the room to find Kristina throwing up in a trash bucket while Emily was draped over the toilet. Lisa threw her hands up in the air and huffed. "This can't be happening!"

Neither player could take their face out of their respective chamber to look at her. Lisa told one of the assistant coaches to take the van and go to the nearest pharmacy for anti-nausea medication, Pedialyte, and saltine crackers. The girls were going to need rehydration and electrolytes when their stomachs finally calmed down.

The girls started crying simultaneously, and Lisa tended to Emily while Athena tended to Kristina, rubbing their backs to try to comfort them. Lisa soaked two washcloths with cold water and handed one to Athena so they could wipe their faces. Lisa called down to the hotel lobby to ask them to have housekeeping bring up a couple of extra trash cans with double liners, and a few extra liner bags.

Lisa and Athena stayed with Emily and Kristina all night, but when the morning came, they had to get ready for their game. Lisa instructed Chris, their volunteer assistant coach, to stay at the hotel with the girls and take care of them.

The whole day felt off-kilter; the rest of the team was upset that their team captain and point guard, Emily, and their starting center, Kristina, weren't going to be able to play. This had been the first time Lisa had ever seen her team look defeated before they even started a game. She had to say something to get them fired up. They were in the meeting room before the game and Lisa started her pregame speech.

"Listen up, Panthers. I know this isn't what we wanted, but there's nothing we can do about it now. With Emily and Kristina sidelined with food poisoning, I need you all to step up, and play the winning game you're all capable of playing. I believe in each one of you individually, and in you all as a team. The question is…are you ready for your season to be over, or do you want to continue your journey, and make it to the next round?"

A few of the players muttered, "Keep playing."

"I'm sorry. What did you say?"

"Keep playing!" they all shouted.

"Give Emily and Kristina an opportunity to keep playing too. Melissa, you're starting for Emily, and, Dana, you're starting for Kristina. Now, let's get our fight on."

The team started out strong, scoring the first ten points. The other team pulled to within two points by the end of the first quarter. The ladies played hard defense and ran their offensive plays efficiently, setting solid screens, making sharp cuts. Everything GU did could have been used in a video on how to play perfect basketball.

Lisa's anxiety eased just a smidge, but she was still pacing in front of their bench, barking out orders. When she stopped, she folded her arms across her chest. When either a good or bad play was made, she'd turn to her team on the bench to make sure they saw that. The players on the bench must have picked up on Lisa's anxiety because they spent nearly the entire game on the edge of their metal folding chairs, arms linked together.

The two teams went back and forth for the rest of the first half, neither team getting ahead by more than four points. At halftime, the two teams were tied at thirty-four. The Panthers were sitting in the meeting room, drinking their sports drinks to replace their electrolytes they'd lost by sweating so much, and sucking on orange wedges to replenish their energy.

"You ladies are doing great." Lisa strode to the front of the room, uncapped her dry-erase pen, and started drawing diagrams on the board. "Melissa, you're doing a great job running the plays and seeing the open player. I want you to try this play in the start of the third quarter." Lisa drew Xs, Os, and lines with arrows to draw up a new play they'd never practiced. The defender on Dana was playing a little too closely, and if Dana could pin the defender behind her, Dana would be wide open for an easy shot.

"I know Emily and Kristina would be so proud of the way you're playing. I have one question, though. You don't have to answer me, only yourselves. Are you giving it your all? Are you leaving it all on the floor? Because that's what it's going to take to win this game. I know you have the hearts of champions. We have twenty more minutes to lay it all out there. Are you ready?"

"Yeah!" everyone screamed and jumped out of their chairs. They huddled up with their arms around each other and started swaying back and forth, side to side, yelling out a chant. When it ended, they ran back into the gym to warm up before the start of the second half.

Their first time on offense, Melissa and Dana ran the new play perfectly that ended in an easy basket. The other team's coach quickly called a timeout. Lisa suspected it was so she could yell at the player that just blew the defense on that last play, but that wasn't Lisa's concern. Her players were giggling that the play had actually worked, and they looked a lot more relaxed.

Despite playing relaxed, the other team just wasn't going away. Back and forth. Back and forth. Trading baskets, getting steals, sprinting up and down the floor. Any time the clock stopped, every single player on the floor was bending over, grabbing their shorts, trying to suck in deep breaths of air. There was twenty-three seconds left, Glassell was down by three, and they had the ball. Lisa called a timeout and knelt in front of the five players on the bench.

"This is it, ladies. This is what we've worked so hard for in our practices, games, preseason conditioning. It's all been for these last twenty-three seconds. We need a three-pointer to send this game into overtime. Mac, I want you to take the shot with eight to ten seconds left. You're going to come off a double screen, get the pass behind the three-point line, and take the shot. If you miss, and we get the rebound, kick it back out to Mac. She's had the hot hand all night. Any questions? Let's do this, Panthers."

The team inbounded the ball, and Melissa kept dribbling until the clock ran down to thirteen seconds and she gave the signal to Mac to run her play. She was wide open when she got the ball, and she shot it. The ball bounced off the rim, but Dana got the rebound and passed it back out to Mac with three seconds left. She took the wide-open shot for three points. The ball hit the metal rim, bounced up, came down and hit the rim again, then bounced one more time before finally missing as the final buzzer went off. The five Panther players stood in shock, looking at the basket as if they were wondering how it could betray them at the time they needed it most.

The other team ran onto the floor, cheering and celebrating while the players from Glassell University mourned the end of their season. Some of the players started crying, hiding their faces in their jerseys, and hugging their teammates. Lisa had to collect them to congratulate the other team. The locker room had been somber, a few of the players still crying silently and sniffing.

"I know you're upset, but we fought hard and we had the shot we wanted, but bad luck happened. It's nobody's fault. But I'm so damn proud of all of you. You played your hearts out from start to finish and you never gave up. We had a great season this year, and I love all of you. Now get dressed so we can go back to the hotel and see Emily and Kristina." Lisa was too choked up to continue her speech. If only that shot had gone in…

The team stood in a group hug, and one last time, yelled out, "Panthers!"

Chapter Twenty-five

Monday morning, Lisa sat in her office making notes on the season and players. She'd meet with every player individually over the coming week to discuss the season and the player's individual play, what they wanted for next year, and how they were going to go about it. Her office phone rang and she picked it up.

"Coach Tobias."

"Hello, Coach. My name is William Thomas, and I'm the athletic director at Northeastern University in Boston. I've been keeping tabs on you throughout the season, and I'm very impressed on how well your team did. With your experience as a player and your coaching style, I think you'd fit in really well with our program. I'd like to invite you out for an interview early next week if you're interested. I can show you the campus, our state-of-the-art facilities, and go over our hopes for the future of our women's basketball team. What do you say?"

Lisa had a death grip on the phone receiver. She'd been hoping for a phone call like this. This was her opportunity to get back into the big leagues.

"I say yes, Mr. Thomas. Let me get my flight and I'll call you."

"Oh, Coach, we'll fly you out here on our dime and set you up in a hotel close to campus. Just let me know what day is good for you."

"How's Thursday?" It was soon, but if this turned out to be a good fit for her, she'd have to let her athletic director know so they could start looking for a coach.

"Terrific. I'll email you your itinerary along with my contact information."

"Thank you for your call, Mr. Thomas. I'll see you on Thursday."

Lisa hung up the phone and stared off into space and had a quick daydream of what it would feel like to be back coaching at the Division I level. She wasn't looking forward to telling Celeste though. Or Athena for that matter. They both knew that this had been her dream so she'd hoped they'd be happy for her. In case they weren't though, she'd tell them later.

Celeste finished lecturing by ending with a corny joke. Her students gave her an obligatory laugh, and Celeste thanked them for their generosity. A few of her students waited patiently to talk with her. When Lisa came through the door, Celeste had held up her index finger to tell Lisa she'd be a little while. It was ten minutes later when she was finally alone with Lisa. Things between them had been a little distant since Lisa got home from the tournament. She'd been upset that they lost, and it seemed over the past couple of days, Lisa had been in her own head. Celeste had questioned herself over and over again if it had been too soon to tell Lisa she loved her. She thought maybe Lisa felt the same way, but she'd yet to say those three words to Celeste. Even now, Lisa looked like she had the weight of the world on her shoulders. Celeste put her papers in her leather briefcase and took a seat next to Lisa.

"Hi. What brings you by?"

"I got an interesting phone call this morning. Northeastern University is flying me out on Thursday to interview me for their head coaching position."

Well, if that wasn't a punch in the gut. Celeste leaned back in the chair and felt her mouth open but no words came out. She cleared her throat in hopes of producing some sort of question or sentence.

"I don't know where that is, but if the name is any indication, I'm guessing it's in the northeastern part of the country?"

"Yes, in Boston."

"I see." Celeste felt deflated. Just when she thought she'd found someone who really liked her, really cared for her, she was going to leave. "Well, this is what you've wanted." Celeste just wished Lisa wanted her more.

"I thought you'd be happy for me."

Celeste sighed and placed her hand over Lisa's. "I am happy for you, honey, but I'm sad for me."

"Even if I take this job, Celeste, we can continue to see each other."

"When? On summer break? I don't want a part-time lover. I'm almost fifty years old. I want someone that wants to be with me and wants to spend the rest of our lives together. Maybe we should just make a clean break now before we get in too deep." As the words came out of Celeste's mouth, her heart broke, knowing she was already in deeper than she'd expected to be.

"Wait a minute. We don't even know if I'm going to get offered this job or if I'll think it's a good fit."

"Come on, Lisa. You know they wouldn't be flying you out there if you weren't already their first choice. It's your decision if you take the job or not."

"Celeste, please don't do this. I'm starting to have feelings for you. I want to be with you."

Celeste felt that she would start crying any minute so she needed to make this quick and get out of there. "Please don't take this as a threat, Lisa, because it's not meant as one. But if you move away, we'll have to break up. Like I said, I want a full-time partner." Celeste stood and cupped Lisa's cheek with her palm. "The proverbial ball is in your court."

Celeste walked out of the room as fast as her heels and dress would take her. She kept willing the tears away, but once she reached her office and locked the door behind her, she allowed them to fall.

❖

That night, Lisa and Athena were having dinner together in their home. She'd told Athena earlier about the interview and Athena had been quiet ever since, only speaking when she asked what Lisa wanted for dinner. This day should have been a happy one for Lisa, but it had turned out to be a shit show. Lisa knew it would be hard to tell her girlfriend and best friend, but not this hard.

"Are you going to talk to me at all?"

"Yes, but just give me a minute. This kind of took me by surprise."

"Why? You knew this was my dream to move up."

"Yeah, but that was before this team and the season we had. And before Celeste. What about her?"

"She broke up with me today."

Athena's fork clanged on her plate. "Are you serious?"

"Yep. Said she wants a full-time partner not a long-distance relationship."

"And you're willing to let her go that easy?"

"Dammit! I don't even know if I'm going to get the job."

Athena rolled her eyes at Lisa and resumed eating. Even Lisa had a difficult time believing that statement. She'd been around long enough to know the excitement in the Northeastern's athletic director's voice that it was her job if she wanted it.

"Well, I guess we'll just wait and see. If you go, I'm really going to miss you."

"You'd stay here?"

"Yes. Stephanie and I are getting closer, and I want to see where it goes."

"Oh, I see." Lisa didn't, really. She knew it was a possibility that Athena would stay. She'd not been shy about expressing how much she liked GU and Old Town. They'd been friends for so long that Lisa didn't want to think about not having Athena on the bench next to her.

"Look, Lisa. I understand why you want to coach at the Division I level, but sometimes there are more important things, and people, to consider. Sometimes, what you thought you wanted turns out to be something entirely different. It's okay if your dreams change along the way."

The next afternoon, Lisa was in her office on the phone when there was a knock on the door. She looked up to see Emily standing in the doorway. Lisa waved her in and ended her call after Emily sat down across from her. Emily looked like someone had died, her face was long and her gaze was in her lap.

"What's up, Logan? Why the frown?"

"Are you leaving, Coach?"

Crap. How did Logan find out? "Where did you hear that?"

"I overheard Professor Bouchard talking with Professor Daniels and telling her that you had a job interview somewhere back East."

"Professor Bouchard said that in front of you?"

"Not exactly. The door to her office was open. They were talking. It looked like Professor Bouchard was crying so I ducked out of sight."

"So, you were eavesdropping."

Emily shrugged. "I guess. Is it true, Coach?"

"Yes, Logan, it's true, but keep it quiet for now, okay? It's just an interview. I haven't decided if I'll take it if they offer the job."

"Can I say something, Coach?"

"Of course."

"I don't want you to go. I owe who I am to you and I want you to help me grow more."

Lisa wasn't sure what Emily was talking about. "Can you explain?"

"Before I came here, I was raised to be quiet and do as I was told. I was taught to be a follower. But when I came here, you taught me how to lead. You believed in me, not only in basketball but in academics. Your faith in me made me want to be a better person. I want to be like you, Coach. If you decide to leave, I'll miss you like crazy, but they'd be lucky to have you. For my sake, the team's sake, and Professor Bouchard's sake, I hope you stay here."

"Logan, about Professor Bouchard."

"I know to keep quiet about that, but it's obvious you like each other. I think that's why she was crying. I think she's in love with you."

"You do, huh?"

"Yep. She's a real catch, Coach. If I was old like you, I'd want her to be my girlfriend."

"Who are you calling old, kiddo?"

Emily laughed and stood, and Lisa came over to stand next to her.

"Look, Emily, I appreciate what you said. You're an exceptional young woman and I'm proud of you."

Emily threw her arms around Lisa and hugged her tight before letting go and walking out.

Well, shit.

Chapter Twenty-six

Northeastern University sent a car to Lisa's hotel Friday morning to bring her to campus. She'd had dinner with William Thomas the night before, and he discussed what her salary would be as well as her benefits. He'd asked her about her playing days in college and the pros. It was a "getting to know you" dinner, and Lisa really liked him. He appeared to be down-to-earth and an advocate for women's sports. He gushed about women's volleyball and the men's and women's ice hockey teams. He'd been at Northeastern University for almost twenty years, and it sounded like he was the person responsible for women's athletics' equality. This would definitely be a good place to be a woman coach for a women's sports team.

They pulled up to the front of the campus and William was standing in front of a long brick sign that displayed the name of the university. Lisa had seen the same picture when she took a virtual tour on the website. It had looked impressive in a picture but even more so in person. She stepped out of the car and shook William's hand, then they were on their way to tour the campus.

He had saved the athletic department for last. He took her to the gym they would play their games in. It wasn't quite as big an arena as she was led to believe by the virtual tour, but it was definitely bigger than GU's. She tried to imagine coaching, and her current team kept popping into her head. She gave herself a little shake to try to dispel the image. *Stay in the moment and pay attention.* He then took her to the locker room. It wasn't much different from the one at GU—the lockers were in good shape, benches between the rows, showers were clean. She exited to find William waiting for her. They made their way to the weight room. It was also impressive. Large. State-of-the-art equipment. But so was GU's. Last stop of the tour was the coach's offices. She was introduced to some of the coaches, who seemed nice enough. The offices were spacious and well equipped with computers and a flat screen TV on the wall. No more watching game film on her laptop or a fifteen-year-old television. It was about twice the size as her current office.

Lisa shook William's hand once more, told him she'd be in touch soon to give them her answer, and left to walk around the area. She had told him she would catch a cab back to her hotel. She'd been to Boston only a few times, so she decided to take advantage of her free trip to walk around and see the sights. She walked by Fenway Park, which was kind of cool given the history of the baseball stadium. She stopped in a little eatery and had a lobster roll and enjoyed the rest of her walk around central Boston. Once she made it back to the hotel, she lay on the bed and contemplated the day's events.

Northeastern University was a gorgeous campus. It had a few different quads throughout, plenty of buildings and trees. Lots of students milling about. There were a few times where she thought she saw Celeste, but obviously it wasn't her. She thought about Athena and her team at times too.

The head coach position was a good opportunity for her though. It would get her back in the coaching ranks of Division I. It was lower-level but still Division I, which meant more money, better equipment, and better travel. It shouldn't take her more than five years to get to a higher Division I school or maybe even as an assistant coach at the professional level. Everything had gone according to plan except for one thing. Falling in love with Celeste Bouchard. If it hadn't been for Celeste, Lisa might have already accepted the job. She went back to what Athena said. That it was okay if dreams changed along the way, and sometimes what she really wanted had been in front of her the whole time.

Lisa had spent her life eating, sleeping, and breathing basketball. She'd known from an early age what she wanted, but was she willing to give up that dream?

She called the number that was newly stored in her phone. "Hi, William. It's Lisa Tobias. I have an answer for you."

❖

Lisa paid the Lyft driver when they pulled up to the front of the house, and she exited the car. It felt like she had been gone forever, but she was excited to make a new start. She'd made a tough decision the night before, but she had to do what was best for her. Now it was time for Lisa to tell Celeste her decision. She knocked on the front door, and Celeste had thankfully answered. Apparently, she was working out on the pole, given the way she was dressed.

"Lisa, what are you doing here?"

"May I come in? There are some things I need to say."

Celeste stepped aside so Lisa could enter. Lisa felt the chill coming from Celeste, and she was hoping she'd be able to thaw her out.

"How did the interview go?"

Lisa hadn't been expecting that question, and from the tone of Celeste's voice, she didn't seem to really care. She probably did, in all honesty, but Lisa knew Celeste was trying to protect herself. She didn't blame her. Lisa decided to be honest and tell her everything. At that point, she'd had nothing to lose.

"It went really well. Beautiful campus, really nice facilities, the athletic director is very supportive of women's athletics, and the salary they offered would be the most I've ever made as a coach. He presented me with a really great opportunity."

"That's nice. Congratulations. I'm glad you're getting what you want."

Celeste turned away from Lisa, and Lisa remained where she was.

"I turned it down."

Celeste turned back around. "What did you say?"

Lisa took her hands out of her pockets and shrugged. "I said, I turned it down."

"Why? I thought that was your dream."

"It was my dream. Turns out I had another dream that I became recently aware of."

"Which is?" Celeste crossed her arms across her body, almost looking afraid of the answer.

"You. You've become my dream come true, Celeste. I love you. I think I fell in love with you when I saw you at Gerald's faculty mixer. From that first moment, I'd been unable to get you out of my head, and now, I can't get you out of my heart." Tears filled Celeste's eyes, and that was Lisa's cue to finally go to her.

"You love me?"

"I do. I love you more than anything."

"Even more than basketball?"

Lisa put her finger on her chin and looked like she had to think about that. Celeste smacked her arm, causing Lisa to laugh. "Yes, baby. Even more than basketball. This little quaint private university grew on me. Old Town grew on me. I love my team and support staff. But most of all, I love you. When I was getting the tour of the campus yesterday, I thought I kept seeing you, Athena, and my players. Then I kept comparing everything to what I have here. I realized last night in my hotel room that what I'd wanted, I already had."

Celeste threw her arms around Lisa and kissed her, letting her know what every day with her would be like.

"I love you so much, Coach. Are you going to be happy coaching at this level?"

"Yes, I had a great time coaching these kids. But I promise, if I decide I need more, I'll only apply to schools in this area. I will never, ever leave you, and I'm going to spend the rest of my life showing you how special you are to me."

"Why don't you start now?" Celeste took Lisa's hand and led her to her bedroom. Lisa happily followed.

❖

Lisa was back in her office on Monday morning. She had texted Athena that she was back in town on Sunday, and Athena had texted back that she was spending the weekend with Stephanie in Temecula wine tasting. She'd said that she would spend the night at Stephanie's and just see Lisa at work. Athena came in about an hour later, looking tanned and rested but also a little nervous.

"How was your weekend wine tasting?"

"It was fun. We stayed at a bed and breakfast at one of the wineries. It was really pretty out there, seeing all of the grapevines lined up. I know way more about wine now than I ever thought I would know." Athena laughed, and Lisa felt the knot in her stomach ease.

"I have to ask you a question about you coaching next year."

"Okay." Athena drew out the word like she was skeptical.

"Would it be okay if I remained the head coach and you stayed on as my assistant?"

"Here? At GU?"

Lisa nodded.

"Hell, yeah, it would!" Athena held Lisa in a bear hug. "What changed your mind?"

"You. I listened to you and thought about my dreams changing. I went straight to Celeste's house from the airport, told her I turned down the job, and that I love her."

"Way to go, Ice. It's about damn time you told her."

"Yes, I know. Enjoy this while you can because it will never happen again, but you were right."

Lisa shoved Athena when she started doing her version of a happy dance in the middle of their office. It was good to have a home that she loved. The knock on their office door interrupted Athena's dancing, thankfully.

"Hey, Logan, come on in and shut the door. I wanted to let you know that I decided to stay at GU, so you'll have to suffer with us as your coaches still."

Emily pumped her fist in the air and joined Athena in dancing. Lisa smiled at the scene and realized she probably wouldn't have this anywhere else. There was something magical at the university, and Lisa was grateful to be part of it.

CHAPTER TWENTY-SEVEN

One Month Later

Lisa and Celeste were sitting near one of the fountains on campus, enjoying a fruit smoothie from the café. The sun was shining and students were walking by them, occasionally waving to them. Emily came along wearing shorts, a button-down Hawaiian print shirt, and a baseball cap on backward. That kid had her own style and Celeste loved seeing her spread her wings and come into her own.

"Hey, Coach. Hey, Professor. What's going on?"

Emily sat down with them, uninvited but neither one minded. Lisa had talked to Celeste about her fondness toward Emily, and Emily would occasionally stop by during Celeste's office hours just to talk about life. Celeste enjoyed their talks, especially being privy to how Emily's mind worked. It turned out that she had a lot of good ideas about politics, history, sports, entertainment, and such. She was going to go places.

"Hello, Emily. How are you?"

"I'm cool. Just aced my sociology exam."

"Atta kid. Keep up the good work. You still going to show the recruits around on Saturday, right?"

"Absolutely, Coach." Emily slung her backpack over her shoulder. "Gotta get to my next class. See you, Coach. Bye, Professor."

"Have a great day, Emily."

A few minutes later, Gerald came by. "Just who I wanted to talk to. I wanted to quickly let you know that Jackie Stone has officially been let go from her position here, and as a condition of no jail time, she's been ordered to attend anger management classes and to stay away from you, Celeste."

"Thank you for letting me know, Gerald."

"You ladies have a good day."

They were finally alone, and Celeste really wanted to hold Lisa's hand and kiss her but instead she settled for smiling and looking into her eyes.

"How about we celebrate tonight, Coach? No more Jackie Stone."

"How about we not give Jackie any more of our energy and we celebrate us?"

"That's a brilliant idea, my love."

"Thanks for taking a shot at love with me, baby. I love you."

"I love you, Coach."

The End

About the Author

KC Richardson attended college on a basketball scholarship, and her numerous injuries in her various sports led her to a career in physical therapy. Her love for reading and writing allows her to create characters and tell their stories. Her second novel, *Courageous Love*, was a Golden Crown Literary Award finalist in the Traditional Contemporary Romance category. She and her wife live in Southern California where they are trying to raise respectful fur kids.

When KC isn't torturing/fixing people, she loves spending time with her wonderful friends and family, reading, writing, kayaking, working out, and playing golf. She can be reached at kcrichardsonauthor@yahoo.com, on Twitter @KCRichardson7 and on Facebook.

Books Available from Bold Strokes Books

Brooklyn Summer by Maggie Cummings. When opposites attract, can a summer of passion and adventure lead to a lifetime of love? (978-1-63555-578-3)

City Kitty and Country Mouse by Alyssa Linn Palmer. Pulled in two different directions, can a city kitty and country mouse fall in love and make it work? (978-1-63555-553-0)

Elimination by Jackie D. When a dangerous homegrown terrorist seeks refuge with the Russian mafia, the team will be put to the ultimate test. (978-1-63555-570-7)

In the Shadow of Darkness by Nicole Stilling. Angeline Vallencourt is a reluctant vampire who must decide what she wants more—obscurity, revenge, or the woman who makes her feel alive. (978-1-63555-624-7)

On Second Thought by C. Spencer. Madisen is falling hard for Rae. Even single life and co-parenting are beginning to click. At least, that is, until her ex-wife begins to have second thoughts. (978-1-63555-415-1)

Out of Practice by Carsen Taite. When attorney Abby Keane discovers the wedding blogger tormenting her client is the woman she had a passionate, anonymous vacation fling with, sparks and subpoenas fly. Legal Affairs: one law firm, three best friends, three chances to fall in love. (978-1-63555-359-8)

Providence by Leigh Hays. With every click of the shutter, photographer Rebekiah Kearns finds it harder and harder to keep Lindsey Blackwell in focus without getting too close. (978-1-63555-620-9)

Taking a Shot at Love by KC Richardson. When academic and athletic worlds collide, will English professor Celeste Bouchard and basketball coach Lisa Tobias ignore their attraction to achieve their professional goals? (978-1-63555-549-3)

Flight to the Horizon by Julie Tizard. Airline captain Kerri Sullivan and flight attendant Janine Case struggle to survive an emergency water landing and overcome dark secrets to give love a chance to fly. (978-1-63555-331-4)

In Helen's Hands by Nanisi Barrett D'Arnuk. As her mistress, Helen pushes Mickey to her sensual limits, delivering the pleasure only a BDSM lifestyle can provide her. (978-1-63555-639-1)

Jamis Bachman, Ghost Hunter by Jen Jensen. In Sage Creek, Utah, a poltergeist stirs to life and past secrets emerge. (978-1-63555-605-6)

Moon Shadow by Suzie Clarke. Add betrayal, season with survival, then serve revenge smokin' hot with a sharp knife. (978-1-63555-584-4)

Spellbound by Jean Copeland and Jackie D. When the supernatural worlds of good and evil face off, love might be what saves them all. (978-1-63555-564-6)

Temptation by Kris Bryant. Can experienced nanny Cassie Miller deny her growing attraction and keep her relationship with her boss professional? Or will they sidestep propriety and give in to temptation? (978-1-63555-508-0)

The Inheritance by Ali Vali. Family ties bring Tucker Delacroix and Willow Vernon together, but they could also tear them, and any chance they have at love, apart. (978-1-63555-303-1)

Thief of the Heart by MJ Williamz. Kit Hanson makes a living seducing rich women in casinos and relieving them of the expensive jewelry most won't even miss. But her streak ends when she meets beautiful FBI agent Savannah Brown. (978-1-63555-572-1)

Date Night by Raven Sky. Quinn and Riley are celebrating their one-year anniversary. Such an important milestone is bound to result in some extraordinary sexual adventures, but precisely how extraordinary is up to you, dear reader. (978-1-63555-655-1)

Face Off by PJ Trebelhorn. Hockey player Savannah Wells rarely spends more than a night with any one woman, but when photographer Madison Scott buys the house next door, she's forced to rethink what she expects out of life. (978-1-63555-480-9)

Hot Ice by Aurora Rey, Elle Spencer, Erin Zak. Can falling in love melt the hearts of the iciest ice queens? Join Aurora Rey, Elle Spencer, and Erin Zak to find out! (978-1-63555-513-4)

Line of Duty by VK Powell. Dr. Dylan Carlyle's professional and personal life is turned upside down when a tragic event at Fairview Station pits her against ambitious, handsome police officer Finley Masters. (978-1-63555-486-1)

London Undone by Nan Higgins. London Craft reinvents her life after reading a childhood letter to her future self and in doing so finds the love she truly wants. (978-1-63555-562-2)

Lunar Eclipse by Gun Brooke. Moon De Cruz lives alone on an uninhabited planet after being shipwrecked in space. Her life changes forever when Captain Beaux Lestarion's arrival threatens the planet and Moon's freedom. (978-1-63555-460-1)

One Small Step by Michelle Binfield. Iris and Cam discover the meaning of taking chances and following your heart, even if it means getting hurt. (978-1-63555-596-7)

Shadows of a Dream by Nicole Disney. Rainn has the talent to take her rock band all the way, but falling in love is a powerful distraction, and her new girlfriend's meth addiction might just take them both down. (978-1-63555-598-1)

Someone to Love by Jenny Frame. When Davina Trent is given an unexpected family, can she let nanny Wendy Darling teach her to open her heart to the children and to Wendy? (978-1-63555-468-7)

Tinsel by Kris Bryant. Did a sweet kitten show up to help Jessica Raymond and Taylor Mitchell find each other? Or is the holiday spirit to blame for their special connection? (978-1-63555-641-4)

Uncharted by Robyn Nyx. As Rayne Marcellus and Chase Stinsen track the legendary Golden Trinity, they must learn to put their differences aside and depend on one another to survive. (978-1-63555-325-3)

Where We Are by Annie McDonald. Can two women discover a way to walk on the same path together and discover the gift of staying in one spot, in time, in space, and in love? (978-1-63555-581-3)

A Moment in Time by Lisa Moreau. A longstanding family feud separates two women who unexpectedly fall in love at an antique clock shop in a small Louisiana town. (978-1-63555-419-9)

Aspen in Moonlight by Kelly Wacker. When art historian Melissa Warren meets Sula Johansen, director of a local bear conservancy, she discovers that love can come in unexpected and unusual forms. (978-1-63555-470-0)

Back to September by Melissa Brayden. Small bookshop owner Hannah Shepard and famous romance novelist Parker Bristow maneuver the landscape of their two very different worlds to find out if love can win out in the end. (978-1-63555-576-9)

Changing Course by Brey Willows. When the woman of your dreams falls from the sky, you'd better be ready to catch her. (978-1-63555-335-2)

Cost of Honor by Radclyffe. First Daughter Blair Powell and Homeland Security Director Cameron Roberts face adversity when their enemies stop at nothing to prevent President Andrew Powell's reelection. (978-1-63555-582-0)

Fearless by Tina Michele. Determined to overcome her debilitating fear through exposure therapy, Laura Carter all but fails before she's even begun until dolphin trainer Jillian Marshall dedicates herself to helping Laura defeat the nightmares of her past. (978-1-63555-495-3)

Not Dead Enough by J.M. Redmann. A woman who may or may not be dead drags Micky Knight into a messy con game. (978-1-63555-543-1)

Not Since You by Fiona Riley. When Charlotte boards her honeymoon cruise single and comes face-to-face with Lexi, the high school love she left behind, she questions every decision she has ever made. (978-1-63555-474-8)

Not Your Average Love Spell by Barbara Ann Wright. Four women struggle with who to love and who to hate while fighting to rid a kingdom of an evil invading force. (978-1-63555-327-7)

Tennessee Whiskey by Donna K. Ford. Dane Foster wants to put her life on pause and ask for a redo, a chance for something that matters. Emma Reynolds is that chance. (978-1-63555-556-1)

30 Dates in 30 Days by Elle Spencer. A busy lawyer tries to find love the fast way—thirty dates in thirty days. (978-1-63555-498-4)

Finding Sky by Cass Sellars. Skylar Addison's search for a career intersects with her new boss's search for butterflies, but Skylar can't forgive Jess's intrusion into her life. (978-1-63555-521-9)

Hammers, Strings, and Beautiful Things by Morgan Lee Miller. While on tour with the biggest pop star in the world, rising musician Blair Bennett falls in love for the first time while coping with loss and depression. (978-1-63555-538-7)

Heart of a Killer by Yolanda Wallace. Contract killer Santana Masters's only interest is her next assignment—until a chance meeting with a beautiful stranger tempts her to change her ways. (978-1-63555-547-9)

Leading the Witness by Carsen Taite. When defense attorney Catherine Landauer reluctantly becomes the key witness in prosecutor Starr Rio's latest criminal trial, their hearts, careers, and lives may be at risk. (978-1-63555-512-7)

No Experience Required by Kimberly Cooper Griffin. Izzy Treadway has resigned herself to a life without romance because of her bipolar illness but wonders what she's gotten herself into when she agrees to write a book about love. (978-1-63555-561-5)

One Walk in Winter by Georgia Beers. Olivia Santini and Hayley Boyd Markham might be rivals at work, but they discover that lonely hearts often find company in the most unexpected of places. (978-1-63555-541-7)

The Inn at Netherfield Green by Aurora Rey. Advertising executive Lauren Montgomery and gin distiller Camden Crawley don't agree on anything except saving the Rose & Crown, the old English pub that's brought them together. (978-1-63555-445-8)

Top of Her Game by M. Ullrich. When it comes to life on the field and matters of the heart, losing isn't an option for pro athletes Kenzie Shaw and Sutton Flores. (978-1-63555-500-4)

Vanished by Eden Darry. A storm is coming, and Ellery and Loveday must find the chosen one or humanity won't survive it. (978-1-63555-437-3)